MW01277270

FAR
Kingdom

*The Chronicles
of Emeraldia*

Casey A. Telling

Casey A. Telling

Other books in the Chronicles of Emeraldia:
Into the Blood of the Sun
Under the Light of the Sun

For ordering information, go to chroniclesofemeraldia.com

Copyright © 2010 Casey A. Telling
All rights reserved.

ISBN: 145281256X
ISBN-13: 9781452812564

ACKNOWLEDGEMENTS

Many are they who have contributed to the writing of this series by their unfailing support and enthusiasm. Maggie Thurston, Dana Quade and her son, Evan, and the host of readers from where I work, such as Nellie, Bonnie, Lisa, Chip and Paul have all given excellent feedback that only made the stories better. My thanks to them all.

Especial thanks goes to my wife, Elvera, for her support through this time of writing as well as for her creative ideas and constructive criticism. Our niece, Emily, has been very helpful in developing the music script for some of the songs in the books. Pastor Harry Fritz has also been very encouraging in his remarks regarding both the story and the marketing of the works. To all of them I owe a great debt of thanks.

CHAPTER 1

Glowing in the darkness that consumed the cavern were two small, red points visible in the distance; the eyes of the Koosti chief, Sarim'tay. Those eyes guided thousands of his subjects inside the deep breach beneath the earth. Even their breathing dared not disturb the silence as Sarim'tay called out to the Dark One. Since the deposing of LeAnre, Sarim'tay had learned the arts of necromancy. His mind was keener than LeAnre's and absorbed the black knowledge of the spell weavers easily. With the infusion of the Dark One's power he gathered more of the Koosti under his sway. Driven by fear, his followers showed greater fanaticism than LeAnre's ever had.

He incanted a spell and a pulsating energy throbbed through the cavern. Streaks and blurs of color swept over the heads of the people, streaming by to congeal into a roiling mass of brilliant effluence over Sarim'tay's head. He called out a second incantation and the colors slowed, shimmering into a three-dimensional picture reaching thirty feet high and fifty feet wide.

The people gasped and worshiped the Dark One, asking that he imbue Sarim'tay with more and more power. Their request came forth when the Koosti chief raised his hands and called for the picture to resolve for all to see. Seemingly from out of great depths appeared a picture of Veranna. She held a sword and fought against Sarim'tay. He repulsed all of her attacks and then drove her back, swinging his own blade with such force that he knocked hers out of her hand. With one swift, fluid motion he then swung and decapitated her, tossing her body to the dogs.

Another vision then arose. This time, Veranna stumbled along as a captive before Sarim'tay, her arms tied over her head and her naked body showing a multitude of marks from terrible abuse. Her emerald-green eyes were no more, having been taken by Sarim'tay and eaten according to the custom of the Koosti. He commanded his slaves to put her into a cage in the middle of his main city where all could see the tortures he would inflict upon her day by day.

A third scenario arose, showing Veranna dead and flown away into the hills by a dragon. It dropped her body onto the ground where it was covered by a landslide and never seen again.

A fourth then swirled and formed. Veranna stood before Sarim'tay and bowed. With a gesture he commanded her to remove her clothes and she did so without hesitation. Before all of the people in the city square he raped her repeatedly until she became pregnant. Her womb swelled and she gave birth. In her misery she adored the little baby, but Sarim'tay took the babe and tore it to pieces in front of her, laughing at her horror and sadness. He did this several times until her mind broke and she cared not how he used her, groveling at his feet and worshiping him as a god.

The image receded into the background and Sarim'tay's voice permeated the silence.

"It does not matter which end the Emeraldian harlot comes to; they shall all result in her total defeat and submission to me. The Koosti shall reign over the Seven Lands and make it part of the Koosti empire. The weakness of our current Great One shall be wiped away and I shall lead us to the glory that is our destiny, a destiny assigned by the Dark One, the Master over all. His servants are many in the different lands who will give their very lives for even the smallest chance to serve him. Already they are in place to do so when I order it."

He raised his hands toward the colors and they returned to the forefront. Another scene emerged full of people in joyous celebration. They were Koosti eating the live and dead captives from the Seven Lands whom they had crushed in a great war. Wine and the flesh of their opponents was a feast lasting for days. Sarim'tay was there at the center and the people bowed down and praised his name.

In the cavern a chant arose. Slowly it gained momentum until it was a deafening roar that shook the very depths of the earth. The gathered people swayed as they cried, 'Let the Dark One have victory; let Sarim'tay be his chosen one to lead us against our foes."

The celebration went on for hours and Sarim'tay ordered prisoners from the jails to be brought forth for the people to consume for a taste of the victory to come.

CHAPTER 2

Dressed in common clothes, Karsten and Treybal pulled hoods over their heads as they entered a tavern in the far northeastern corner of Tolemera. The tavern was known for serving many of questionable character and those allied with underground smugglers.Many of the men wore the tatoo of a crime worthy of the death penalty on their right upper arm. It was a head split in half by a sword, with three drops of blood dripping from the blade. Karsten and Treybal knew they were among the scum of the world and sought to give themselves a small amount of separation from the others, finding a table in a dimly lit corner while sipping tankards of poor-quality ale.

Outbursts of raucous music overrode the hushed conversations of the clientèle, while lusty serving girls coaxed them to spend more. Treybal kept track of those entering and leaving while Karsten concentrated on picking out bits and pieces of conversation, hoping to find even a single word that would help Veranna gain some leverage against the Erains.

Treybal leaned across the table and whispered to him, "Do you see the fellow walking over toward the table in the corner? I am sure that I saw him with several members of Erain Households. It might prove useful to see that his mug is never empty."

Karsten eyed the man and nodded his agreement, then instructed the barkeeper to regularly refill the man's mug. They took the opportunity to move closer to the man's table, keeping to the dim light along the wall.

It took close to an hour before the steady consumption of ale loosened the man's tongue. His speech evinced a slight slur and greater volume while his ego protruded all the more.

"I'm tellin' 'ya Vig, you can break your back and labor all the rest of your pitiful life; you still won't earn anythin' near what I got me now. Ya just needs to know the right people. How do ya think I just got the tatoo and not the noose?"

Vig, a man of average height but heavily muscled, thrust his bulldog face forward and pointed at the man's nose.

"Just remember where what you have got came from. You'll have to lie low for years and wonder if your 'backers' will expect more. Maybe they will start wondering if you know too much and have to be gotten rid of. Besides, you don't have sense enough to hold on to any money. Dag, you will be broke and begging before the year is gone."

Dag set his mug down hard on the table and spat out his reply. "You always think you knows how things work, but look at you; a tiny, rotten shed for a house and hardly two coins to rub together."

Vig looked him over and shook his head slowly, wondering at how foolish people could be. "Dag, you won't understand a word I am about to say, but you got to listen up if you want to live a while. I got nowhere under that murderous thug, Weyland, who called himself a duke. Since the empress came along, things have been better. I don't worry about my money being stolen through taxes and conscription, and I am able to expand my blacksmithing trade and make an honest day's wages. The empress has been honest with us and we prosper by being honest in return. If you had even a shred of sense in your head you could see that the future lies with her."

Dag laughed at him and spilled ale on himself. "Empress, hah! She will be gone and won't be back; where's your future in that? The Erains are returning and won't appreciate your lack of loyalty. When you are hanging from the city wall by a rope around your privates, just remember who warned you." He stopped and leered at Vig's wife who sat across the table. "I'll even attend to your wench and daughters when you are gone."

Vig's right hand slammed into Dag's nose, sending him back in his chair and onto the floor. In the next instant the whole room erupted into chaos as fists flew without care in all directions. Vig took several blows and returned better as Karsten and Treybal fought to keep from getting injured. Ale made many of the men slower and witless, but they did not feel as much pain when struck. Treybal shouted at Karsten to start maneuvering toward the door to keep anyone from escaping. It seemed forever before the shrill whistle of a constable sounded over the din. Captain Cody, of the City Guard, led a dozen constables into the room, their batons rapidly reducing the melee until all fighting ceased. Cody's baton was more like a surgical instrument in his hand, felling one rough-neck after another. He barely managed to avoid knocking Karsten across the forehead, recognizing him in an instant and changing the arc of his blow to impact Karsten's assailant. A few moments later and the room gained a semblance of order, but for the moans and groans of the injured.

Karsten flashed Cody a hand signal telling him to avoid reveal-ing his identity. The captain was quick on the uptake and hurried to divert attention to routine matters, his strong voice carrying through the room.

"I want to know who started this fracas, and why; if you are reluctant to cooperate I will have you all jailed until you are ready to talk."

One man near the bar hurried to speak up, stumbling over his words due to the pain in his jaw. Of average height, he had a lanky build and bony face of sharp angles. Pointing toward the man, Vig, he glared accusingly.

"T'was 'im, cap'n; he up and knocked some guy in the pate, then we all had ta' defen' ourselves."

Cody pointed his baton at Vig and raised an eyebrow to urge him to speak. Vig stood and shook his head to clear it a bit.

"Captain, it be true I struck first. However, that swine, Dag, in-sulted my wife and threatened my daughters."

Several voices sounded 'ayes' to his words and Cody had to raise his hand for silence.

"If what you say is true I won't fault you. The empress, however, along with her lords, has stressed the necessity of civil order. Violators must appear before a magistrate and be judged."

Vig hurried to speak up. "Captain, this idiot, Dag, made comments about the empress being gone soon and the Erains taking over. Shouldn't he be required to face the magistrate and explain himself?"

A hard edge came into Cody's voice. "That he shall. Did anyone else hear these words of Dag?"

Treybal and Karsten kept their hoods over their faces as they raised their hands and grunted. Cody understood their desire to remain anonymous and motioned for them to exit.

"You two, into the wagon; you're going to the castle for questioning. The rest of you are to help the tavern owner clean up this mess, and you will all share in reimbursing him for damages." He scanned the room and a puzzled look came over his face. "Which one of you is Dag?"

Vig responded, "He is not here, Captain; he must have run off in the midst of the fight."

Cody hurried outside and looked around. He glanced at Karsten and Treybal and spoke discretely. "It would help if I knew what this fellow 'Dag' looks like."

Karsten shook his head in frustration. "I do, and I do not see him anywhere. We must find him and squeeze the truth out of him. Captain, get us back to the castle, immediately. Lord Treybal and his Rockhounds are going to revisit their days as thief catchers."

Cody nodded briefly and ordered the wagon driver to return to the castle. After taking down the names of the people in the tavern he and his men started patrolling the streets. Guards watched all of the roads out of the city while the patrols crisscrossed the city blocks in hope of drag-netting their prey.

Karsten was anxious for the capture of Dag. Webs of subterfuge were growing steadily with the ongoing efforts of the surviving Erain houses to undermine Veranna's rule. They were so used to wielding power that peace and prosperity were inconceivable in light of their lust for tyranny. The idea that evil thoughts and desires held tyranny over them simply did not penetrate their consciousness. Dag was likely one of their insidious spies bent on attaining his own position of power in a revived Erain hegemony.

A thought congealed in the young Genazi ruler's mind, one that had been flitting through it for some time. A spy network of their own would come in mighty handy; but they could not afford to spend time with lengthy training regimens. They would need to use people already familiar with the craft, and Kreida would know who might fit the requirements.

Two hours later he paced back and forth in a large meeting room deep in the castle's underground. He wondered if his trust was misplaced in thinking that Kreida could find the right person for the job he had in mind. The fiery Genazi woman had her own way of appraising people and situations. His thoughts were interrupted when a muffled struggle in the hallway preceded a knock on the door.

"Come in."

The door swung open and two burly guards entered. They ushered in another person who was bound and had a sack drawn over the head and down to the waist. The person writhed like a snake fighting capture.

Kreida followed them into the room. Her loose fitting tan pants and top showed smears of a scuffle, and her voice carried a note of satisfaction as she presented the mysterious person to Karsten.

"This is the one; just take a moment to gather your wits before saying anything. I have had the pleasure of taming the badger's tongue a bit."

She pulled the sack off of the person and Karsten blinked in surprise. He wondered if Kreida was playing one of her ridiculous jokes. Before him was a woman from the remote northern reaches of the Boar's Spine Mountains. Her caramel skin was typical of some of the northern Genazi who had taken mates from nomadic tribes beyond the border of the Seven Lands. Large brown eyes and milky white teeth contrasted well with her thick, shiny black hair that hung down to her shoulder blades. In height she was slightly shorter than Kreida, but she was every bit as lean and mean.

Karsten shook his head slowly. "I cannot believe my eyes. Nisha Jamir, the rising star of Wolf Tribe; have you been out of confinement very long?"

She gave Kreida a nasty glare before turning to Karsten. Her face transformed in an instant to one of violent lust.

"Ah, Karsten, I knew that you would one day send for me. Your parents were too stupid to make a marriage pact with mine, but it was only a matter of time before you desired me for your satisfaction. Kreida was an obvious loser, and this weakling from far away that you married will never be woman enough to please any man."

Karsten's eyes blazed with anger, but before he could say anything, Veranna entered the room and gave him a quick kiss. She turned to Nisha and smiled confidently.

"'Any man' may be your goal; however, I have only one, and you will do well to remember it."

Nisha paused for a moment and then sneered. "I take what I wish; you will stay out of my way or I will crush you before I tear Kreida's arms off."

Veranna disconcerted her when she put her hand to her mouth and chuckled. "Oh my, Kreida, she reminds me of someone else who needed a lesson in civility."

Kreida and Karsten both knew that she referred to another Genazi woman named Falona. The woman had staked a claim on Karsten and been rude to Kreida before challenging Veranna to a combat contest. Veranna easily defeated and humiliated Falona.

Kreida chuckled at the memory and said resignedly, "Yeah, and nothing but the same type of lesson will get anything into her head."

Nisha snarled, "If these guards weren't holding me back I would give you a lesson you would never forget."

Veranna, Karsten and Kreida exchanged knowing looks and then moved the table and chairs to the periphery of the room. Veranna, dressed in a teal blue cotton blouse and a long, black skirt gave Nisha an overly sweet smile.

"What you say has some merit; and, for your sake, I hope you are a good teacher."

Nisha returned a vicious smile as she anticipated the beating she would give Veranna, followed by knocking Kreida unconscious and claiming Karsten for her own.

Veranna nodded to the guards and they cautiously released their grip on Nisha. The young Genazi woman leaped at Veranna, her hands reaching out to grab her by the throat.

Veranna hardly seemed to move. Her left hand deflected Nisha's hands while her right hand came up and under Nisha's arms, striking with the butt of her palm on the underside of Nisha's chin. Nisha's head and shoulders flew back while her feet swung up and over her head. She landed flat on her back on the stone floor, the air knocked out of her lungs. Pain radiated through her body. Nearly unconscious, she could hear one sound: Kreida laughing hysterically and slapping the surface of the table.

Veranna reached down and grabbed Nisha's ear, twisting it hard to force her to her feet. Still in shock at how easily Veranna had subdued her, all she could do was comply and ease the painful twist of her ear. Ever since she was twelve she was dominant over her peers, and won the Championship of the Woman Warriors of her clan at the age of fifteen. That Veranna held total mastery over her rattled her to her very core.

The empress kept her voice calm, an exasperated, motherly tone coming through.

"Now that the lesson is over with, I want you to listen very carefully. Kreida thinks that you are well qualified for a mission of great importance. She is certainly correct about your appearance; you are a rare beauty. But the role we have in mind requires a quick and deep mind."

Kreida drew herself up haughtily and stepped in front of Nisha. "For that they would have chosen me, but I am already too well-known for the job."

Veranna looked at Karsten and rolled her eyes, covering her mouth to keep from laughing. She could not afford to undermine Kreida.

"The Lady Kreida is correct. As the princess of the Genazi, and a ruler of your people, she is known by virtually everyone. We need someone whose face and name are unlikely to be recognized. The role will be dangerous; however, you would be doing your land and people a great service."

Embarrassed by defeat, Nisha did not make eye contact as she spoke. "What do I get out of this mission? Am I simply to obey and be thrown away when it is done?"

Veranna's patience was wearing thin, but she tried to hide it. "Of course, you will be well paid. Also, you would have the respect and gratitude of your people as well as that of the Seven Lands. You would also know the satisfaction of obedience for that which is good; that would be invaluable."

Kreida eyed Nisha coldly. "Besides all of that, you won't have to suffer the whipping I am dying to give you."

Nisha's eyes smoldered as she looked at Kreida. However, she knew that Kreida was both able and willing to do as she said. Lowering herself to one knee, arms spread wide, she bowed her head and spoke clearly.

"I, Nisha of the Wolf Clan Genazi, swear to obey and do as you request."

Veranna tried to dispel some of the tension in the room. "My first request is that you arise and embrace me as a partner. Since all authority is grounded in the Creator, and we both must live in obedience to Him, we labor for a common goal. We simply have different stations."

Nisha looked confused and wary, but gave Veranna a quick embrace. The empress smiled and gave her a brief inspection.

"Lady Kreida will see to your raiment and bath after which you will be instructed in your mission by Lord Karsten. You shall have a room provided for you in the best inn of the city, as well as jewelry. Practice acting like a lady so that it starts to come naturally."

Nisha nodded and started to walk away, but Kreida's voice stopped her.

"That is not how you respond to the Great Mother of our people, or the empress of the Seven Lands! Show some humility, girl."

Nisha's eyes blazed, but she managed to control herself. After several seconds she turned and bowed to Veranna before Karsten took the empress by the hand and they exited the room.

The Genazi woman from Wolf Clan felt as though the world had turned upside down. Staring out at the now vacant hallway, she spoke to Kreida, her frustration punctuating every word.

"How can you put up with this way of life! Genazi are free to live as they choose and take whom they will."

Kreida snorted derisively. "You could not even take a woman you thought soft. In case you have been deaf the last couple of years, I will tell you that the empress is the greatest fighter you will ever meet. She moves as smoothly as silk but can knock you on your butt harder than a mountain goat. In the very first fight she ever had she nearly killed me along with three others." Her voice turned to ice as she moved directly in front of Nisha and placed her finger on her chest. "One other thing; the empress is as a sister to me, so if you ever insult or disrespect her, you will be doing it to me. I will not be slow to tear out your tongue and throw it to the dogs."

Nisha wanted to attack Kreida and give her a good beating, but the Genazi princess had a great reputation as a warrior. Besides, certain principles held true for all Genazi, even those of mixed ancestry such as herself. The Great Mother of their people had given her a command and Kreida was still the acknowledged Champion of all the Women Warriors. To violate these laws was to abandon being Genazi. She lowered her eyes and calmly said, "Yes, mistress."

Seeing Nisha's submission, Kreida turned and headed for the door. "Follow me. You will prepare my bath and then take one, too. You stink, and nobles resent a good sweat. Perfume and powder are some of the things you will need to get used to. These lowlanders have strange ways; you must learn them. They call it 'refinement,' even if it seems more like suffocation." She spun around and resumed her way down the hall. "These lowland women do not have enough sense to realize what an honor it is for a Genazi woman to pleasure her man."

Nisha nodded and wondered what she had gotten into. *At least Kreida still has sense in some things.*

✣ ✣ ✣

CHAPTER 3

Lady Gelangweil made her way through the castle corridors with ease. Having been here many times before Duke Weyland was deposed, she knew it well. This new empress had destroyed not only Weyland, but also the Lady's husband, Dalmar, who had been emperor. It was good to get him out of the way, since he came from such a rude and incompetent household. However, it was sore humiliation that the Lady suffered, due to his defeat, at the hands of an upstart. The Lady had no doubts about Veranna's Emeraldian ancestry, and could even appreciate the fact that she demonstrated high style. It was irrelevant, though, since the Emeraldians had been conquered by the Erains at one time and would be again. She, Lady Gelangweil, of House Erain, would see to it that the Emeraldians were subdued once more and served her will.

Familiarity with the castle brought her no comfort today, since she was under the scrutiny of adversaries. The pressure showed in the flush of her cheeks and strained breathing. The conventions of etiquette would have to be observed and it galled her to treat her enemies with deference.

In her gown of midnight blue she strode into the dining hall next to the pavilion and chose a table in a corner where a number of nobles, sympathetic to her, dined. They arose and bowed as she sat down, one man in his forties moved over to the chair next to her. His hair and beard were only just beginning to show signs of gray, but his build was still hale, even if his waistline showed a slight bulge.

"My lady, it is good to see you. Are you getting along well enough?" His smooth voice set her at ease and his close proximity excited primal instincts. Tall and secure in his own person, he imbued her with longing and confidence. His predatory gray-brown eyes watched everything while managing to center in on her. She reminded herself to address him according to the dictates of noble parlance lest any eavesdropper sense more than friendly concern.

"My lord, baron, I am doing as well as I am able under the circumstances. Memories of my past keep coming to the fore of my mind, making me realize how much I have lost."

He put his hand on hers and spoke comfortingly while slipping a note through her fingers. In one deft movement she placed it into her bosom and continued as though nothing had happened. She ordered a serving girl to bring some fruit and sausage, and then turned back to Baron Ciclanno to speak just loud enough for any spy to overhear.

"Arve, I have been so distraught by the death of my husband that I find it difficult to concentrate on my responsibilities. My two daughters rarely come around to console me; they claim that their husbands allow them little time for personal matters. With slavery no longer allowed, they have so many chores to deal with. I do not see how they will ever realize the stations to which they were born."

The baron recognized the coded inferences in her words: She was relieved that Dalmar was gone, and kept herself busy with her scheming to regain the imperial throne. Her daughters, married to lords loyal to House Erain, were hard at work helping her with plans. She already had a good idea of how and when she would see her daughters raised to positions of high status, with as many slaves to serve them as they wished. In like manner he responded.

"My lady, I am so sorry to hear of your distress, and would that I could help you more. Alas, I am bound up in my duties on the far northern border. The nomads are proving themselves more than a distraction, and the lords of the new empress want a steady stream of reports on their movements and doings. As I have estates far to the north, I have been selected for this duty."

The lady raised her eyebrows to indicate that she understood his reply: He was devoted to her cause and had infiltrated the nomads to bring them in to help. The reports he sent to the empress would be close enough to the truth while leaving gaps that would prove decisive.

"I do hope, my lord, that you shall find some reprieve from your strenuous labors once things settle down. Is there anything I might do to help?"

He affected a gracious smile and hurriedly vanquished a lustful gaze. They had been enjoying an affair for years; tonight would bring another episode. They planned each encounter with the greatest care, and covert meetings with their allies would leave even a fox unaware of their trail. Veranna Emeraldia would not know what hit her.

Kreida set two plates of food down on the small table in her room. Nisha eyed them and started forward when a firm voice brought her to a stop.

"Hold!" Mrs. Gruntun, Veranna's personal servant and main custodian of the castle, frowned and motioned for Nisha to move back. Gray hair in a bun, and wearing a black dress over her plump form, she cast a strong impression of mature authority. "You look like a starved wolf pouncing on a fresh kill." She saw that the illustration pleased the Genazi woman. A bit frustrated, she took a calming breath and proceeded. "What I mean is that you should not act like an animal. Even when hungry you must control yourself and act civilized. If you are dining where there are other nobles you must wait to be seated.

Nisha sneered. "I can pull my own seat and eat; I am not a child."

"I agree. However, you are learning how to behave like a lady, and a noble lady allows a noble man or servant to pull her chair out. She then sits and calmly dines while helping to make the meal a pleasant time for those around her. Many things you hear at the table you will not hear elsewhere. Learning manners is like learning a language; they help you to communicate with the rest of the world."

Nisha scoffed at the notion. "Food is for the stomach just as desire is for the bed. Why should I wait to devour either of them?"

Mrs. Gruntun snapped back, "Because either of them can destroy you. Unbridled passions have been the cause of death and destruction from the beginning. Encouraging such behavior leads to selfishness and irresponsibility. The rules exist to preserve life and happiness by promoting love and respect for one another."

Nisha looked to Kreida for help, but the Genazi princess remained neutral. "Just do as she says; it is important for your mission."

Nisha's face showed her consternation. "Mission? I do not even know what it is. All I know is that I am suffering a bunch of pig manure for no reason."

"Be careful using reason around them; they will always be ahead of you." Kreida walked down the hallway to find Treybal, a vision of Mrs. Gruntun holding a blacksmith's hammer in her right hand running through her mind. With her left hand she held Nisha on an anvil, the Genazi woman glowing red. Down came the hammer, pounding away to fashion a blade of usable quality. Kreida mused, *I am glad that I was never that stubborn.*

CHAPTER 4

Nobles and their advisers scurried through the ancient halls of the castle in Tolemera. The empress, Veranna, the last of the purebloods from the line of Ergon, of the Emeraldian Empire, summoned them to hear their reports on the state of the empire. Two months had passed since she wed Karsten, of the fierce Genazi clans, and the need to assess the empire's strengths and weaknesses forced itself upon her. Her training in the Academy, in Clarens, had prepared her for economics and politics, but the regular cycle of meetings with counselors and advisers left her longing for her private, little room in the school. However, Clarens was all the way on the other side of the empire, and the Academy would only be an escape at this point. Her destiny, one laid out for her from before she was born, allowed few exceptions; the needs of her people had to come first.

Tall and slender, in her dress of deep blue silk with a top of white satin brocaded with red roses, the empress moved with a natural grace that inspired those around her to act accordingly. Having recently cut her hair from a long braid to just under her shoulder blades, she marveled at how such a simple action could cause so much change in her own mind. Her habit of pulling on the braid showed up often when she was in deep thought or nervous. Her best friend, Kreida of Clan Torreo of the Genazi, teased her in her typical, raucous manner. Walking along the portico outside of the castle pavilion, the two of them traded friendly barbs.

"Girl, I am just warning you; do not cut your hair much shorter or the Genazi women might think you are being punished for fooling around on your husband. That is how we mark a woman who violates another woman's marriage, aside from the black eyes and split lips." Kreida was a couple of inches shorter than Veranna, and the lean, athletic lines of her muscles gave the impression of a compressed coil ready to spring. Dressed in a sleeveless top of black leather, with a long Genazi-style knife mounted on her belt, her unkempt hair warned everyone that she was not to be trifled with.

Veranna just shook her head and gave her a wry smile. "So why are you not bald and broken?"

The Genazi warrior woman gave her a lugubrious smile in return. "They would have to find some proof that I did something to earn it. None of the men wanted to risk my not enjoying some time with them again, so they kept their mouths shut. Quality has its rewards."

Veranna arched an eyebrow and looked at her accusingly. "In case you do not already know, that is *not* what one would call quality; in fact, just the opposite. Don't ever let me catch you trying to spread your 'qualities' around here, or I shall look the other way if Treybal decides to relieve all of your samplers of their ability to test your qualities. Remember, you are a representative of the throne, and need to exemplify true quality."

Kreida smirked, "Well, since there is some question as to your quality with Karsten, I am simply making sure that we have proper representation."

"I am afraid that I have a quality in that way that you will only know after a long time of being wed to Treybal." She imagined the stalwart Rockhound leader laboring mightily to gradually form Kreida into a more cultured creature. Treybal was a study in contrasts, able to move among nobles and commoners alike. Although one of the toughest and fiercest fighters in the empire, he could appreciate the finest works of art and lowliest of men.

Honor preceded him, and those who followed in his wake could not help but be affected for the better. "You know, Kreida, too much joking around about serious things can bring others to discount the fact that you have a brain. There is already a steady debate over the question, and I am tired of having to…"

She stepped into a shaft of light beaming down through an archway in the portico and suddenly found herself looking at a goldsmith pounding on a piece of gold. Blow after blow carefully formed the piece of gold into a fine statuette. She then turned to her right and saw a worker in an orchard digging out weeds from the soil and pruning branches from the trees. Turning even further, she saw a shepherd training a dog to herd the sheep. Over and over the shepherd ran the dog through drills until it performed its tasks without error. Turning back around she saw a warrior training recruits. He set them hard tasks and pushed them to the limits of their physical abilities, and then asked for more. Pain showed on the faces of the recruits, but when it was over they stood in formation in fine uniforms.

Veranna shook her head and heard Kreida's voice ringing in her ears.

"Girl, are you even listening to anything I have been saying? You must have been a hundred miles away, just now."

The empress felt disoriented for a moment, but slowly her surroundings came back into focus. "I am sorry Kreida; I just had the strangest vision."

Kreida's shoulders slumped and her face twisted into a sickly mask as she groaned. "Oh no, not another vision! Every time you have had one of those we have been in for trouble. We are not yet recovered from the last round of fun and games after your vision at Dufuss's café. The only good thing that happened after that was the chance to kill Koosti."

Veranna was annoyed by Kreida's blatant savagery when it came to Koosti. They had been a scourge on the Seven Lands, and done them all terrible suffering, but a truce had been reached and diplomatic envoys now made regular exchanges of correspondence. Veranna ruled a Koosti province as recompense for the damages wrought upon her and her empire, and the former ruler, LeAnre y'dob was now her servant and charge. The empress reminded herself that while Kreida had shown improvement in some things, she still had a long way to go before she could abandon some of her distasteful ways. Veranna tried to get her disapproval across with sardonic humor.

"I am so sorry that your entertainment was so limited. Maybe I can arrange something else that will satisfy your longings."

"Yeah, well, that sounds good in theory, but Treybal would not like my going to the soldiers' barracks every night."

Veranna gave her a strong glare. "You are terrible! Is there nothing else that can occupy that incorrigible mind of yours? I should have you chained to a dog house for such a comment."

Kreida affected a lascivious smile and voice as she cooed, "Oh, chains and dogs; you are learning more every day."

Veranna started to respond with a sharp comeback, but Karsten came around the corner and greeted them.

"Good day, my ladies. Are you wandering about just to pass the time until the Council of Lords' meeting? We still have time for some refreshment if you like." He put his arm around Veranna's waist and gave her a quick kiss. She leaned against him and laid her head onto his shoulder, finding great comfort in his sure strength. All she could think of now was running away to some place private.

"Some refreshment would be very much appreciated, my love, especially after suffering through Kreida's version of a good time. The dining chambers should have some food ready since many of the nobles are here."

As she spoke, several members of noble houses passed by and bowed as they greeted her, Karsten and Kreida. The courtyard was abuzz with all of the unloading taking place, and Veranna asked her companions to hurry their pace so as to avoid the delays associated with all of the etiquette involved in royal greetings.

"I suddenly feel all the more hungry; let us hurry and get to the dining hall."

After a quick meal they headed for their private chambers to change, then proceeded to the throne room for the Council meeting. Veranna walked in and brought everyone to their feet and into a bow as she stepped up onto the dais and sat down on her throne. Her dress was a simple, but elegant pale-green silk, and all she wore on her head was a tiara with one small, deep-green emerald.

The meeting commenced with Karsten reciting events and numbers concerning the state of the empire, along with policy changes made by the empress regarding labor practices. Many of the nobles were anxious for news about the truce with the Koosti, as well as the progress made in pacifying the province formerly ruled by LeAnre. The official discussion time ended, but another hour was taken up with social affairs and introductions.

Veranna made the rounds to greet various lords and ladies, especially those from fiefs of which she had little familiarity. Most of the stories the nobles related to her were grim, but there was also a note of hope. The Koosti war had cost them all dearly, leaving them to despair. However, once peace had been restored they found a deeply seeded courage that helped them face the future with optimism, and to trust in the people of the empire. Those nobles from, or aligned with, the Erain Houses were cool toward her, even if polite, the tension obvious under a façade of etiquette.

The empress reminded herself that change came slowly, especially in attitudes. The late emperor's wife had come from the leading Erain House, and could not disguise her lust to recover her previous status. Veranna greeted her warmly and hoped that some of the icy barrier between them might melt.

"Good afternoon, Lady Gelangweil; I hope that all is well with you and your House."

Although shorter than Veranna, and tending toward a plump figure, Lady Gelangweil tried to draw her posture and face into an intimidating pose. Condescension radiated from her and her followers. After a slight curtsy, her voice came out in accusatory sweetness.

"I am doing well enough under the circumstances...your highness...however, you should have foreseen the consequences of deposing my husband. We would not have had any difficulties with the easterners if you would have simply minded your own business and been content with your status. One does not enter a plough horse into the races and expect to win."

Kreida bristled and started to retort angrily when Veranna held up her hand to signal her to stand down. The empress then renewed her pleasant smile and forestalled any more hostile exchanges.

"I am sorry that you feel that way, Lady Gelangweil. I would think that we are running the race together, for the eastern tribes are notorious in their disregard for agreements made with those they believe to be inferior. We hold certain principles to be inviolable, which they do not. The freedom to make a living and transcend the strictures of caste is basic to our outlook on life. The Koosti will require a good deal of time to learn to appreciate such a concept, and it seems that the Creator is using us to exemplify it."

Lady Gelangweil gave her a smile bordering on pity. "You poor, naïve girl; you have so much to learn. You give too much credit to people and think you know how the Creator operates in the world. Winning a few battles or making a treaty are shaky grounds for any repository of hope that you have divine approval. You may turn out like me and suffer great hardships to learn very simple lessons. Do not presume to know what the Creator's designs may be."

Realizing that lady Gelangweil was still too entrenched in her opposition to the new regime, Veranna decided not to continue the discussion. "Thank you for your advice, my lady. I hope that your journey home goes well for you. Good day."

Lady Gelangweil knew she was being dismissed and felt a surge of resentment. She had hoped to lure Veranna into a heated verbal battle to disrupt her composure, but saw that the young empress had sense enough not to do so in public. She curtsied briefly and stepped quickly out of the room.

Kreida rounded on Veranna, "How could you let her talk to you that way! If she had said any of that to me I would have cut her tongue out. Now she will think that she can treat you with disdain anytime she wants."

Veranna took Kreida's arm in hers and walked toward the exit. "I am hoping that I have established a new basis for her to relate to us. If she cannot predict our responses according to her preconceptions, then we will have succeeded in disrupting her game plan. She is used to demonstrations of power and political maneuvering, so we take those elements out of the contest and force her to adapt. Those who cannot adapt are less likely to survive. If she does adapt, then we have moved her closer to our own position."

Kreida wagged her finger in front of Veranna's chest, as she looked her sternly in the eye. "Just make sure you know which hand holds the knife before you try to disarm her."

"Yes, ma'am!" Veranna laid her arm over Kreida's shoulders. "I am glad that I have you around to remind me of such points."

Just then, Karsten bade a nobleman good day, and turned to join Veranna and Kreida on their way out. "Did I notice a bit of frost between you and the Erains?"

Veranna took his hand in hers and continued into the corridor. "Yes, but it was to be expected. Kreida admonished me to cut off their tongues."

"Is that all?"

"Yes, although I daresay she would want more if the mood took her."

Kreida snorted, "I do not have to be in a mood; common sense tells you not to treat an enemy like a friend. That woman would slit your throat in a heartbeat just for revenge."

Veranna frowned in puzzlement. "Revenge? I do not think there is any sadness in the woman at the loss of her husband."

Kreida pretended to faint against the stonewall of the corridor. "Oh, woman, when will you ever wise up? The stones here are not as thick as that skull of yours. She wants revenge for the loss of power she held. Her whole Household will be scheming to see how they can prune your authority and then cut you down altogether."

Karsten spoke up before Veranna could respond. "She is correct in her assessment, my love." He looked around to see if anyone was within earshot before continuing. "I will be meeting with our spies to see what they have to say concerning the movements and interactions of the various Erain Houses while here in Tolemera for the last week. We can begin drawing up lists of Houses that seem favorable to them, and insert spies in those Houses to gather more information."

The empress groaned and rolled her eyes. "I hate political skulking and in-fighting; so much of it is simply contesting petty desires and stoking overblown egos." She said a silent prayer to the Creator that Tesra's work in the Academy of Clarens, way on the other side of the empire, would be done so that she could return to Tolemera and help with her sagacious advice.

Karsten grinned affectionately. "That is why the Creator established you as empress, so that you can help restore some depth and honor to the Seven Lands. It might even spill over to other nations in ways we cannot imagine."

She responded with playful sarcasm. "Oh yes, I am the only one the Creator has available for such tasks." Sounding weary at the thought, she said shallowly, "We will be lucky if we can influence Loreland for the better in the next twenty years."

"Unbelievable!" Kreida shook her head and spread her arms wide to indicate her disbelief. "You are saying that hardly anything has been accomplished since you gained the throne? Just look around, girl, and take notice. You have fought two wars and won, effectively neutralized our worst enemy, have the masses in love with you, increased the markets, danced with peasants and managed to marry a Genazi. What more do you want?"

Veranna smiled and gave Karsten a tight hug. "True, I do have my Genazi husband, and the rest can fly away for all I care."

Kreida frowned and looked at Karsten. "I hope that you can find a way to get some sense into her head. If not, we will either be dead or collecting chamber pots in Erain castles."

Karsten chuckled a moment, and said, "I do not think we have much to worry about. Look at how she has changed since her days at the Academy. Can you claim to have changed as much as she?"

Kreida looked at him as though he was a total dunce who had missed the obvious. "I have had to settle for only one man! That is not just change; that is a huge sacrifice."

Veranna's tone was dry as she said, "I will be sure to point that out to Treybal when next I see him." She turned to Karsten and her face lit up. "Do you still want to go with us for a picnic? Kreida and I are going to take some children from the town school for an outing a couple of miles southwest of the city. We can relax in the sun, or soak our feet in the stream, while the children play in the fields or woods. We plan on leaving the castle after midday."

His eyebrows rose, and he said, "That sounds like a wonderful idea. I will not be able to stay the whole time since I must return to the castle for the meeting with the spies. I take it you will be back around dinner time, and the meeting should be done by then."

"Well, then, let us get ready. Kreida, we will meet you at the front entry, shortly."

As she and Karsten walked toward their private chambers, Kreida said, "Do not keep us waiting. If you are late, everyone will be guessing about what you are doing."

Karsten shot back, "At least with us it is still a guess."

Kreida frowned and walked to her own room.

A half-hour later a wagon pulled up to the front entry of the castle, with two mounted guards in front and two in back. Kreida greeted the driver and then helped six children up and onto benches placed along each side of the wagon bed. Alicia, who was now near ten years old and the eldest of the children, looked after her cousin, Elly, and Tyrzah, a little girl of four years old. Three boys of seven and eight years of age sat on the bench opposite the girls and pretended to ignore them. When Karsten emerged from the castle and climbed into the driver's seat, the boys started asking him questions about the Genazi, and how old one had to be to serve as a warrior.

A couple of miles southwest of the castle, Karsten halted at a clearing in the surrounding woods. A stream flowed along the western side of the clearing, and paths were evident in the grass. The boys immediately jumped to the ground and started exploring the area, all but ignoring Kreida's shouts not to go too far away.

Karsten and Veranna chose a spot near trees to spread a blanket and set out food and drink. Kreida ate a large serving of bread, ham and cookies before setting off to playfully terrorize the children by pretending to be a lioness hunting prey. The children loved the game, their screams erupting after each attack. The fearsome Genazi woman pounced and gave them a ferocious tickling. After a time for refreshment, the children huddled together for a minute before scattering into the clearing. As they ran, they yelled back that Kreida could not get them now that they knew what to expect. They taunted her with dares and accusations that she was too slow and stupid to find them.

Veranna could not resist a bit of taunting of her own. "Gosh, Kreida, you are getting along wonderfully with the children. I am glad that you found some people on your own maturity level."

Kreida gave her a mean look. "Before you go smarting off, you should take a better look. I am helping them learn how to plan an attack and scare the stuffing from their opponents. Genazi train their children in tactics from the day they are born."

Karsten nodded agreement with the statement and then stood. "There is some truth in what she says, my love. In fact, she has been attacking men for years and cannot understand how they all learned to flee so quickly."

Veranna laughed, but Kreida threw a dirt clod at him. "Go ahead and make fun all you want; just make sure to thank me when they grow up to serve as warriors." She turned and looked out over the clearing, then crouched down and crept into the tall grass to stalk the children again.

Near the stream the girls rustled the tall grass and giggled a bit, then went still and silent once more. Kreida spotted them, then crept closer. A few feet away, she roared and launched herself at them, watching their faces for signs of fear and surprise. Instead, their surprise was mixed with anticipation. Too late she saw movement to her right. The boys jumped up from hiding spots and pushed her hard. She tumbled through the gooey mud on the bank of the stream and rolled into water, drenching her from head to foot.

She hurried to get out of the stream, but slipped and went down again. She regained her footing and stepped carefully out of the water. The children laughed and teased her for being a klutz, then ran back to the picnic spot. Kreida growled and sped after them, but they reached the spot first and were safe.

Looking like a swamp rat, Kreida yelled, "You no-good little brats; look what you have done; I am a mess. You just wait, you pack of..."

Veranna and Karsten could hardly control their laughter. The empress paused long enough to say, "Well, Kreida, what lesson have you taught the children today?" Another wave of laughter rolled over her.

Karsten calmed himself and gave the children a nod of admiration for their craftiness. "You did very well; knowing the difference between being the predator or the prey is one of the most important keys to survival. You should thank the lady Kreida for such an effective demonstration of this point."

The children laughed again and Kreida gave Karsten a jab with her elbow.

"Thanks a lot! Get that snotty look off your face and get a fire going so that I can dry off. Don't be slow."

He performed a mock bow and said, "Yes, my lady," then asked the children to help him gather some firewood. Ten minutes later they had a crackling fire going. Karsten, after readying the extra horse they had brought along for his use, gave Veranna a kiss.

"Do not be out too much longer, my dear; the evenings are still a bit too cool and it will be getting dark soon."

"Yes, my love. We should be back by the time you finish your meeting with the spies. We are going to roast some sausages over the fire and sing some songs, then be back a little after dusk."

"Good. Have fun and enjoy yourselves."

She gave him a sly wink, and said loud enough for only his ears, "I plan on enjoying myself into the night."

"Indeed? I will have to see to it that you are not disappointed."

Veranna's face blushed and she smiled self-consciously. "You had better get going."

He turned and climbed onto his horse, waving as he rode away. "I will see you later."

Veranna watched him ride out of view. Kreida smirked, "It looks like you have your own plan of attack in mind; we had best not let you get tired out."

Veranna absent-mindedly gave her a questioning frown. When the import of her comment struck home, her face turned red again. "Kreida, you have no sense of decency, especially around the children." She jumped over the fire and chased her across the clearing.

After working up a bit of a sweat playing with the children, a cool breeze floated by and gave her a chill. Her travel clothes were made of strong hemp fabric, but sitting by the fire helped her to warm up before continuing eating. The sausages were wonderful after some roasting, and the children gobbled them down like hyenas. Kreida stunned them all by eating more than anyone else. The children teased her and she let out a ferocious roar.

"Alright you little twerps, you have been giving me sass all day. It is time I taught you a lesson." She jumped to her feet, contorted her face into a savage, maniacal look and pulled her knife. "Now, it is my turn!"

The children screamed and ran off in several directions, with Kreida hot on their trail. A few minutes later she returned with Alicia over her shoulder.

"Hah ha! The little fawn thought she could escape the lioness, but here I have her." Kreida growled and pretended to bite Alicia's neck. The girl tried to scream, but it came out as a giggle because the bite actually tickled. Kreida set her on the ground by Veranna and then ran off to get the others. After about twenty minutes she had captured the two boys and Elly. The little blond girl sat on Veranna's lap and leaned her head back against her breasts, trying not to fall asleep.

The empress saw the girl's eyelids drooping and asked the guards to help get things loaded onto the wagon. It was almost nighttime, but her special night vision allowed her to see easily in the dark. She had the boys retrieve water from the stream to douse the fire and then sat down in the driver's seat. "Is everyone ready to go?"

Kreida, holding the sleeping Elly, nodded, as did the boys. Alicia's eyes suddenly went wide with alarm.

"Tyrzah is not here."

Veranna jumped to the ground. "Blessed Creator! I totally forgot about her." She and Kreida told the children to stay in the wagon while they took two of the guards to look for the little girl. They stayed within hearing distance of one another as they searched the areas where she would likely be. After ten minutes of furtive searching they still saw no sign of her.

"Kreida, you head east and search that end and I am going into the woods on the south end."

"I can hardly see anything, now. If we do not find her soon we will need to get Yanbre and his knights out here to search in the dark."

"True. Go east and circle around to the wagon, then race the children back to the castle. I will keep looking."

Kreida nodded and moved off to the eastern edge of the clearing, while Veranna, and the guards, headed into the woods. The young empress was desperate to find the little girl, knowing how fears suffered in youth could stay with a person even into adulthood. She thought that she could make out a trail through the grass and leaves. A great feeling of fear suddenly came over her, but she could not find any reason for it. About a quarter of a mile into the woods she came to another, smaller clearing and found Tyrzah sitting on the ground beneath a tall tree, whimpering in terror. At the sound of Veranna's voice, the little girl broke out in full-scale crying and held out her arms to be picked up. Veranna lifted her off of the ground and held her tight, whispering words of comfort into her ear.

Just as Veranna turned to call back to the guards, something landed on the back of her neck. Before she could swat it away, there came a sharp, needlelike pain into her spine. The pain exploded to excruciating and she was knocked to her knees, dropping Tyrzah onto the ground. She tried to scream but her voice was gone. Panic overtook her being. She could not move and felt nothing as she fell flat, face-down to the ground. A large, black and white-striped spider jumped from her back into the grass. Tyrzah screamed and stomped on it, breaking its legs and sending it to a slow death.

The pain in Veranna's neck turned into a burning sensation and spread quickly down to her tailbone. There was no sign of her guards as desperation pulsed through her being. All she could manage were short gasps while darkness filled her mind, her last thought a prayer that the Creator would keep Tyrzah safe.

Two men emerged from behind trees further south. Tyrzah tried to run, but one of the men grabbed her and slapped her hard, knocking her unconscious. The other man rolled Veranna's body onto its back and looked it over, the unseeing eyes staring straight up. He pulled at her clothes to inspect them for money or other valuables. The only things he found were gold earrings with a small diamond, and her wedding and Academy Sisterhood rings.

The man holding Tyrzah leaned over and scanned the body quickly. "C'mon, Bergy, take the rings and let's get goin'. Likely someone'll come lookin' for her any time, now." His dark brown hair and black clothes made it hard to distinguish his features in the darkness, but the totally callous attitude toward killing was as clear as the day. Greed was all that came through in his tone.

Bergy, a greasy, heavy-set man in his later forties, shook his head. "Listen, Farne, Sarim'tay said he wants to see the body before he pays us even a copper. The rings will help him identify the body, or all our work'll be for nothin'. Besides, with what he will pay us you'll be able to buy more rings than you can imagine. Now, summon the dragon."

Farne let out a sharp whistle and a moment later a large, deep-brown dragon glided into the clearing, setting down a few feet away. The two men tied Veranna's body to its back and tied Tyrzah next to it, then climbed onto the huge beast and hunkered down. Farne whistled once more. The dragon took a few quick steps and beat its wings, lifting into the air with ease. East they flew under the canopy of clouds to receive their pay.

CHAPTER 5

Kreida hurriedly removed the children from the wagon and raced to find Karsten and Yanbre. Both of them were in Karsten's office studying some old books about the ancient empire. Kreida's eyes were a hard glare and her mouth twisted into a snarl.

"What are you two doing sitting there looking at books? We have a lost child to find, and Veranna is alone out there."

Karsten rose and tossed the book onto his desk. "Alone? What are you talking about?"

"The little girl, named Tyrzah, ran away from our site and we forgot about her until we were about to leave. After some searching, Veranna told me to drive the children back and get Yanbre and his knights to help with the search. She stayed to keep looking."

Karsten dashed out of the room toward the stable, barking orders to servants along the way. Kreida followed him while Yanbre went to summon a hundred of his knights, and ordered servants to bring torches. Just as Karsten and Kreida mounted their horses, dozens of knights in their special armor poured into the stables to ready their horses. Even with the amazing speed with which they accomplished their tasks, Karsten urged them to move faster. In five minutes he, Kreida and Yanbre led them down the road.

Karsten hoped to find Veranna walking along the road with Tyrzah in her arms. When they reached the picnic spot and still did not see her, the Genazi warrior growled with frustration.

"Everyone, be quiet!" He cupped his hands around his mouth and yelled for Veranna, but no answer came. He jumped off his horse and started for the south end of the clearing, holding his torch close to the ground.

Yanbre directed his men to spread out in pairs, with one man reporting back every fifteen minutes. Two hours later they all regrouped in the clearing, Karsten looking anxiously at each pair of returning guards. "Yanbre, all I can see is a faint trail that she might have made. With all of the footprints from the day's outing, it is hard to identify a clear path."

"True. I hope that she did not fall into the stream and get swept into the river. That is a long ways away, and the stream is swift. I have sent a man back to the castle to alert more knights and to send riders along the stream to search for her."

"Good. Tell the men to get a large fire going and set up a camp here. We will search all through the night if we have to."

"Yes, my lord."

It was not much longer before they found the bodies of the dead guards. Each had a heavy arrow protruding from his throat. The arrows had penetrated into the spine, killing them instantly. Karsten's teeth ground as he cursed the darkness that kept him from seeing more of the clearing.

Dawn broke through the partly cloudy sky and still no sign of Veranna or Tyrzah could be found. More men from the army joined in the search, as well as many people from the city of Tolemera. Fear and tension showed clearly on the faces of many in the castle; fear for their beloved empress and for the fate of the empire should she be dead. The political ramifications could easily tear the empire apart in a great civil war.

LeAnre y'dob, formerly the Great Lady of the Koosti, opened her chamber door and sensed the emotional climate immediately. She was accustomed to the routines of servants and knew that some type of disruption had altered their performance. Many of the women were near to tears as they scurried along with hardly a glance at her. Suspicion and resentment had been the norm. However, with her belly swelling with child, she started receiving more attention. She headed toward the dining hall for breakfast and was amazed at the few people present. A serving girl hurriedly asked what she desired for breakfast, mentioning a half-dozen items available. LeAnre's face turned to a curious frown.

"Where are all of the people, and why are you all so quiet?"

The girl looked at her as though irritated. "Do you not know, my lady? The empress is missing after an outing, yesterday. No one can find a trace of her since last eve. The knights and troops have been out all night looking for her and a little girl." She straightened her dark blonde hair and closed her eyes for a second. "Please, my lady, choose your food quickly, for we are in a rush to send food to the searchers."

LeAnre was too surprised by the news to be offended with the girl's disrespect for her noble status. She requested ham, with biscuits and honey, and a large cup of tea. The girl had said that Veranna was missing, meaning that no body had been found. If the soldiers had been out all night and not found her, then she was either hidden very well or removed a great distance away from the area quickly. She would not just run away, so someone had to have taken her. But who? Doubtless there were any number of people who would want her removed from power, and they would gladly work together to accomplish that goal.

After eating quickly, she returned to her room and changed into some clothes suitable for riding, and then went to the stable to get a horse. Only a few were left, but the stableman found a smaller, plain, brown mare for her. After asking where the searchers had gone, she trotted out through the gate and down the road.

Fifteen minutes later she arrived at the site. Kreida, Karsten and Yanbre frowned when she approached, and the Genazi woman slowly drew her knife halfway from its sheath.

"What are you doing here, witch woman! You have not been granted leave from the castle."

LeAnre tried not to inflame any hostilities by ignoring Kreida.

"My lords Karsten and Yanbre, I am here to help. What may I do?"

Karsten took a moment to consider her request. "I doubt that there is anything you can do; the search has been very thorough in this area, and we found nothing. Search if you like, but do not get lost."

She could see easily that he was holding a great deal of frustration in check, so she made sure that she showed proper respect. "Thank you, my lord." She then started walking slowly into the clearing, pausing every now and then to consider how a child might proceed through such an area. She also noted how Kreida followed at a distance to keep an eye on her.

After an hour of meticulously studying the ground along the path leading southward, she came upon the second clearing where Tyrzah had been. Although the soldiers had trampled large parts of the clearing, she still could make out a pattern of impressions in the grass that sent a note of alarm through her. Knowing that Kreida was hiding nearby, she spoke loudly and clearly.

"My lady, Kreida, please summon lord Karsten; I have found evidence that his men have missed."

Kreida was furious that LeAnre knew she was hiding nearby, but did not want to allow her the satisfaction of knowing where. She crept stealthily and quickly away, then returned with Karsten and Yanbre a few minutes later.

An embarrassed frown on her face, the Genazi woman pretended not to have seen LeAnre for a while."Well, there you are, witch; we thought you had gotten lost. Did your demon-vision help you in any way?"

A slight smile curled LeAnre's lip. "Only in identifying another demon." She quickly dismissed Kreida from her mind and looked at Karsten. "My lord, I believe that I know why you have not found any trace of your wife."

His voice showed irritation at what he assumed was a wild goose chase. "We have been over this area many times and found nothing. I am in no mood for wasting time."

LeAnre bowed, impressed with how he controlled his anger under the circumstances. "My lord, if you look over the clearing toward the south, you will see a definite pattern in the grass. I am not referring to those made by your men."

He scowled at her, but took a deep breath and looked where she pointed. After concentrating for a few moments, he did see a pattern emerge. However, he was unable to interpret it in any meaningful way. Large, elongated depressions with four distinct sections on one end and a long trailer on the opposite end fit nothing in his experience. Two parallel sets about four feet apart headed southwest from one large trampled area.

LeAnre helped bring meaning to the evidence. "Your men would not have noticed this pattern during the night, especially since they would be unfamiliar with what things could make such tracks. Some type of large, flying beast was here and flew out of the clearing toward the southwest. We will not likely find any other tracks of humans since your men have trampled the area."

Karsten felt a moment of relief at the explanation, but his mind now worked extra hard to figure out who would do such a thing. "We know that Koosti use dragons, and Veranna and I flew aback two great eagles. Who else uses such creatures?"

LeAnre gestured as though the list was long. "Many lands use them, my lord. Emeraldia was kept safe from them before the empress opened the Curtain of Power. Since then the dragons have multiplied. North, south and east of you there are lands that have used them for centuries. Smugglers and slave traders use them as well. They move swiftly."

Yanbre tried to sound encouraging. "My lord, this is good news. If someone simply wanted her dead we would have found her body. Since they took the trouble to transport her, she must be worth something to them. It is likely we may receive a ransom note soon."

Karsten looked at Kreida who shrugged her shoulders, and then at Yanbre. "In that case, recall the soldiers. We must return to the castle and consider what we can do. LeAnre, you will write a list of all the lands and people who utilize dragons or giant birds."

The Koosti woman bowed and said, "Yes, my lord. May I look a little longer through the clearing and see what I can find? The empress is such a formidable fighter that I cannot help but believe that there must be some sign of how she was subdued."

Karsten agreed and motioned for her to continue. Ten minutes later, under a large tree, she stopped and pointed down at the ground.

"Here is the explanation."

The other three ran over to her and looked where she pointed, but had trouble recognizing anything under the trampled grass. LeAnre warned them not to touch what she uncovered.

"All of the tiny hairs on the limbs of this spider are poisonous. If I may use your knife, my lord, I can remove it from the grass." She did so and soon had it out on a sheaf of grass for examination. It was slightly larger than a man's hand, with black and white stripes on its legs and body. A dozen eyes stared out lifelessly while a small torn spot from just above its mouth oozed body fluid. LeAnre pointed to that spot.

"The stinger is gone. This is the way they hunt, letting the poison in the stinger continue to flow into its prey. The spider then grows a new stinger in a few days. You can see that someone with a small foot stepped on it and crushed it. That must have been the little girl. Someone then removed her and the empress on a flying creature."

Yanbre asked the dreaded, obvious question. "Are these spiders deadly?"

LeAnre looked at the ground and spoke softly. "Yes, almost always. However, that depends on the person stung and the amount of poison given."

Yanbre saw Karsten's jaw harden and his eyes smolder. The faithful castellan moved closer to him and spoke only loud enough for him to hear. "Karsten, I believe that she is alive. Her death would have come through my armor clearly, but I have felt nothing."

Karsten looked him in the eye and then placed his hand on his shoulder.

"Thank you, my friend. That is the only hope I can muster. Tell your men to return to the castle and rest. You and I must meet with the spy masters and get our webs working to gather information." He then turned to LeAnre. "Thank you for your help, but I must ask for more. When we return to the castle, I need you to write up a description of how these spiders are used."

She bowed and immediately started thinking about her past life when she seemed to know every spell and potion possible. It could prove crucial for her own survival since Veranna's death would end the protection she enjoyed from the Genazi fanatics, but even more so, from her own people. Ambitious chiefs or powerful men would rush to claim her, as well as anything belonging to her. Veranna's life was the only thing keeping her from certain death, or worse.

CHAPTER 6

Four nights later the brown dragon of the assassins landed in the hill country on the easternmost limits of the Koosti Empire. Dragons were a common sight in this part of the world, and one more would rouse no attention. Nevertheless, the assassins kept the darkness close about them; their livelihood depended on it.

Set against the base of a nearby slope was a modest-sized tent nearly invisible against the background of scrub bushes and rocks. The barest flash of dull light escaped as the entry flap opened a fraction of an inch.

The assassins unloaded Veranna's body and carried it into the tent, but they placed Tyrzah into a bag after making sure that she remained unconscious. Inside the tent stood one man in plain warrior's attire. He motioned for the assassins to lay the body into a wooden box next to him, and frowned when they told him what was in the bag.

"This is not part of the mission I assigned you. You should have tossed the child into the hills and avoided complications."

The assassins outnumbered the Koosti man two-to-one, and were larger. However, the voice and posture of this warrior intimidated them. They felt no shame at that fact, for this was no common warrior; this man was the chief of a large Koosti province. Sarim'tay, a Master of War among the Koosti, tried to keep emotion from his expression, but his voice showed both his displeasure with the assassins and anticipation at seeing the body revealed in the box.

He lit more candles and leaned over it. A wicked smile spread over his face as he studied the body. The hair was right, the height was correct, as were the eyes, and the rings on the left hand were exactly as reported. The face, limbs and breasts had swollen to twice their normal sizes, but this was typical of those killed by use of the spiders. He wanted to laugh in victory; this stupid girl had thought she could oppose him, but now she was simply a memory in the course of the world.

He straightened up and told the men to put Tyrzah into the box, tie the lid down, and then carry it out to a hole dug into the slope. After covering it up with dirt the three of them returned to the tent to settle their affairs.

Bergy bowed, and said, "Great Chief, we are done, now. We must be away before dawn, and request our payment."

Sarim'tay kept his expression inscrutable, as well as his voice. "You have done well and shall receive great reward." He half turned and reached for a bag full of something heavy, then handed it to Bergy. The assassin opened it and smiled with total greed.

"Ah, pure gold coin! Thank you, master. If ever you need our services again we will be more than ready." The two killers bowed again.

Sarim'tay snorted derisively as he said, "Your services shall not be required anymore." With one blur of motion he pulled his sword and sliced through the throats of the two men. Their eyes popped open, but a moment later they fell like sacks to the floor.

Sarim'tay extinguished the candles and walked out into the darkness. Letting out a soft whistle he saw a large, black form about fifteen feet away, move. Yellow eyes glowed as a dragon arose and lumbered over to him. In seconds he was on the beast's back and flying north to his province.

Another set of eyes peered cautiously from behind a large boulder forty feet from the tent. They followed the silhouette of the dragon against the dark clouds until it was gone from sight. A few more minutes of waiting and watching convinced the person to move closer to the tent to see what was going on.

While dragons were not uncommon in these parts it was the norm for them to utilize the town called Pullay, which was about four miles to the south. The town had been built for just that purpose centuries ago. Some, however, did not care for the presence of other people much, and would set down outside of occupied areas for a night's rest. This night brought little rest to the onlooker.

Standing up, the man's bushy beard and tall frame showed the tough physique of a veteran dragon rider. After listening for even the slightest noise from the tent, he decided to risk peeking in through the entry flap. He could see nothing in the total darkness and presumed the two men were asleep. Creeping in more carefully than a ferret, he reached down and touched the heel of a boot. No movement could be felt, not even that of breathing. The smell of blood wafted up and the man's pants felt wet. Taking a great risk on a hunch, the dragon rider pulled out an expensive item acquired in the far distant land of Seacorro, called a fire stick. Finding a smooth stone on the floor he pulled one end of the stick across it and a small flame sputtered to life.

Except for the two men, who were plainly dead, no one but the dragon rider was present. He lit the candles and saw the dark stain of blood over the floor. He extinguished the candles and allowed his eyes to adjust before exiting the tent, then went to the slope where the men had done something. Quickly finding the half-buried box, he guessed that the men assumed that the natural process of dirt and rock falling down the slope would bury it further. He risked another fire stick and saw the body of a woman lying in a fetal position, and a small girl laid near her feet. The girl breathed! She could be sold to the slave marketers in Seacorro for a decent price. The dead body had rings on the left hand; he would need to get it home to try getting them off, for the flesh was swollen around them tightly.

He turned and hooted like an owl, and what had looked like a huge rock unfolded into a large, dark-brown dragon. It glided down from a ways up the slope, landed and quickly lay on its belly.

The man lifted the dead body from the box and secured it in a narrow basket on the back of the dragon. The girl he tied to the saddle and then commanded the dragon to fly southeast. The beast complied easily, which was one of the advantages of the dark-brown line. They were nearly as strong as the blacks and far less cantankerous. They also had greater endurance in flight, making them excellent transports.

By midmorning he saw his home nestled in a hollow of the mountains and set down in the dragon stable yard in back. The beast was not really tired; however, a little sleep would do it good.

Lifting his cargo into his timber frame home, he laid the body on a table and placed the girl near the fireplace where large coals still glowed. Fresh wood soon crackled and gave some light as the man examined the body. He surmised that it must have been dead only a short time since no putrid odors were detectable, and the blood veins were noticeably dark and full. He lit a candle and tilted the head back to look into the mouth and nose. There were no bits of gold on the perfectly formed teeth, so he held his knife in front of the nose to reflect the candle's light up inside. There were no gems or precious metals; the only items of value were the rings on the left hand. After cutting off the fingers he could remove the rings and throw the corpse to the dragon for a treat.

Just as he started to pull the knife away he thought his eyes were playing tricks on him; there was a momentary dulling of the light on the blade. He held it in place for a few more seconds and, sure enough, a very faint steam on the cold blade dulled the light again. The body was alive! He pulled the shirt down from her chest and placed his ear over her heart. Very slow and shallow, he could barely make out the sound of a heartbeat.

He rolled her over and looked along the spine. Finding what he expected, he grabbed hold of the spider's stinger after wrapping a thin piece of leather around it. With one crisp, hard yank he pulled it out of the spine. The body jerked and went flaccid again, but the breathing was a bit stronger.

The man knew about the spiders and realized that they preferred to keep their victims just on the side of life so that the juices would not spoil before they had a chance to be sucked out.

The bones would be softened and gradually turned to gel by the poison, as would most of the other parts of the body. Now that the stinger was out, the body would try to fight the poison. Heat and more gelling of the tissues were the result, with survival highly improbable.

The man held his hand against her forehead and noticed that her temperature was already increasing. The only chance he had for selling her at a profit was to get her to Seacorro, where they had experience treating those bitten by the spiders. Their slave market was also one of the busiest, and the little girl would make him some money. She awoke from her drug-induced slumber and cried, after which she ate some food and drank water. She bothered the man with her crying, so he placed a small amount of sleeping potion in her milk.

The flight to Seacorro could take nearly a week. He readied his supplies and took a nap, then loaded his human cargo onto the dragon. After placing the woman in the carrying basket he put a tube to her mouth and she unconsciously gulped down some water. Her fever was high but he could do nothing for it.

Off he flew into the east, planning what he would do with the money from the sale of two slaves.

CHAPTER 7

On the far southwestern corner of the Empire of the Seven Lands, sat the city of Clarens, where the empress had grown up. It flourished more than it had for several hundred years now that the ancient rulers of the line of Emeraldia were in power once more. Veranna and her representatives had opened up the Lands for greater trade and collaboration, effectively undermining the stranglehold that the guilds had imposed for generations. Free markets boomed with the rise of new business, and the need for trained workers and clerks grew every day.

That need was keenly felt by the woman sitting behind the Head Mother's desk in the Academy, for which the city of Clarens, was renowned. Tesra, the only known Mother of the Academy to have survived the murderous raid of the late Duke Weyland, contemplated the staff and supplies the school would need to train more girls for business. The school had centered on raising and training orphaned girls, but there had always been those sent by a noble house for their education. Whereas the school had depended on the good graces of the people for sustenance, the Academy now had to charge the businesses fees for training workers.

A young girl in the dress of a student walked quickly up to Tesra's office door and knocked softly. The middle-aged Mother responded without looking up from her papers.

"Yes, what is it, Chalane?"

The girl curtsied and entered the office, her large, brown eyes scanning anything available to view. Her long braid of light brown hair hung down across the right side of her chest, which rose and fell quickly since she had run through the halls to the office.

"Mother Tesra, a pigeon just arrived with a note for you; it is marked 'urgent.'"

Tesra nodded for her to place the note on her desk. "Thank you, dear. Make sure that you do not miss any of your classes."

The girl curtsied and then hurried out the door and down the hallway.

Tesra stared at the note, an inexplicable sense of foreboding made her loath even to touch the imperial scrap. Ever since coming across the ancient volume, *Mysterium Konsequenter Ergonum*, in Veranna's castle bed chamber, she wondered if she had worried herself over nothing. The book recorded events that followed those times when the Curtain of Power was opened. Veranna had opened it more than once and accomplished great things. However, those openings had consequences that were unpredictable; when and how they would come could not be foreseen.

She finally lifted the scrap of paper and examined it. It looked like Karsten's handwriting and was clearly written quickly. As she opened the note and read the contents, a tear dribbled down her cheek. Her beloved adopted daughter, Veranna, was missing and presumed abducted by an enemy or slave traders. With her was a little girl named Tyrzah. Karsten requested that Clarens, along with every other city in the Seven Lands, activate their spies and informants to glean any information they could about her whereabouts. He was frantic to find her. LeAnre had identified a spider used by assassins and slavers that was most likely deadly. Two guards had been killed with arrows.

Fear and rage filled the Mother of the Academy. She wanted to fling the old book of *Mysterium Konsequenter* onto the fire in hope that it would end any of its influences. However, that would not stop the terrible consequences; the book was simply a record and commentary on events.

She got up from behind her desk and went to the door, then yelled for Leighana. A few minutes later the young woman walked in, a puzzled look on her face.

"Yes, Mother Tesra; you called?"

Tesra refused to break down and sob. Leighana was now a Sister of the Academy, and a good one, too. She needed to see Tesra controlling herself. Leighana had been through her own time of hideous abuse by Duke Weyland, and had a soft spot in her heart for anyone else so treated. Tall and slender, with long, blonde hair in an Academy braid, she had a core of steel beneath her fair appearance.

"Yes, I did. I need you to keep things in order around here while I am away for a few days, if not longer." A sniffle broke through before she could continue. "Veranna is missing and feared kidnapped. No one knows where she might be, so I am going to start inquiries with some of the contacts I've made over the years. I may be gone for quite a while if I come up with anything."

Leighana gasped and sat down heavily in a chair, her mind reeling with emotions. "Who would want to do this; she has made life so much better for us all. Are there any clues?"

"No; only a poisonous spider not native to the Seven Lands, and evidence of some type of flying beast. No enemy has yet sent a ransom note and it has been nearly a week since she disappeared. I agree with her husband that slave traders took her and a little girl. We must pray that Veranna and the girl are still alive."

"Yes, Mother; Didi and I shall see that everything stays on track here. I pray that you find Veranna and the girl; if they are harmed I pray that the Creator will fill our troops with strength."

Cold as ice, Tesra looked out through the window as she said, "If either of them are harmed, the dogs that have done so had better hope they run faster than I." She took a deep breath and turned toward the door. "I am heading to the city center, but I will be back before going anywhere else."

Leighana curtsied and bade her success, then watched her step quickly down the hall and out the main entry. When she was gone the echo of her steps still pulsed through the school.

Tesra went straight to the mayor's office and spoke directly to him, Baron Theodore Lenard. After relating the information, Tesra obtained permission to arrest and detain anyone who she felt had information relevant to Veranna's disappearance.

For the next week she moved among the circles of underground traders to try and catch even a word of any transaction dealing with slaves. Slavery was illegal in the Seven Lands, but that did not stop its practice in some quarters.

No information came forth; it was as though Veranna had never existed. The traders lived in a world unto themselves and had little regard for the policies of any particular land. This frustrated Tesra, for riff-raff usually knew what other riff-raff were up to. After thinking on it a while she realized that there was something useful in this lack of information. If there was no word among the domestic traders, then someone from outside the empire must be involved.

Escorted by six veteran Rockhounds, she headed east for Grandshire, hoping to glean something helpful from the underground forces there.

✡ ✡ ✡

CHAPTER 8

In the predawn the Koosti dragon rider set down in the low hills about an hour's ride from the city of Seacorro. Smugglers and slavers utilized small encampments for their business, for the Seacorran policy regarding dragons was combative. They believed that dragons were the spawn of strange demons that required destruction. Slavers were seen as a necessary evil in that they brought people to Seacorro who were obviously under the curse of the Creator by being given over to slavery.

The journey from the eastern part of the Koosti Empire had taken more than a week. The dragon rider had to stop many times for water along the way, for Veranna, even though unconscious, drank a great deal. Her flesh continued to swell as it battled the spider's poison and her temperature remained high.

Making sure that both Veranna and Tyrzah were secure on the dragon, the rider headed for an inn at the center of the encampment. It was made mostly of thick poles and heavy canvas in order to be dismantled rapidly should the Seacorrans send a raiding party after them. It had not happened for a long time, but the smugglers knew that the threat was real.

As the rider walked inside and his eyes adjusted to the candle and lamp light, a throaty, low-pitched woman's voice called out from the long bar across the room.

"Pren-ye, come over here and sit down; it has been a while since we last saw you."

The woman was shorter than average, with an ample bosom and a slender waist. Short, stubby legs protruded past a knee-length wool skirt. Her bright, white hair straggled down to her shoulders, contrasting with her swarthy, oily skin tone. She pulled out a stool for him along the bar.

Pren-ye nodded and sat down heavily, his dark gray eyes matching his beard. "Hello, Marlenye; it has been a while. However, business has been slow and routine, so I have not had reason to come this way."

Marlenye let out a deep chuckle that sounded as if it came from a hollow barrel. "I was thinking you had been so worn out by my girls last time that you had fallen from your dragon and cracked your neck." She paused and clapped her hands three times. From behind a thick curtain came two women wearing sheer cotton shifts that evidenced a lot of use. There was nothing remarkable about their features except a devious, seductive look to the eyes. Marlenye barked two quick commands to them. Pointing at one with dark blonde hair, she said, "Fetch food for our customer." To the other, a woman with slick, black hair, who already looked old due to too much servicee, she said, "Relieve the knots in his back and shoulders."

Pren-ye leaned onto the bar as the woman started massaging him. Long hours on the dragon had made him stiff and sore; the woman's strong hands soon had him feeling relaxed and limber. A few minutes later the other woman set a plate of hot meat, squash, potatoes and eggs in front of him. After he finished, Marlenye sat next to him.

"If you have come this far you must have some business."

"I do. I need to find a slave trader. Are there any around?"

Marlenye smiled coyly. "Oh, yes, there is one with some of my girls right now. It should not be long before he is finished. Go sit by the fire and rest until he comes out."

Two hours later a tall, burly man with a modest beard of gray and brown, stepped out from behind a curtain that hung over the opening to a passage leading to the back of the inn. He rubbed a beefy hand over his pockmarked face and small, black eyes.

Marlenye handed him a warm, wet washcloth and then served him a cup of tea. "Well, now, Arigush, did my girls serve you well?"

Arigush grunted and shook his head. "Yeah, Mar, they did. I wish I had more time; I am due back in Seacorro before midday and must ready my latest stock for display at the market."

Marlenye put an arm around his back and smiled. "So, you will have some extra money to spend. I can help you do that. My girls are always eager."

A short bark of a laugh shook him as he turned toward her and gave her a quick peck of a kiss. "'Eager' is not the right word, Mar. They have the manner of wild dogs in heat. I am not complaining, especially since the women in Seacorro are so restrained by their idiotic religious ideas."

Marlenye gestured toward Pren-ye. "This man is named Pren-ye. He is here on business and may be able to help you increase your profits. Then you will not have any excuse for staying away."

Arigush turned his gaze on Pren-ye and studied him for a moment. The early morning light helped illumine his features. "He looks like one of them Koosti vermin. What could he have that I might want?"

Pren-ye rose and walked over to Arigush's table. "I am, as you have noted, from the great empire of the Koosti. However, I will take no offense at your presence since we have something in common. I speak of two slaves to sell, a woman and a girl. I do not know if they are mother and daughter, but they were taken together. The woman has been bitten by a spider..."

Arigush shook his head and waved his hand for Pren-ye to stop. "You are out of your mind if you think I am stupid enough to buy a dead woman from you, and little girls are hard to sell since they need so much training and tending by others."

Pren-ye nodded his admission of Arigush's point, but hurried to make his own. "What you say is obvious; however, the woman is a value even when dead for she wears two rings that look to be quite costly. Simply selling her for the rings would be a great profit. If she survives, then the owner has a useful slave, as well. The girl is a bonus."

Arigush eyed him as he considered the offer, wondering what risks he might be taking if he accepted. Finally, he stood and headed toward the door. "I will take a look before I decide."

Pren-ye nodded and led him out to where his dragon rested. Opening the lid to the cargo box, he was surprised at Veranna's appearance in the morning light. Her body was now a light blue and the swelling of tissues had transformed her into what looked like a small hippopotamus. Her mouth was pinched into a round hole resembling an octopus' sucker, while her emerald green eyes were fiery red, and her breasts had swollen to over twice their normal size. Tyrzah lay beside her like a limp rag.

Arigush had seen the effects of the spider poison on others, but not to this degree. "Won't be long before she is dead; it is amazing that she has lived this long. Why did you not just chop off her fingers and take the rings?"

Pren-ye just shrugged. "That can be done by whoever has her, dead or not. If she lives, then she can be sold again for profit."

Arigush took a moment to ponder his potential profit margin. As the Koosti had said, there was every reason to expect a favorable trade. "Fine; I offer you fifteen hundred kranys for both."

Pren-ye frowned. A krany was roughly equal to a Koosti gelde, and half the value of Emeraldian stadia. While it was a sizeable amount of money, he had expected more. It was obvious, however, that the slaver would not budge on his offer, and Pren-ye could not waste time trying to locate another.

"So be it, but you know your offer is near robbery."

Ten minutes later and Arigush drove his wagon toward Seacorro, with his cargo stretched out in back. Pren-ye headed back into Marlenye's inn for a day's rest, purchasing the services of two girls. After exhausting his sensual pleasures he lay down to sleep. He did not awaken in this world, and Marlenye added his money to her own. She increased it by selling his body to another dragon rider with a hungry dragon.

✿ ✿ ✿

CHAPTER 9

Arigush drove his wagon into the main slave trader's depot in the bustling city of Seacorro. The city was ancient and its architecture showed a variety of styles and materials. Piers extended into the river and sea harbor, with many ships in and out for trade. Warehouses of whitewashed plaster and stone operated day and night to accommodate trade, and the streets near the docks were dotted with inns and cafes.

The clear sky of mid-morning was full of gulls and bright sunlight that lit up the central display platform of the slave market. Men, women and children stood tied to strong metal turnstiles that allowed buyers to easily inspect their bare bodies. Slaves were brought in from many lands including Koosti, Deeri, Felinii, Randalian and other far-flung places. Black, white, yellow and reddish skins were further differentiated by eye and hair color, as well as bone structure and facial traits.

Veranna lay on her back on the platform, too miserable to know what was going on around her. Even on the cold stone her temperature made her sweat. The swollen tissues of her body made her feel as though she would burst, and her eyes could only open into tiny slits. Noises sounded as though underwater, and her body ached terribly, especially when she tried to move.

Arigush was a master of bartering and before long doubled his money with the sale of Veranna and Tyrzah. He spotted a wealthy man well known for trading in jewelry and centered in on him. The man was in his later fifties, tall, of medium build with a short beard and sea gray eyes. His fine linen pants and shirt were black, as was his felt hat. His questions to Arigush were direct, no nonsense inquiries that Arigush dared not lie about, for the man had the reputation of a keen mind able to see through falsehood.

Arigush bowed respectfully as he responded, "My lord Knoxun, I do not know where the woman comes from. The effects of the spider poison make it difficult to gauge her features, and the trader I bought her from did not mention where he got her."

Knoxun glanced at him, and then asked, "Where was the trader from?"

"All I know is that he was Koosti."

Knoxun spat on the floor. "Bah! Koosti; may they burn in the fires forever, along with their Master. If one of them brought her, then she is likely a whore rewarded with gaudy rings. She is under the Creator's curse and must suffer purging before death. Load her into my wagon; the little girl is obviously under the curse of something her parents did. You will have to find another buyer for her." Tyrzah was now awake and struggled against her bonds. As Veranna was loaded onto Knoxun's wagon and driven away, the little girl cried hysterically. A sharp slap from a handler dazed and quieted her.

Knoxun did not care for slave traders. They simply performed a necessary function in delivering those condemned by the Creator to special punishment. Atonement and rehabilitation were only possible under harsh discipline. The Creator had assigned this woman to a fate whereby mercy might be possible in the next life; in Seacorro they knew that their fate was to serve the Creator's means of punishing and reforming these heretics and moral cesspools enough for the Creator to deal with them more gently.

A half-hour later they reached a large estate nestled in the low hills of the northern sector of the city where the nobles and rich people lived. High walls of stone and plaster surrounded large houses that served as winter homes, with most owning huge estates in the country, too. Sandstone was readily available and used for many buildings and walls, while the wealthy purchased granite and marble from quarries east of the city.

Knoxun instructed his driver to halt near the rear gate after they made their way across the grounds. The gate opened onto a well-traveled alley used by delivery services, vendors and slaves going about their tasks. The nobles and wealthy often used it as a by-pass route when traffic was heavy on the main roads. Before reaching the gate, Knoxun ordered another slave they passed to retrieve a poison rack. The man threw down his rake and ran to do as told.

A few minutes later, Knoxun ordered his driver to place Veranna onto the rack, front side down. The rack sat just inside the rear gate, over a metal sewer grate. The crossbars of the rack were padded, with one crossing under her collarbone, one at the bottom of the ribs, one supporting the hips and leather straps to hold her arms and legs. She looked to be on hands and knees just above the ground, with her head held by a padded leather harness.

Knoxun gave more orders to the servant who had brought the rack. "Do not put on her clothes, just cover her bottom and privates with a shawl. The direct sunlight will help to reduce the effects of the poison, and she will be burning with fever. Douse her with water at least twice an hour, and do not let the insects lay eggs in her eyes, mouth or other places. Adjust the angles of the rack several times a day so that she does not get sores from irritation. Make sure that none of the children throw things at her or hit her with sticks or whips. Let me know if and when she starts to recover; she will regain a desire for food and be very hungry. Feed her only warm chicken broth; her mouth will be too tender for solid food."

He walked back to his house for his midday meal and religious studies, wondering if this new slave would survive.

For Veranna, everything was a blur. Her head ached and she felt like she was in the middle of the hottest desert imaginable. Objects failed to resolve in her vision, a thick haze obscuring the different colored blobs moving past her narrow-slit eyes. A strong feeling of pressure caused terrible pain in her abdomen, and loud noises were dull echoes in her ears, leaving her unable to detect anyone's presence. Her underside from the bottom of her chin to the top of her knees was now chalk white, and in the direct sunlight her backside from her neck to her calves turned an inky, dark blue. She did not realize that she was naked; all she knew was the agony of her afflicted body.

The shock of cold water could not bring on a tensing of her muscles because of the poison, but the relief of her temperature felt wonderful. A moment later a tube was in her mouth and cool water trickled down her throat. Whoever was giving the water to her also poked the middle of her back, sending a spear-like jolt of pain through her. She could not reflexively gasp or scream. Sheer agony danced through her head, as her hair was pulled tight. A sharp snipping sound echoed in her ears and her head felt a little cooler.

For all she knew years had passed. The only thing she could remember was a momentary satisfaction when doused with water. In reality only a few hours had gone by when some loud yells registered on her hearing. Vague forms raced in and out of her field of vision, seeming to approach and then hurrying away. Something poked her left cheek, then another poke jabbed into her chest, followed by several to her buttocks and legs. Multiple voices were just beyond her ability to take in and the poking grew into a feeling of fire on her skin. A panic rose up in her as she finally understood that she was naked, exposed for all the world to see.

"I am telling you, Tarn, it is a swamp beast! Look at the size of it. I bet it could eat one of us without any problem."

The voices seemed to all come at the same time, now. Three blobs of different colors passed her vision, and more poking increased the panic welling up in her mind. She managed to turn her head toward the blobs and let out a raspy exhalation that resembled a dragon's hiss.

The blobs screamed and ran out of sight. One of them darted past and gave her a hard slap on her right buttocks, sending excruciating pain through her. Soon a cacophony of voices circled around and hard slaps impacted her bare skin at virtually every point.

"It is tied down...It cannot get you if you do not get too near its mouth...The tongue is probably poisonous; do not let it sting you...It looks like a female ready to lay eggs. It will fill the city with deadly beasts."

The yelling went on and on, increasing the pounding in her head. Not being able to scream made the pain ten times as bad. She passed out before hearing the loud voice of the slave tending her. He yelled at the boys to stop their abuse of her and go away.

The next thing she knew was another dousing of water. It helped reduce the pains from the beating of the children, and gave her temporary relief from the fever. Her vision was still blurry but her hearing had improved with the slight reduction of swelling around her ears. She could even make out a tense exchange going on to her left.

"You are a servant and should know better than to ever yell at your masters. My son has every right to punish anyone so cursed by the Creator." The woman's voice had an odd accent, but conveyed pride and derision. She took a step toward Veranna and slapped her viciously just below the left shoulder blade. Veranna's muscles tried to tense; however, only a wisp of a shrill yelp managed to come from her.

"This is not a swamp beast; this woman is clearly a heretic, an evil brute who must be beaten into submission. My son and his friends were helping your master by initiating her training."

The servant bowed and strove to keep his voice in check. "My Lady Aquaneh, you are correct; however, my master gave me strict orders not to let anything damage his property. He wants this slave to recover and be saleable. I am sure that you recognize the difficulty of my position, my lady."

Aquaneh snapped back, "Moral and legal principles are beyond slaves, so never presume to share your ideas of enlightenment with me." She took her son, Tarn, by the hand and moved closer to Veranna. "You did right, my son, to punish this sinful woman. Remember her well, for this is the punishment given by the Creator to heretics and sinners." She glared at Knoxun's servant and then walked quickly back to her own home a ways down the street, taking Tarn with her.

The servant, Beneto, shook his head in relief as she walked away. It had been over forty years, since his early twenties, that he had served Knoxun. Many years of resistance had accomplished nothing for him, so at age fifty he surrendered his will out of a sense of total futility and was granted permission to wear the earth brown of a reforming servant. Veranna would wear the plain gray that signified abject slavery. Whereas Beneto had a measure of freedom to enter the city unaccompanied, Veranna would always be monitored. Everyone knew that un-reformed slaves had to be beaten into submission to drive the evil from them, and that being a slave meant you were under a curse from the Creator.

Beneto poured another bucket of cold water over Veranna, noting that the blows given her by Aquaneh and the children left scrapes and bruises. He also realized that the inky blue of her backside was less dense. He surmised that she was a woman with strong recuperative qualities, as well as a strong will. He felt sorry for her already, knowing the pain and humiliation she would suffer as they methodically reduced her to nothingness.

Two more days of agony passed. The skin along her backside necrotized and cracked, leaving hundreds of sore and itchy spots. Beneto washed her down with soapy water and rubbed on a thick salve that reduced the cracking and itching. She still could not move her limbs, but she could turn and raise her head a bit.

The next day she regained her hearing, and her vision cleared. The skin along her backside started peeling, leaving new, pink skin exposed to the sun. She found that she could grunt to answer questions Beneto asked. He applied more salve to reduce sun damage and saw that her front side skin color was returning to normal. He was amazed at the speed of her recovery.

The first few attempts at swallowing chicken broth resulted in vomiting, but slowly she was able to keep more down than spit up. The next day her appetite was voracious. Not only broth; bread and boiled vegetables were a feast that seemed incomparable to anything she had ever experienced.

In the late afternoon, Tarn, and four other children from the neighborhood, passed by on the opposite side of the street. He pointed toward Veranna and said to one of the girls with him, "That is what I was telling you about; that is the heretic."

The girl fixed her gaze on Veranna and crossed the street to stand in front of her. After studying her for a moment the girl slapped Veranna's face and yelled, "Slut." She then ran back to the other side, laughing and jeering.

Beneto heard the commotion and walked out through the gate to see what was happening. He saw the children mocking and reviling Veranna, but was too late to stop Tarn from throwing a clay and rock clod at her.

Veranna saw Tarn throw the clod but could do nothing to evade it. All she could do was try to shift her head to avoid having it strike her eyes. It impacted on her eyebrow over her right eye and sent a sharp jolt through her whole body. She screamed in pain and lost track of everything around her. When she came to her senses she had trouble seeing through the blood oozing from the wound. The throbbing pain pounded in her head and she prayed for loss of consciousness.

Beneto moved in front of her and yelled at the children to stop damaging his master's property. The girl who had slapped Veranna clenched her fists and stomped purposely across the street to confront him.

"You, slave, are never to speak to me like that again. I am a princess of House Faresea, and will do as I please. If I wish to tear out this evil woman's eye and feed it to a rat, you will not dare to stop me. You have caused your master great difficulty already; my father will deal with you both."

With that she turned and rejoined her friends, speaking with them clandestinely. A moment later, all five of them began a barrage of clods. Beneto blocked most of them, but a few still got by and struck Veranna on the back and legs. She yelped and cried, a great deal of her misery stemming from the fact that she could not move to evade the clods or defend herself. She did notice that Beneto took quite a pounding before the children stopped and walked away. He calmly brushed debris from his clothes and cleaned Veranna's wounds.

The next day her fever broke, leaving her feeling chilled from the ocean breezes. Beneto washed her down with warm water after brushing her skin to loosen up the dead tissue. It hurt and felt great at the same time. He raised her into a sitting position and, at first, it was difficult for her to keep her head up. She managed to steady it uprightly and looked around as far as her eyeballs could move, glimpsing the sea between buildings down below and many pines and madrona trees. Ornamental gardens lay resplendent on the hillside estates, and the buildings were painted in bright red, green, blue, tan and gray. The roofs were made of gray or brown tiles. Servants and merchants scurried about, some driving wagons and others on foot.

Beneto used a wet rag and gently washed her face, clearing away the crusty buildup from around her eyes, ears and nose.

"Are you able to control your body well enough that I can move you indoors?"

She tried to say 'yes,' but all that came out was a grunt.

He gave her a fatherly smile. "Good; I went to the market and selected a slave dress that should fit you while leaving room for growth. When the last of the sickly waters is gone from your body you will be skinnier than a stick. It will be quite a while until you are able to use your limbs; I am amazed that you are even alive and able to keep your head up. Mighty warriors die from the spiders very quickly. Please forgive our leaving you naked in the sun, but it is the only way to combat the poison of the spiders. Somehow, the light of the sun neutralizes the poison. It is the only known way to save one so bitten."

He unfolded a simple, gray cotton dress and placed it on her. Veranna felt so much relief at being clothed once more. However, a soul-wrenching sense of humiliation and shame at having been naked for all to see brought her to break out in hoarse sobs. How did she come to such a terrible situation? Why was she here?

Beneto felt terrible for her. He had gone through much the same experience many years before and still had to control his emotions lest his rage get the better of him. He dried away her tears and hugged her close, stroking her cheek as a kindly father would a heart-broken daughter.

"I know, dear child, I know," he said softly. "I will try to help you through this horrible time so that you can recover your dignity. They will look upon you as a worthless slave, but to me you are more noble than one of their queens."

Veranna tried to shake her head affirmatively to his comment, but he did not understand.

A curious look on his face, he asked, "Are you trying to respond to something I said?"

She could only answer with a grunt.

"Ah, about your dignity?"

She shook her head 'no' and gave a short grunt.

"Are you saying you are a slave?" After another short grunt of 'no' his eyebrows rose and his eyes opened wide.

"A queen?"

She sloppily bobbed her head 'yes.'

"Dear Creator!" He studied her features to see if they might spark a memory. "I have met virtually all of the queens of noble houses, even of those of Faresea's allies, but do not recall seeing you before. Are you newly married to a ruler of a far distant province?"

She grunted negatively, frustration building since she could not communicate easily.

"Is this not a wedding ring on your finger?"

'Yes.'

"Were you sentenced to slavery for cheating on your husband?"

A hard grunt of 'no' came back from deep in her throat.

Beneto was at a loss as to how to place her. He was always hearing snatches of news and gossip in the marketplace, but nothing that would apply to this woman. He decided to try a slow, but hopeful, method of getting more information.

"Are you literate?"

'Yes.'

"Then, I will slowly mention letters and you will respond when I say those that spell the name of your realm."

He uttered the alphabet until he came to the letter 'e,' when Veranna grunted. He came then to 'm' and she grunted again.

When the word 'Emeraldia' was spelled out, Beneto gasped silently and felt sorry for her.

"So, that is why you are here; your mind has snapped and you imagine yourself a queen of legendary people from long ago. They hope to punish you to the point where you abandon such fantasies."

Veranna hung her head and wept again. This man, the only one to show her kindness, thought her insane.

"Do not worry, you poor woman; I will shield you as much as I can. However, I implore you not to mention this to anyone else, if you are not asked. They will think you a heretic worthy of sore treatment and death. Besides, your brown eyes do not match the tales of the Emeraldians. I know something about that topic since I was an academy lecturer before my enslavement."

Veranna awkwardly bobbed her head toward her left hand and stared at it. Beneto understood that she wanted him to look at it, too.

"Your hand? The rings?"

'Yes.'

"Your wedding ring certainly looks like one that a woman from a noble house would wear, but the other is very interesting." He saw that the ring had a ruby on it, shaped like a dagger with a hilt designed like a feather plume. Letters in an archaic script wound around its circumference. He was astonished as he read and interpreted them. On the outer face was written, 'Through knowledge do we comprehend the Creator's wisdom.'

Sliding the ring off of her finger he studied the writing on the inner face. 'By the Creator's wisdom give we reverent service.' He carefully slid the ring back on her finger and looked at her with wonder. "Those words were the foundation for all of the ancient academies in this land, and rings like these are given only to those who are certified teachers in them. Are you an instructor in an academy?"

She grunted another yes and felt another round of frustration welling up inside. The ability to communicate at this level was a horrid tease that left her mentally exhausted.

Beneto sensed her travail and lifted her from the rack. "You are tired and need rest. I will move you into the slave quarters where these nasty children cannot abuse you. You are so light that I have no trouble carrying you. Today I will give you solid food and fish; tomorrow we will practice getting your limbs to work. It will take time, but the poison will eventually be gone from your body. I can hardly wait to hear what else you might tell me, even if the poison has befuddled your mind. You are either a tragedy or a total loon."

He gently laid her onto a cushioned mat on the floor of the slave quarters. The building was positioned against the back wall of the estate, about two hundred feet from the main house. The room he placed her in had no window, but along the top of the wall ran a ventilation opening. Five other mats lined the floor and showed recent use. The walls were plain plaster and the doorway had no door. The floor was made of well-set, dressed sandstone, and each mat had only one plain cotton blanket.

Beneto straightened and looked around the room, then shrugged his shoulders. "I know that it is not much to speak of, but it is better than being outside. Get some more rest and try not to soil yourself. I will be back in a few hours with food and drink."

Veranna felt safer now that she was away from the street, but fear for her condition, as well as Tyrzah's safety, brought her to tears once more. Her heart ached for just one soft word from Karsten, and she wondered if she would ever see him again. Even Kreida's obnoxious manners would be a gift from above.

She now understood the terrible agony that Tesra had experienced when taken captive by the Koosti and turned into a dragon wife. The sense of loneliness and despair was overwhelming, especially when her own body would not respond to her will.

The later morning sun glanced through the ventilation space and landed softly on her eyes. Spots remained in her mind as she closed her eyes and her exhausted body drifted off into sleep. A dream arose in her mind. A bright sun shone on the crests of tidal waves in a vast ocean. The waves crashed onto a shoreline of hard stone and barnacles, washing them clean. The waves continued further inland to scour an old city, carrying away many in their currents while others rode them without fear. New life arose in the city and the waves receded, leaving the land clean for those who remained.

The dream shifted to home and the sunspots turned to roiling vortices and flares. Tolemera was shaken by a great, horned beast with twenty-four razor sharp claws. In the city the people strove against one another, angry that they were subject to sinister forces once again. Karsten walked alongside Yanbre down the main street, a wicked gash above his left eye. In many other cities of the empire chaos strove to overtake them. Red lights darted among the hills of eastern Loreland and also in the Boar's Spine Mountains. They turned into flames and barred the passes, blades of fire cutting down any who ventured in.

Next, a stream formed when rain fell from the sky onto the castle in Tolemera. The rain issued from an opening like a curtain. The water was emerald green and carried all of the ills to the ends of the empire. Veranna tried to staunch the stream, but it only spread into unforeseeable directions, along with its consequences. She threw up her hands and screamed to the Creator in total frustration. The dream ended with the stream flowing on.

CHAPTER 10

The sun shone brightly over the city of Grandshire, but Tesra hardly noticed. Tromping up the stairs of the *Red Tailor* inn, she simply pointed at the large lump of abused flesh sitting by the door, and said, "Get inside Jerban; we need to talk." She found a private nook in the dining area and waited for the innkeeper, Rita Caterman, to come to the table with Jerban.

In a minute, Rita strode up to her table and greeted her. Tesra motioned for silence and requested some tea and scones, then spoke softly and purposely.

"I have very bad news. Veranna has been abducted. We do not know who did it or where she is. No ransom note has been sent to Tolemera, nor has any person or group claimed victory over her. All we know is that a dragon was involved in the abduction and that a spider not native to this part of the world was used to poison her. We have been told that the bites from these spiders are almost always fatal."

She brushed a tear from the corner of her eye and paused. Jerban's mouth hung open in shock while Rita's face flushed with horrified anger. Her voice was a hiss as she asked, "Is there anyone who might be a suspect? If so, bring him, or her, here and we can tear them to shreds to get the truth out of them."

Tesra was surprised at the vehemence in Rita's voice, but recalled how Veranna and Rita had bonded closer than sisters when they first met.

"That is one of the difficulties; Veranna has many who would see her dead or deposed. Gelangweils and Erains are still furious about being removed from power over the empire, LeAnre y'dob holds a deep grudge, various Koosti chiefs are very resentful of her and many guild leaders are angry at her economic policies. The forces of evil are always plotting as to how they might resist the Creator.

"Jerban, I need you to keep a steady surveillance of the underground groups in the city. You never know when one of them will let slip a word or sentence that may be helpful.

"Rita, I want you to discretely contact the other innkeepers and ask them to monitor who stays in their inns. It may be that one of their clients has some knowledge of what happened to Veranna. Detain and hold for the duke's men anyone who has the slightest drop of information. Tomorrow I am leaving for Tolemera to establish information gathering there, as well. Remember, the timing and means of the abduction tells us that someone provided the abductors with critical information as to where and when Veranna would be at a given location. Someone knows something and likely received compensation. Thieves and cutthroats are prone to bragging, especially after drinking wine. Be on the alert."

Rita and Jerban both nodded and their faces were grim. Although feeling nearly helpless to contribute toward Veranna's return, they gained some small satisfaction by participating in the search even in such a limited manner.

In a purposely casual voice with undertones of cold steel, Rita picked up the plates from the table and said, "Tesra, if you encounter anyone involved in the plot against Veranna, let them know that they are fortunate that you got to them before me." She turned and headed toward the kitchen.

Tesra took a sip of tea and said to Jerban, "She would make an outstanding Sister in the Academy." She paused and looked directly at him. "Old friend, be very careful. We do not know whom we are dealing with nor how many. If you find some thug hesitant to divulge information, assure him, or her, that much can be forgiven or overlooked if Veranna is safely returned. Otherwise, mercy is not an option."

The huge lump of battered and scarred flesh shook his head in silent agreement, then said, "Most of our old net of spies is still in place. If anything comes up we will be sure to find out."

Tesra smiled briefly. "I know that you speak truly, my friend. It does seem rather odd that having a just ruler still requires clandestine measures like those we used under the Gelangweils. However, the whole world must be shown that evil cannot serve them well; evil has its own aims and will use its followers without any thought for their situation. We must always be vigilant."

Jerban stood and took his leave. "I have some old friends and acquaintances to see; I will check back with you before you go."

Tesra watched him walk out through the doorway, amazement striking her once more. Jerban moved like a carriage down the street, but no one could tell you when, or where, he had gone. He was one of the best infiltrators she had ever met, and could be stealthier than a cat.

She downed a large bowl of hearty stew and a few more scones before setting off for the castle to speak with the duke. She missed Veranna all the more since learning of her disappearance and took solace in the fact that the duke would also pour himself into finding out what had happened. His informants in the business sections, both legal and otherwise, could prove invaluable.

Duke Russell Heilson, of Grandshire, was a smart and reasonable man unfettered by the snobbery so prevalent in noble circles. As the leader of a large, commercial duchy, he had long ago learned to place character and productivity above heredity. After bowing respectfully he gave Tesra a friendly hug.

"It is wonderful to see you again, Tesra, although you typically show up when trouble is at hand. Do I guess rightly that this visit has to do with the disappearance of the empress?"

She had to control herself to keep tears from obscuring her vision, and then answered quietly. "It does."

For the next half-hour she laid out all that she knew regarding Veranna's absence, as well as some of the steps she took to find out more.

Heilson shook his head wearily and sighed, "I have been hounding every contact I know to see if any word has been heard about Veranna. Apparently, secrecy was a strong requirement for whoever planned this mission. If that is the case we might not have any braggarts wagging their tongues over the deed."

Tesra looked down at the floor. "What you say is true, but I cannot believe that she could be captured without someone giving the captors exact information about where she would be. If you want to have someone fall into a trap you have to know where to place it. The informant would not even have to harbor ill-intent; all he would need is a big mouth."

The duke agreed. "If there was ill intent, then be on the lookout for anyone of limited means suddenly having a good deal of means."

"My thoughts exactly. That is why I am in a hurry to get to Tolemera. I am leaving tomorrow morning on a fast skiff that will take me to Chenray. From there I will head north by the imperial coach service."

Trying to sound positive, the duke smiled and lifted his teacup in salute. "The weather has been excellent, so you should make good time. If I can do anything else for you, do not hesitate to ask."

She returned his smile and thanked him, then walked back to the Red Tailor inn. Everyone came under her discreet scrutiny as she looked and listened for any clue about Veranna. The tension took its toll on her body. When she arrived at the inn, she felt famished and ordered a large portion of mutton, potatoes and vegetables. Raspberry pie with whipped cream followed, leaving her more than satisfied. She chose a comfortable, padded chair by the fireplace in the common room and relaxed with a deep mug of mulled wine. Rita joined her but said little, fearing to interrupt her thoughts. Rita's husband, Malcolm, brought her a lute, and soon the room was filled with sweet music. Rita knew many songs and had an excellent voice. Tesra closed her eyes and hummed along, for she knew many of the songs, too. The inn's patrons requested songs as the evening wore on and Tesra hardly noticed how dark it had already grown outside. Rita asked if anyone else had a request and a teenage boy asked for a song from the ancient realm of Emeraldia.

Rita paused to recall one, and then said, "I do not know the original tune for the words of this song, and so I made up a tune for it. I found the words in an ancient book given to me by Lord Karsten, the husband of our dear empress, Veranna. The book contains many poems and songs, mostly about the rulers of old."

With her nimble fingers striking the strings, Rita's voice carried them out of their world and into another time long ago when heroes undertook great quests. Tales of the ancestors of the founders of the Empire of Emeraldia were a favorite of all.

By roads all unknown we traveled afar.
Leaving our homes we followed a star.
To the west lay the lands all foreign and new.
Before us flew eagles of green and gold hue.

The old lands lay mired in ways all untrue.
Their lusts turned commands of the Creator askew.
They built halls of stone and plaster to Him.
Not knowing their eyes for His will had grown dim.

The faithful departed, a Household despised.
Their hearts full of sadness at hearing the lies.
Of power and wealth to expect as their due.
Of lowly and slaves to unloose their shoe.

The Creator then blessed us with skills to survive.
He led us through lands to a home where we'd thrive.
The Curtain of Power now answered our call.
Accomplishing great feats, but that was not all.

The green throne shall rise like a tremor of earth.
The dormant and sleeping shall rise to new birth.
In chaos and turmoil the Lands brief will be.
The old lands shall hear the one calling them to see.

The song brought a hearty round of applause from the guests, but Tesra felt all the more anxious about Veranna. The young woman had fulfilled many prophecies and defeated gruesome terrors, but if she was not caught up in another fulfillment it would not end until those involved suffered greatly.

She wanted to show faith in the face of her fears. However, tears and trembling were only a heartbeat away. She sighed and folded her hands beneath her chin, a simple prayer being all she could muster. "Dear Creator, I will trust in Thee."

✵ ✵ ✵

CHAPTER 11

The morning air brought a chill to Veranna. Already the clouds were breaking up, having unloaded their rain during the night. Bright sunlight struck her eyes causing her to shield them with her hand. She gasped as her mind registered that action. *I lifted my hand and moved it correctly! Dear Creator, bless you for your mercies.* She flexed her fingers and found that she could move each of them independently. Beneto had told her that it would take time for the spider's poison to wear off. To be able to see it actually happening gave her a thrill of encouragement.

She realized another improvement just then. Her hand did not bob around like a ball on the water. She could lift, bend, turn and twist with full control. The thought came to her that the recovery was progressing from her head and down to the rest of her body. Breathing deeply she tried speaking and found that she could pronounce words, even if their articulation was not perfect. After another deep breath she managed to work through a voice lesson she had practiced many times at the Academy.

Next, she exercised her arms by lying flat on her back and raising them in front of her, trying to touch the fingers of one hand lightly to the other. Several repetitions helped improve their coordination, but it would still take time to regain full control.

The sound of a footstep in the entryway of the building startled her. She lowered her arms and pulled her blanket up to her shoulders. A man in reform servant's clothing walked in and leered at her. His head was shaped like a splitting wedge, and a long, slender nose resembled a bird's beak. Stringy shoulder-length graying hair hung in oily sheen from the sides of his head while the top was bald. Taller than average, his lanky frame indicated someone used to a regular schedule of physical labor.

"Ah, so this is the new slave. At least you are not ugly like the last one. I enjoyed her a lot before she was sold, and I miss that. It is good you are here to take her place. Hurry up and heal so that the spider poison won't affect me when I enjoy you."

He eyed her again and slowly licked his lips. Beneto walked in just then and gave Veranna a concerned look before speaking to the man.

"Leave her alone, Iyan; she is healing. Master Knoxun does not want her harmed."

Iyan did not even bother to glance at Beneto. "Shut up, old man. You know as well as I that slaves like her are at any man's disposal. It is part of their training. Applying training is not going to harm her." He grinned and then exited the building.

Beneto knelt and studied her face. "You do not look too scared, but you should be. Iyan is a vicious criminal even though he pretends to the reform. He is the type to simply take what he wants without regard for anyone else." Beneto nearly jumped back at the sound of Veranna's voice.

"I have encountered others like him, and am not as easy as he presumes."

Beneto's eyes were wide open. "At last you speak! But I warn you, say nothing rash; Iyan has the choice to take you for his pleasure since you are under punishment for being a whore."

Veranna's teeth ground together as she said, "I am not a whore. I have a husband and he is the only man I have ever been with."

Beneto shook his head sorrowfully. "Even if what you say is true, it makes no difference. You have been sold as a slave, and slavery only happens to those under the Creator's punishment. For women it is always assumed that they have been whoring, besides other offenses."

She looked at him in disbelief. "You told me that you used to be an instructor in an academy. How can you agree to such simplistic reasoning?"

Her words caused a stab of pain in his mind; he had said the same many years ago. He took off his shirt and turned around slowly, bringing a gasp from Veranna. "I have learned, girl, to adapt just to survive. The scars you see on my body came with great pain. However, the lash could not penetrate as deeply as the anguish of pouring myself out in vain to move the Seacorrans to think. My wife and children were taken from me and given to others. I have not seen them for almost forty years."

She could not imagine how much he must have suffered and it made her feel emptier than she could ever remember. She looked down and apologized. "I am sorry, Beneto; I did not know."

He put on his shirt and smiled wistfully. "Of course; how could you know? Besides, you have been suffering from poison and delusions."

"Delusions?"

"Yes. You may not remember it now, but you told me that you came from the kingdom of Emeraldia. Such tales are myths that we tell our children to scare them to good behavior. Everyone knows that the Emeraldians were simply renegades who fled the country and died in the wilderness far to the west. Those tribes called Koosti either destroyed or absorbed them. The Kingdom of Faresea tried to exterminate their heresy."

Veranna wanted to say so many things that she hardly knew where to begin. She decided that a simple, straightforward approach would be best.

"Beneto, you could not be more wrong. My ancestors were not destroyed nor absorbed by the Koosti. They made their way through that land after transforming it in ways, and then migrated west to found what is now the Kingdom of the Seven Lands. I am, as far as I know, the last of the purebloods from the ruling line."

Beneto studied her for a moment, amazed that she spoke with such sincerity. He hoped that reason might break through her madness.

"Dear girl, the ancestors you claim were said to have bright, emerald-green eyes. Yours are mostly brown with only a few specks of blue and green. This would argue that at best your line is a common, mixed heritage."

Veranna was puzzled and her mind raced to find an explanation. Most of her life she had brown eyes. However, they had changed to emerald green when she first arrived at Tesra's house about three years ago. It had been a sign from the Creator that she had been chosen for the task of leading the restoration of Emeraldia.

"Beneto, the only thing I can think of is that the spider poison has affected my eyes. Every other part of me is affected, even if it is slowly abating. But I swear before the Creator that Emeraldia lives and knows His blessings."

He looked around quickly, a sense of fear overcoming him. "Dear girl, speak not so freely; you could be skinned alive in the city square for speaking such words."

She stared at him, unable to appreciate the fear he lived under in his own land.

"Beneto, is there no room for dissent in this country? Are people so blind that they cannot even allow a shred of reality to threaten their idea of the world?"

He took a deep breath and let it out slowly, remembering days long past. "You sound like me many years ago. I was seen as subversive to the realm since my ideas were interpreted as challenging the ruling caste's right to power. They guard their place with the utmost vigor and enforce the concept of particular destinies down everyone's throats. They believe that the Creator has absolutely ordained them to rule as they will. Freedom only exists as a hypothetical concept. Determinism is the dogma used to enforce their claims."

"That is simply an excuse for despotism. I had to battle despots to gain my throne, and fought off Koosti despots to keep my people from being killed and enslaved. In fact, the Great Lady of the Koosti, LeAnre y'dob, is now my servant. Although painful, I can see the Creator's hand moving events while people act freely."

Beneto let out a quick chuckle. "Even if you are a bit touched I can see that you are full of interesting stories." He moved closer and helped her get to her hands and knees. "This may not be the most dignified, but it will give you some exercise for your limbs. Come, I will help you to the washroom; you should be able to get yourself cleaned up now."

She felt a stab of exasperation at not being taken seriously and realized that she would be seen as a rebel and heretic for her views. Once her mobility returned there would be more she could do to escape. However, simply crawling to the washroom caused great fatigue. Moving her legs felt more like swinging tree stumps. Oh well, at least she could move them.

In a mirror in the washroom she saw that her hair was growing quickly, nearly reaching her ears. Her eyes were mostly brown, but tiny points of green twinkled as though through a mist. Her skin felt baby-soft and had no sign of any scars. Having lost a good deal of weight left her ribs and collarbone protruding; her appearance reminded her of the prisoners rescued from the dungeons of the late emperor Dalmar Gelangweil.

A woman walked in and interrupted her thoughts.

"Huh, you must be the new one. Heard you are a whore from some northern province and got stung by a tiger spider." She was on the tall side and had golden-brown hair. Slender but sturdy, her eyes were large, round and a melting, soft brown in color. Veranna was reminded of a doe. "Course, I can't say as I have ever heard of someone surviving the spiders. From the way you look survival might be the worst part."

Veranna reacted to the idea that she was a whore, but could sense that the woman meant nothing offensive.

"My name is Veranna, and I come from the Empire of the Seven Lands which, I am told, is far to the north and west of here. One thing must be made clear: I am not a whore and I do not come from anywhere in this kingdom. I am married and faithful." She paused and looked the woman over again. "Do I guess rightly that you come from the people called Deeri?"

"Yeah; my name is Jennafah. How did you know I'm Deeri?"

"I have met one of your people before. Her name is Ghijhay and…"

Jennafah's eyes smoldered. "We thought she was dead! The bloody Koosti killed almost all of us. I was a slave to them when a Faresea army attacked and destroyed one of their towns. I thought that I was going to be free, but the Fareseans told me that I had been made a slave in order to be punished. They say they must continue the punishment to fulfill the Creator's will."

Veranna sighed and shook her head sympathetically. "I am so sorry, Jennafah. The Fareseans follow a very misguided and self-serving philosophy. I only ask that you do not give up hope. The lady Ghijhay was a slave of the Koosti and served their ruler as a concubine. I helped her overcome their rigid laws and be free. She is now the wife of their ruler and my regent over an entire Koosti province. She and her husband proclaimed a total non-aggression command against the Deeri. Ghijhay's brother, Gai-jhan, performed my wedding ceremony."

Jennafah's eyes watered and stared at Veranna, her mouth agape. "Thank the Creator!" She embraced Veranna, a shiver of excitement running through her. "You have given me a reason to live and hope for freedom. It may be that someday I will find some other members of my family and herd still alive."

Veranna smiled and thanked the Creator that at least two people in this strange land showed her kindness and sympathy. "Jennafah, never give up hope. Always remember that our Creator works everything for the best. Even the evil of men will accomplish His purposes."

Jennafah smiled and wiped her eyes. "Very true." She then stood and tended to her hair and clothing. "You had best hurry and get ready; High Lord Knoxun awaits us down in the city center. I am to be raised to reform servant status and sold to a northern lord. You will likely be evaluated for worth. The higher your value the quicker you can rise from the pit of total slavery."

Veranna felt a surge of anger at the idea of anyone being sold as a slave. "Where I come from all people are equal before the

Creator and have inestimable value. This land is no better than the Koosti."

"That may be, however, I warn you to hold your tongue. Punishment is both severe and swift. Come on." She helped Veranna along to the slave quarter door where Beneto waited with a wheelbarrow to take her across the property to the wagon he would drive to the city center.

The air was warm and high clouds floated lazily along. Citizens lined the streets going in and out of the city, intent on business. The city center buzzed with buyers and sellers trying to bring attention to their wares. Children scampered through as they chased one another, and dung sweepers in slave attire followed any horse brought into the center.

Beneto stopped in front of a sturdy building made of large, dressed stones and plaster. Over a side door hung a sign that read, 'Punishment shall be your deliverance.'

Inside milled dozens of people waiting to witness those slaves appointed to reform status and those new slaves to be evaluated. The new slaves tended to have cuts and bruises from the time of their capture, and all of them stared out vacantly in their despondency. A few resisted when they were tied up to posts in a display area. With arms spread wide and feet placed at shoulder width they looked like fencing along a farmer's field. A small loincloth barely covered their privates, regardless of gender.

Veranna looked on them in horror knowing that they would likely be slaves until the day they died. Abuse and public humiliation would be the norm. Some had obviously been starved to deprive them of strength; their captors probably had a hard time controlling them. It would not be long before cruel punishment and debasement brought them to conformity.

Jennafah turned to Veranna before proceeding to another part of the building. "I thank you once more for giving me hope, and pray that the Creator will give you strength. Goodbye."

Veranna felt abandoned as her newfound friend was herded away. Before disappearing around a corner, she turned and gave Veranna one last look.

A moment later a group of men and women in workers garb stepped purposely toward her, their white tops and sea blue pants marking them clearly. A stout man in his mid-fifties barked orders and two women started removing Veranna's slave dress.

"No," she yelled as she grabbed the hands of the women and manipulated their joints to cause them pain. They stepped back, surprised, and looked to their foreman. Veranna braced for another approach but realized that she could not fend them off for long since her strength and coordination were well below normal.

The two women closed in again, each grabbing an arm and pulling it over her head. The foreman bound her wrists tightly and lifted her off the wagon, then carried her over to the display area. He tied the rope to an overhead support beam, giving her enough length to sit on the floor.

Beneto bowed and begged for the foreman to treat her gently. "Master, she is not well; she has been bitten by a tiger spider. She is a kindly and rational woman."

The foreman snorted derisively, "If she were gentle and rational she would not be under the Creator's punishment. She nearly broke the arm of Grata," He pointed at the blond-haired woman on his left, "...and I can tell you that she did not learn her skills in a ballroom. Whores know those techniques, and Lord Knoxun's paperwork on her lists her as a whore. Now be quiet and step aside."

The foreman retrieved a knife from a shelf and started to cut off Veranna's dress when the whole room went quiet. Everyone stopped what they were doing and bowed to a woman who walked in through a side door. Her dress was made of sky blue silk with a silver fringe, and on her head was a circlet of mirror-bright silver. Tall and slender, her shiny, porcelain complexion made her blue-green eyes stand out like jewels. A slight smile held her face even when she frowned.

The foreman spread his arms wide in obeisance as he addressed her. "High Queen Sreba, all is ready for your review. We have many examples from which to choose."

She nodded regally and motioned for him to proceed. At the furthest end of the display area from Veranna, he showed her each of the captives and listed their offenses, strong and weak points. After a brief inspection of her own, Sreba announced the slave's value and punishments.

When they came to Veranna, Sreba asked, "Why is this slave not standing, and why is she not undressed for inspection?"

The foreman bowed and said, "Great Queen, she was bitten by a tiger spider and has not recovered the use of her legs. I was about to remove her dress when you walked in. She gave us some surprising resistance when we attempted to remove her dress before you arrived."

"Really? What is her offense?"

"Whoring, your highness."

"Well then, it will know no shame in its nakedness. Remove its dress, now."

The foreman reached out to cut the shoulder straps, but pulled back when Veranna said, in a very commanding, regal tone, "No. I am no whore nor do I deserve any of this treatment. As the Creator lives, you will not touch me."

Sreba flinched as if struck, her porcelain complexion shattering like a smashed vase. Anger took over in the next heartbeat. She stepped forward and slapped Veranna's cheek. The blow was painful, but Sreba was a thin, pampered woman, and hurt her own hand, adding to her rage.

"You are a slave and will not speak unless commanded. The Creator has sentenced you to punishment and given you to me for training. Nothing happens apart from His will!"

Veranna's own anger flared, not only at the abuse she suffered, but also at the abuse of the knowledge of the Creator.

"If you applied your wits for even a moment you would see through the absurd fatalism you espouse. Think! If the Creator directly ordains every action, then no guilt can be charged to those who simply perform His will. Law and responsibility would be nullified, and your own torture or death would be no crime."

Sreba's body jerked with rage. She finally found her voice and yelled, "Take this heretic to the post in the square. Let her punishment be seen by all."

The people in the display area exploded into a frenzy as they responded to her command. The rope tied around Veranna's wrists was loosed from the support beam and retied around a pole that two men placed across their shoulders. They stood up straight and lifted Veranna just enough that her knees did not drag along the ground as they carried her into the public square outside the building. Word of her punishment spread in an instant, bringing hundreds of people to the punishment pole located in the middle of the square. Veranna desperately screamed for mercy, but her voice went unheard against the din of the crowd calling out curses upon her.

The punishment pole was set on a platform raised three feet up from the ground and had a short crossbeam at the top. Many had been hung to die from this pole, some quickly, while others agonized through days of suffering before death. The two men carrying Veranna to the pole tied the rope binding her wrists to the crossbeam with enough length that she could stand on her knees with her arms stretched up and over her head. A small mob of crazed citizens grabbed pieces of her dress, ripping it from her body, leaving her bare. As if an unspoken command had been given, the people started spitting at her. She could hardly breath or open her eyes.

White-hot pain burst through her body as a two-inch wide strap lashed across her back. She burst out in a hideous, high-pitch scream and her whole body spasmed in rigid convulsions. She fought to draw a breath when another blow impacted across her hips. Her scream pierced the din of the crowd and rallied them to more cursing and jeering. Her eyes felt on the verge of popping out. Everything was now a blur as her muscles reluctantly collapsed. Her lungs burned for air that would not come and her arms felt detached from her shoulders. A third blow landed across her shoulder blades. Her body convulsed again, but the pain did not register as directly through the fog in her brain. A vision of Karsten and her on their honeymoon filled her failing consciousness. *Karsten, my love, I am here. Come, take me and never let go.*

A fourth blow struck below the shoulder blades, but delirium blocked her senses. One last pathetic attempt at a breath and she was gone, her body hanging limp from the rope around her wrists.

CHAPTER 12

Nisha made her way through the modest ballroom projecting an air of self-importance and seduction. Mrs. Gruntun had drilled her on the fine art of how to greet nobles and flatter them for an advantage or dismiss them as lowly vermin. With her quick wit and exotic beauty she enjoyed toying with them. However, the older ones were the preferred targets. They stood the best chance of being in on any of the secret plots of the Erains. She spotted one and carefully walked close enough to him and his coterie of followers that he could not help but notice her. In a purple silk dress cut teasingly over her cleavage, and mesmerizing dark-brown eyes, she easily drew his interest. He made a deliberate effort to engage her as she passed by.

"My lady, I do not believe that I have had the pleasure of meeting you before."

Nisha stopped and turned toward him in one elegant, effortless maneuver. She then curtsied and bowed her head while making sure that he would notice an ample amount of her bosom.

"My lord baron, I am honored that you address me. My name is Nisha, of House Kimo. But of you I have no need of introduction, for your name is known throughout the Lands. House Ciclanno has long been an ally of House Kimo."

The baron's eyes and posture took on an aggressive, anticipatory set. "Indeed, and we are proud of our interactions with your House. Tell me, does your house still hunt down and destroy the northern nomads?"

"Of course. We must have blood to color our cloth." She recalled the information that Karsten and his advisors gave her about the baron. He was a bold man and appreciated that quality in others. She flashed him a provocative smile and stepped forward as though they were old friends, putting her arm around his. She then turned him away slowly from his fellows and walked casually through the hall. "With the new empress we have found ourselves hampered. We used to make a great profit from selling the slaves we captured from the nomads. After breaking they made obedient and strong slaves. However, this empress put an end to such commerce in the empire. Now, we must operate clandestinely and smuggle them over to the Koosti. They pay far less for a slave, and this hurts our income."

The baron nodded his understanding. It gave him a thrill that this woman was not just a pretty face, but had a sharp, ambitious mind as well.

"We all feel the impact of these mindless policies. Hopefully they will not last long."

They wandered through the hallway as Nisha chatted with the baron. He suddenly realized that they stood in front of the doorway to his private chambers. Eyes full of desire, he gestured toward the door.

"Would my lady care to join me in my chambers for more, uh, intimate conversation?"

Nisha nodded slyly, "My lord is too kind. This hallway is a bit drafty, anyway."

Once inside, the baron ordered his servants to bring a large pitcher of fine wine and two goblets. "My lady, I hope that the wine helps to drive away the chills you feel."

Nisha chuckled flirtatiously. "I am sure it will, my lord. But worry not; we northern women learn early on how to generate… substantial heat." Her eyes glowed temptingly, raising the baron's pulse.

A serving girl arrived with the wine and goblets. The baron was so excited that he dismissed the girl before she had a chance to pour the wine. He stepped over to the tray to do the job himself when Nisha stopped him. Placing her hand on his upper arm she gave it a teasing squeeze as she spoke in mock chagrin.

"My lord, please do not shame me so. I am here to serve you." She imbued the sentence with undertones that sent his mind racing.

"Forgive me my lady; I anticipate your every service."

Nisha turned to the tray and reached for the pitcher with her right hand. On her left middle finger was a ring with a disk mounted on the palm side. With her thumb she deftly slid the cover from the disk and emptied its contents into one of the goblets. Just as deftly she slid it closed and poured wine into both goblets. Holding a goblet close between her breasts she turned back to the baron and nodded submissively, a feral, sensual smile reaching out to engulf him.

"Your wine, my lord."

He cared not the least for the wine. All he could think about was what she would look like without her clothes. He emptied his goblet in one swift gulp and set it aside.

"Enough with the wine; it is time for you to serve me far more fully."

Her voice and posture were totally submissive as she turned around for him to unbutton her gown. It fell to the floor, revealing sheer lace undergarments wrapped strategically around her figure. The baron quickly lifted her in his arms and laid her onto his bed. She let out a desirous moan and slowly writhed on the bed. The baron tore off his clothes and flung them away, then jumped onto the bed and on top of her. He kissed her savagely as she rubbed her fingers along the sensual points of his body. He drew back onto his hands and knees and went motionless as his eyes glazed over. Nisha wriggled out from under him and put on her dress, amazed at the effectiveness of the 'geistlos' powder that LeAnre gave her. It numbed the mind and blocked the memory. The wretched Koosti woman was good for something, at least, especially for her knowledge of herbs and substances used to influence people.

She took a moment to calm down and review Karsten's instructions. She thought it a shame not to enjoy the baron now that he was at her disposal, but Karsten was adamant that she put the good of the empire and the Genazi people ahead of her lusts. He had grown so soft since the new empress came along. Even after they married, he never bragged about her ability to please him. Was there any Genazi left in him?

"Ciclano."

"Yes, mistress?"

"Is there a plot to do the empress harm?"

"Yes, mistress. Erains and certain Koosti want her out of the way."

"Which Koosti?"

"I do not know, mistress. The empress," referring to lady Gelangweil, "only tells me what she thinks is necessary for me to know."

"Does the man called 'Dag' have more information than you?"

"Yes, mistress, but only concerning the mercenary slavers. I know not how they are involved."

"Where is this man, Dag?"

"He was smuggled out of the city in a cargo container and is heading for Grandshire. After that he is on his own."

"Do you have any idea of how the Erains or Koosti will harm the empress?"

"No, mistress. Several Koosti chiefs want her dead simply out of revenge. Others want her for their harems. The Erains simply want her gone so that they can resume their control of the empire. I am responsible for practical arrangements for our agents."

Nisha realized that he did not know any more about the Erains' scheming. Her own ego drove her to ask different questions.

"Are you intimate with Lady Gelangweil?"

"Many times, mistress."

"Is she a worthy partner?"

"Not very, mistress, but she is a powerful woman and can help me advance my own cause."

Nisha raised an eyebrow at this. "Do you think that the present empress is desirable?"

"Yes, mistress."

"Do you desire her over me?"

"Yes, mistress."

Rage flared up in Nisha. No other woman was her equal when it came to men. Her teeth ground together as she glared at him.

"Listen well, Ciclano. I am the only woman you truly desire. The Gelangweil tramp you will use, but only for the sake of keeping close to her for information. You will know that I am the best, even though you do not mention me at all. Your only memory of tonight will be that I pleased you into utter bliss. You will always treat me kindly. If I call you my 'little bear' you will fall immediately into this trance and do as I say. Is this clear?"

"Yes, mistress."

"Now, lie down and take a nap. If Gelangweil wants to use you tonight, imagine that it is me and do your best."

"Yes, mistress." He immediately slumped onto his side and fell fast asleep.

Nisha looked around for any documents relevant to her mission, but found none. She grabbed a sharp knife from a servant's tray left in a corner and hid it in her bodice. Stepping quietly into the hallway she made her way down to a junction where she could turn left and proceed out of the Erain wing of the large inn. Just as she came to the junction, two guards suddenly stepped out from the hallway that crossed the one she was in. They held up their spears to bar her way.

The one on the left called, "Halt! State your name and your business, my lady."

Nisha stood up straight as she adopted the manner of a noble-woman used to getting what she wanted. "My name is Nisha, and I am a princess of House Kimo. My business was with Baron Ciclano, and I will not describe any of it to you, corporal."

The guard hesitated before saying, "No disrespect is intended, my lady. We have orders from the Grand Duchess Gelangweil to monitor all who pass through this hall."

The tone of her reply let him know that she thought him an idiot for having stopped her. "You have done your duty; now, let me pass."

The guards hated getting caught between the opposing wills of nobles, but they did their duty as best they could.

"Yes, my lady. Grand Duchess Gelangweil may wish to speak with you. Where shall I say you are lodged?"

Nisha replied angrily, "At the Excelsior. Now, bother me no more!"

The guards backed up a step and bowed. She passed by as though neither of them even existed, making her way down the hall, but puzzled when she heard a slight echo of her footsteps. It did not seem right since the chairs, rugs and other objects should absorb the noise. Also, her shoes did not have hard soles.

When she came to the entryway there was no sign of the carriage assigned to her. She had finished her task sooner than expected and would just have to wait. Judging the direction from which she thought the carriage would be coming, she walked along the sidewalk, keeping to the shadows.

Again she thought she heard footsteps behind her, wondering if her imagination played tricks. Her instincts said otherwise, and memories of moving along the trails in the northern Boar's Spine Mountains played out in her mind. Mountain lions often stalked so silently that you had to depend upon instincts to aid your senses.

She turned into an alleyway between buildings and melted into the shadows. Pulling the knife from her bodice she covered the blade in her dress lest it reflect light. Breathing deeply she probed the darkness with her senses. After a few minutes waiting to see if someone followed her she took a step back toward the sidewalk.

Seasoned reflexes served her well. She barely ducked a fist speeding toward the left side of her head. Nevertheless, the forearm of the attacker hit hard just above her temple with a good deal of force, pounding her into the wall of a building to her right. She bounced off and fell backwards, forcing herself not to lose hold of her knife. She rolled and came up in a fighter's stance trying to catch sight of her foe. A deeper black against the darkness loomed up in front of her, with the dull sheen of a blade showing a knife ready to strike. A cruel voice hissed from behind a cloth covering the mouth.

"Stupid girl, do not even think about resisting me. I can kill you quicker than a snake, and enjoy it. But first you will tell me what I want to know. If you cooperate I will make your death virtually painless. If you decide to make things difficult, then great pain shall make seconds seem like days."

Seeing his silhouette and the way he held his knife, Nisha knew whom she faced. A cold tremble shook her bones and panic arose in her. She forced it away and cleared her mind, knowing that she was a dead woman.

"Listen to me, Raven's Blade," she growled, "I have no fear of death and will do everything in my power to see to yours."

The Raven's Blade chuckled softly, "I can tell by your accent and speech pattern that you are Genazi. That makes no difference; you always were pathetically inept." Raven's Blades prided themselves on being the best of killers. Some of them approached the skill level of the Swordsmen of Randall when it came to the use of the sword. In close combat they were premier with the knife. Psychology and language skills made them masters of espionage. Many of them now served those nobles willing and able to pay their high fees. Since the late emperor Dalmar's execution they had been disbanded and forced to find their own employment. Some had formed partnerships to establish their own secret training camps for assassins. Funding was a problem without imperial support, but a superior product could overcome that setback.

Nisha attacked, surprising the man as she slashed horizontally at his knife hand and chest. He blocked the blow and swung his left hand up to hit the nerve in her right armpit. She quickly trapped his hand under her arm and jabbed her left hand into his eyes, following up with a knee to the groin. The man reacted automatically and turned his torso to evade the knee as he brought the butt of his knife down on top of her head. She was stunned and fell to her knees. Desperation gave her enough strength to stab her knife at his chest. Her blade bit into the flesh over his left ribcage. Still emboldened by adrenaline, she launched herself at his midsection, intending to reduce his ability to swing his blade by restricting his arm movements. She nearly lost consciousness as her head impacted his hard stomach. She brought up her knife in a tight arc and cut into the backside of his right thigh. He grunted in pain and slammed his left hand down onto her back. The air rushed from her lungs and she landed on her front side on the ground, gasping for breath.

The man tied her wrists together and then wrapped the cord around her ankles, hog-tying her into immobility before grabbing her around the back of her neck with his right hand. He lifted her up to stare into her eyes as he spoke.

"As you can see, all efforts on your part are pointless. You will tell me what I want to know or I will begin by ripping out your eyeballs with my teeth. If that does not convince you, then fire and cold steel will give you exquisite pain." He paused to take hold of her left eyelid to lift it out of the way. "Now, start talking."

Nisha could hardly breath and tried to make herself pass out. A few moments went by and she saw the assassin's teeth reach out to bite down on her right eye. She tried to scream but could not since his right thumb pressed against her windpipe. His teeth touched her eyeball; however, he delayed biting down to increase her terror and induce her to talk. His hot breath dried and irritated her eye. She tried to blink but could not. He paused to let out a sinister chuckle, enjoying the torture of his helpless victim. Nisha braced herself and tried to force her mind away from registering any pain.

Two thuds sounded and the killer tensed straight. A moment later and he dropped her to the ground, then fell on top of her. A second later and he was grabbed by two men and lifted off of her. Two arrows protruded from his back.

She saw two men from Lord Treybal's secret team search the assassin's body and find nothing. One of the men cut her bonds and gave her a quick inspection. She nearly cried with relief. When he removed the Raven's Blade ring and handed it to her she knew that her life had turned for the better. She helped kill a Raven's Blade! She was now a hero among her people.

The two men hurriedly helped her into their carriage, which was outfitted to look like a noble's. After careful false turns and double-backs, they quickly smuggled her back to the castle before disposing of the assassin's body.

A healing woman looked over her wounds before Treybal's men started questioning her. After giving all of the information she could recall, she collapsed on her bed and slept.

CHAPTER 13

Beneto entered the slave quarters with a basket of fruit, two loaves of bread and some fried fish. He headed straight for the room where Veranna slept for the last two days since her punishment in the city square. He hoped that she would awaken and take some nourishment. The five lashes she took were more often lethal due to the total shock sent to both the mind and body. Her back and thighs looked as though they had been through a farmer's harrow. The blood covering her body had hidden her nakedness, and Beneto assumed that she was dead. But air still moved in and out of her chest and her heart kept beating. All through the bathing and tending of her wounds she did not regain consciousness. She had to be made of tough flesh to survive.

However, these oddities paled in comparison to what had occurred yesterday morning. He walked into the room and found her wrapped in a faint green nimbus that persisted for several minutes. When it faded, all of her wounds were healed! No sign of any injury could be found. But strangest of all was the beatific smile glowing on her face as she slept. How anyone who had suffered as she could smile, revealed great depths of mind and soul.

He set the basket down on the floor and knelt beside her. It took several shakes of her shoulder to get her to stir and awaken, even if she did not open her eyes at first. When she did, he gasped, *Dear Creator above.* Her eyes gleamed in pure, vibrant emerald green. Only the highest echelons of the nobility had such eyes and he had never seen one of them with such intensity as hers. The combined beauty of her face and figure was stunning.

Veranna sat up and looked around. "Beneto, what is wrong? What is it you fear?"

"No…nothing, Veranna; I am amazed at your eyes. They glow greener than the king and queen's. They were not that way three days ago. I thought it unlikely that you should be a slave, but I was far from any idea that you would bear the signs of the ruling class."

She smiled and took his hand. "Dear Beneto, I told you who I am. Do you believe me now?"

As if his head were slowly being drawn downward he touched his forehead to the floor. "Yes, your highness. However, I cannot begin to guess at what this will mean for your life. The rulers will likely seek to destroy you since they will see you as a rival. The queen saw you beaten to a bloody heap, yet here you are without a mark on you. I saw them all disappear as you slept."

"The Creator has some plan in mind for me, Beneto. I do not serve my own will; the Creator moves me to do His."

"That is the main reason they will fear and hate you. I advise you to be discreet in all your words and deeds. Keep your gaze lowered or your eyes will give you away. I ask of you only one thing: If you find a way to escape this dungeon, take me with you. I will serve you gladly."

Veranna stood and bowed her head as she curtsied formally. "You have my word that I shall try my utmost to see to your freedom. I am in your debt for all of your help and kindness. First, I must locate the little girl who was brought here with me. Her name is Tyrzah. Only then can we try escaping. I must…" Her eyes grew large as she looked down on her lower body. "Beneto, I am standing! Look, I can walk. It is as though I were never injured. Thank the Creator."

He watched as she moved around the room with total confidence and grace. "Surely the Creator is with you, your highness. He has healed your body, but He also has healed my heart. I thank

Him and you for giving me a purpose to live. Serving the Creator is the greatest freedom." A quiet moment passed before he asked, "How is it that you are not brimming with anger and hatred toward the queen? You suffered terrible abuse and almost died."

Veranna's smile faded. "Anger is one thing that remains, but I will not let it interfere with clear thinking. Hatred diffuses once you realize why others, as human as yourself, do evil things. I am sure that Sreba has been bred to think she may act as she does. Do not be surprised if the Creator breaks her habit."

"Now, that would be a miracle." He smiled and motioned toward the basket next to him. "Come and eat; you must be very hungry."

Veranna plopped down and grabbed a pear. "Hungry is an understatement. Beware lest my teeth grab for anything with flesh."

They both laughed as she devoured every item in the basket. An hour later, Beneto took Veranna on a tour of the grounds. She wore a plain, straw hat with a wide brim to help shield her eyes. Various servants were totally uninterested in simply another slave added to their ranks, but a few sought to intimidate her by threatening they would speak with Master Knoxun if she did not obey those senior to her in the slave order. She lowered her head and tried to look humble, hoping to win some small morsel of comradely loyalty she might use to her advantage at the right moment.

The day passed quickly with laundry and landscaping work. The nobles kept their properties immaculate and saw any short-comings as a sign of irresponsibility. Veranna enjoyed the work since it helped get her body in shape. When they stopped in the evening, Beneto gave her a suspicious look. Over their evening meal, Veranna asked what was bothering him.

"Veranna, you make it hard to believe that you are of noble heritage."

"How so?"

"You work like the best of servants without complaining. No noble I have ever encountered would be so able. You even seem happy."

She smiled and shook her head wistfully. "I was raised in an academy for girls and knew nothing of noble life. My parents were killed when I was a very small child, and they both lived secret lives as commoners until they were betrayed. I did not know of my heritage until just a few years ago. I have always enjoyed work as a gift from the Creator since it strengthens both body and mind."

Beneto's mouth hung open for a moment as he looked at her. "You are definitely not of this land. Work is often synonymous with punishment, and most slaves seek to find a way to escape the doing of chores. Since I taught in an academy, I had contact with many nobles and can tell you that they prize their positions above all. You must be very careful."

She thanked him for his concern, and then asked, "Is it possible that we might take the wagon through the city? I want to get a better idea of its layout."

"Soon. We must first have a valid reason from Master Knoxun for getting use of a wagon. When kitchen supplies run low will be our chance. Many shops strung along the streets will provide a good excuse for us getting around."

Veranna agreed that it was wise to wait for a plausible moment. On their way back to the slave quarters she looked around to see if anyone was watching and then snatched a pair of black cotton pants and shirt from a clothesline. Beneto's head twitched back and forth as he looked for whoever might rush forward to accuse them of theft. Such a charge could get him demoted in the slave hierarchy.

Veranna noticed his agitation and hurried to calm his fears. "Do not worry, Beneto; I made sure that I was not seen." Seeking to provide him with a useful excuse, she smiled and said, "Besides, I needed a change of clothes."

Later that evening, Beneto summoned her to help with cleaning up in the main house after dinner. Lord Knoxun had returned from a visit to a fellow noble's house and brought several guests back with him. Large amounts of food were prepared and eaten, leaving great stacks of dishes, glass and silverware. Veranna worked quickly and steadily, gaining the respect and thankfulness of the house staff. They would not need to work far into the night and get little sleep before rising to work again.

Clouds diffused the moonlight and the stars did not shine through, but Veranna saw her way back to the slave quarters as though walking under sunshine. Someone moved just inside the doorway to the slave quarters. She saw the build, height and hair of the person and knew it was Iyan. She took a moment to consider going elsewhere, but quickly decided to confront the letch directly. Stepping purposely through the doorway, she pretended not to know of his presence, allowing him to grab her by the hair with his right hand. As he pulled her towards himself she turned into his grasp. He had no chance. She struck a lightning-quick, spear-handed blow to his windpipe, then immediately into the middle of his right bicep. The blows were not strong enough to do serious damage, but they worked well to stagger him. She kept hold of his right wrist with her left hand and twisted his arm until he fell to his knees. Applying a painful chokehold around his neck, she spoke as threateningly as she knew how.

"Never think that you will try abusing me again. I will end your putrid life faster than you can blink. I will let you live now since you have the mind of a brute and needed this warning. Now leave, and do not bother either me or any woman here. Have I made myself clear?"

Iyan felt unconsciousness approaching and knew he could not escape her. Gasping for breath he shook his head to acknowledge her warning and fell onto his chest when she released her hold. As quickly as he was able he crawled out of the building, then lumbered into the night, clutching his temporarily paralyzed right arm.

Veranna took a deep breath and let it out slowly. After thanking the Creator for the fighting skills He had given her, she went into the room to her mat and saw three other women sitting on mats. One small candle burned at the back of the room, showing fear and admiration on their faces. The woman nearest to her left, whose curly black hair was pulled back and tied with a piece of string, looked her up and down before speaking.

"You are a dead woman, but one we will remember. Iyan will take vengeance in any way he can find. We all fear going against his wishes; rumors say that he was, or may still be, an assassin for some nobles."

Veranna thought for a moment about the best way to garner the loyalty and friendship of these women. They had to be given something to hope for and have confidence in her. The boldness of Tesra and Kreida came to mind.

"Iyan will either come to a change of mind or I will make him regret abusing anyone. If any of you are raped or beaten by him, let me know and I will see to his punishment."

The woman in the middle, who had dark, silky hair and a bronze tint to her skin, snorted in disbelief as her blue eyes stared at Veranna.

"Pah! You were lucky against that dung heap; he was caught off-guard. He will be brutal the next time he comes for you."

Veranna found it distasteful to speak of having to beat up another person, but knew she had to keep up appearances. She chuckled and waved her hand in dismissal. "Iyan would need a whole cohort of attackers to get to me. By himself he can do nothing."

The woman's head jerked back as her face screwed up into a look that said she thought Veranna mad. "Do not speak to me of such foolishness. I come from a people born for battle and know how cruel they can be. You will only know great suffering before you die."

Veranna gave her a serious look, her left eyebrow rising in stern warning. "I have led my people in two wars: One where Koosti aided my enemies and one against LeAnre y'dob, who is now my servant. DeAndre y'dob is a tentative ally and his wife is the ruler, under my supervision, of LeAnre's province."

The woman was still not convinced. "That is outrageous! The empress of the Emeraldians is a mighty ruler, not a slave. A hundred veteran warriors could not prevail against her."

Veranna shook her head and sighed. "I was not overcome by warriors, but by trickery. Someone used a strange spider to subdue me when I was looking after children."

"Then why are you here? If you are so great a fighter you should escape."

"I cannot. One of the children I was responsible for was brought here and sold to someone. I must find her before I can leave."

"If you are the empress, which of the slaves went with you to your land?"

Veranna's simple answer shook the woman. "Reyiya, her name is Reyiya. She is no longer a slave and leads a life of her own choosing. She gives the best massage of anyone I have known."

The woman was speechless for a protracted moment. "Maybe what you say is true; I will not believe you until I see a Leopard's blade in your hand."

"A Leopard's blade? What is that?"

"Those called Leopards are the elite guards of noble houses. Master Knoxun does not use them since we are close to the city. Further out they are used to protect against bandits. They are well-trained and outmatch most Koosti warriors."

In a very business-like manner, Veranna asked, "How far away is the nearest estate employing these guards?"

At first the three women thought she was blustering. Seeing the serious look on her face they looked at one another as they thought about her question. Finally, the Koosti woman spoke up.

"House Merchana lies near the edge of the city, about a half-hour walk to the north. But you won't make it past the police patrols; they are authorized to kill any slaves seen on the streets at night if they are unescorted."

Veranna retrieved the dark clothes she had stolen from the laundry and began changing as she replied. "They are the least of my worries..." She stopped and looked at them when they gasped at her in astonishment. "What is wrong?"

The Koosti woman held the candle up and motioned for Veranna to turn her back toward its light. "Are you not the one given the flogging only a few days ago? You should have terrible wounds covering your body, and be totally broken in your spirit."

Veranna pulled the dark shirt on. "I am the one. The Creator healed both my mind and body. That is the way I know that He is with me. Otherwise, I would be the sorriest of slaves, or dead."

The Koosti woman held the candle up to see Veranna's face. "Your eyes are as the reports claimed of the foreign empress; emerald green. Too bad they do not see clearly in this matter."

Veranna headed for the door. "I will not scold you for your disbelief; in your place I would probably react the same way. Proof is a valid demand, so I shall provide you with some."

With that she turned and went to the doorway. Looking out she saw no one nearby and headed to the right where a large tree grew next to the estate wall. Springing up, she grabbed a branch and pulled high enough to swing her legs over the wall and then pushed away from the limb. In a second she landed on the walkway along the alley. She saw no one nearby and darted over to where deep shadows lay. After taking a moment to scout the best path to take her to the north side of the estate, she hugged the shadows and sped off.

✷ ✷ ✷

CHAPTER 14

The sun was nearly gone for the day when Kreida walked into the castle infirmary. Nisha lay on a bed near a fireplace, her head and neck covered with bandages. She had slept for a day after Karsten and Treybal questioned her about her mission, and in true Genazi style she gobbled down a large quantity of food. Approaching the bed, Kreida tried to sound as upbeat as possible.

"Hey kid, wake up. A good fight should fill you with loads of energy."

Nisha's head turned toward her, the one exposed eye focusing slowly. "Give me a knife and some Erains to kill; I will have no lack of energy."

Hands on hips, Kreida shook her head and said, "Yep, I know what you mean. Who can stand boring! That is why we Genazi women are so far above any others; we know how to have a good time. By the way, I have something that belongs to you. You would not let go of it even when we had to tend your wounds when you were unconscious." She reached into her cleavage and pulled out Nisha's Ravens' Blade ring.

Kreida continued on in her happy-go-lucky manner. "Too bad you won't get to flaunt it right away. We have to get you back to the

Excelsior, right quick, otherwise your new lover boy might grow suspicious of your identity."

Pride overcame her aches and pains as Nisha sat up and moved her legs from under the covers. She saw Kreida hold out her hand for her to take, but refused the help. Her head throbbed all the more as she took a few steps to loosen her limbs.

Kreida's voice penetrated the fog in her mind. "Your leaving the castle will have to be kept secret so put on common clothes. We will wrap you in a blanket and stow you on a hay wagon for the ride into the city. You can change at the inn. If baron Ciclanno visits you, make sure that he sees how injured you are; you can tie a man's leg around his neck with sympathy. Put it into his head that someone attacked you in your room and that your servants saved you at the last moment. Say that he wanted to know the wealth and number of troops in your household. That will throw a big twist into their scheming."

Nisha cracked a sorry smile. "After all the trouble I have gone to, does this mean I get to enjoy him in my bed?"

Kreida cocked her head as if in thought. "Naw, you better not. It could make it more difficult when its time for you to break his neck. Besides, Karsten is even stronger in his idea that we should not enjoy a few simple, well-earned pleasures if we are not married. Can you believe he and the empress ever got married?"

Karsten sat at the head of a conference table deep inside the keep of the castle. Yanbre, Treybal, Reiki, Captain Cody and Kreida discussed their plans to nab the man named Dag. Karsten's style was more curt than they were used to and he paced more often around the room. The others knew the reason and tried to set him at ease. Yanbre, especially, was able to calm him with his sure, fatherly style.

"My lord, we shall have this man any day. He will find his movements hampered at every turn by our patrols, and the loyalty of the people to their empress will ensure that he finds few willing accomplices."

The young ruler slipped momentarily into Genazi mode. "If any aid or abet this man, see to it that they die slowly." Kreida smiled approvingly while the others frowned. "Forget that; any accomplices are to be arrested and thoroughly interrogated. Nisha's report leaves me no doubt that the Erains are planning some type of uprising. This man, Dag, is our only sure lead at this point. Make sure that our search patrols are well supplied; I want them to bring me this man. I will tear every ounce of flesh from his bones until he tells me where Veranna is."

Treybal squeezed Kreida's hand, thankful that she was safe. His love for the fiery Genazi woman flooded him with empathy for Karsten. He resolved all the more to help his friend and ruler.

"Our network is still a fledgling, but we are already realizing some gains in our knowledge of the Erains and militant Koosti. Their chief, named Sarim'tay, still harbors deep enmity toward us, especially the empress. Every bone in my body tells me that he had a hand in her disappearance. However, evidence is hard to come by. We know that the Erain and Gelangweil houses had dealings with Koosti in the past; it seems that has not changed."

Karsten tried to relax and think more clearly. Images of Veranna suffering at the hands of Koosti torturers plagued his mind. He felt as though he might explode if something helpful did not happen soon.

"Bring me Dag. If you have to set fields on fire to scare him out of the brush, do it." He paused and took a swallow of mulled wine. "Bring in LeAnre."

Kreida held her tongue, but shifted her body to allow unhindered motion should LeAnre do anything suspicious. Yanbre and Treybal were fixed in inscrutable stares and Karsten's face turned a bit redder.

The Koosti woman kept her gaze lowered as she stood near the door. At a signal from Karsten she took a seat at the far end of the table. Her shoulders were stiff with tension, knowing that any of the others would end her life at the slightest provocation. Veranna had refused to do so since LeAnre was pregnant, but that was a delicate technicality for Genazi. In her appearance she had changed a great deal since her capture. Whereas her skin had been discolored and patchy from having ceased bronzing, now it was smooth and tan. Even with her belly swollen with child she kept an attractive shape and her hair was simply, but appealingly, tied back.

Karsten did not let appearances sway him. "LeAnre, you said before that you think Veranna was captured by someone using a special breed of spider to paralyze her. What more can you tell us about these spiders?"

She bowed her head before responding. "My lord, all I can say is that most people die from being stung. Obviously the spider was detached from the empress before it had time to start drawing out the juices of her body. However, the stinger holds enough poison to kill many people. Various breeds of the spider are used for different effects. The Koosti medicine woman you requested from my province will know the effects of the poison from the particular breed we found."

"How will that help me find my wife?"

"If you know the breed, then you know where it comes from. Knowing this will help in finding out who bought one recently. They are rare and expensive; a seller will remember the buyer."

"Where are the sellers of these spiders located?"

"In the far southeast of my province in the mountains along the border with another land. Dragons are the preferred method of transportation."

Yanbre's brow furrowed in concentration. "What is the name of this other land?"

"Seacorro."

Not even Karsten recognized the name. A lingering tease deep in his mind was all that came to him. He put it aside for later consideration.

"Will the sellers be reluctant to divulge the names of buyers?"

"Yes, but Koosti respond to authority. Should my brother command them to give up this information, they will."

"What will your brother do to any Koosti involved in my wife's abduction?"

She smiled faintly as she recalled the punishment of those guilty of heinous crimes. "After an extended period of gruesome torture, he will have them hung upside down and skinned alive. Great festivals are held on such occasions."

Karsten nodded and said grimly, "Woe be unto them if I get to them first. Koosti torture will be as leisure by comparison."

CHAPTER 15

Veranna stopped to catch her breath and consider the best approach onto the grounds of House Merchana. Standing in the darkness under a large tree, her night vision made it easy to see the wall around the property and the guards. A half-dozen of them paced routinely past the main gate, their leopard skin pants and shirts marking them easily. None of them were short and they all had well-defined, honed muscles. The sides and backs of their heads were shaved while the hair on top was about an inch in length. Veranna smiled since they reminded her of pickle jars.

She made her way further up the street on the west side of the wall and crossed where the light was dim, then hugged the wall and cautiously proceeded back toward the gate. Pausing until the guards were dispersed furthest from the gate, she crept just to the side and counted out four seconds. She darted toward the bars of the gate and punched just as a guard's head came in range. Struck clean and hard on the temple, he fell to the ground. Veranna reached and grabbed the keys from his belt, then hurriedly unlocked the gate. Slipping inside, she took the guard's sword and placed it outside the gate, then found a sturdy baton on his belt; it would come in handy. Using his knife to cut strips of cloth from his clothes, she tied his hands and feet, and then gagged his mouth.

The closest patrolling guard walked casually alongside the wall; nothing much happened here, so it would not hurt to save his strength for when he got home. He thought he must have been imagining things when a deeper shade moved through the darkness before him. Before he could give it another thought, a hard fist hit just below the separation of his ribs, knocking him breathless. He doubled over and a stick whacked across his right shin, causing blinding pain. A split-second later and a stick hit just below the back of his skull and knocked him out.

Veranna handled three more guards just as easily, but the sixth one must have gone to another part of the estate. She crossed the wide lawn by darting from tree to tree and found a rear door to the main house. It was locked. She tried the keys taken from the first guard until one of them worked. Stepping slowly inside, she could hear piano music echoing through the halls. She steered clear of that area and went upstairs. Room after room was either empty or had only one person asleep. The large children's room held seven sleepers, but Tyrzah was not one of them.

She crept past the servants and out through the rear door, making sure to lock it before heading off to search the slave quarters. Rounding a corner of the house, she saw the slave quarters twenty yards to the east. Seeing no one, she trotted over to them, when suddenly the sixth guard stepped out from behind a tree and held up his sword.

"Well, well; we have a visitor. When I checked the door a few minutes ago I found it open. Since no alarm has come from the gate I figured that it must be a slave using a smuggled key to steal some food. And, here you are running back to your bed. Too bad for you that your sleep will be permanent."

Veranna realized that the man was unaware of his comrades' being neutralized. The situation called for caution; the guard had to be subdued quietly lest he alert anyone else and complicate matters. She went down on one knee as if surrendering and spread her arms wide in a plea for mercy while hiding the baton by aligning it against her arm.

The guard spoke contemptuously. "You slaves have no sense of honor. Herding you sheep is boring; I should give you some painful wounds just for the fun of it."

He stepped forward and swung his sword casually at Veranna's left upper arm. In one quick lunge she went under his swing and punched him in the groin. He gasped and doubled over, and then fell to the ground when Veranna brought the baton down on the back of his head.

She took a moment to see if anyone was nearby, then headed for the gate. The guard there was still unconscious and nobody else was in the vicinity. She grabbed the sword she had left there and darted into the darkness.

Reaching Knoxun's slave quarters without incident, she laid the sword down by the Koosti woman and then changed clothes, hiding the black garments under her mat. Sleep came upon her quickly and a dream formed. She saw a large haystack shaped like a thimble in a wide field. She approached the stack and was surprised that she could lift it. She gave it a good shake and saw two shiny needles fall from within. One needle she placed in her sleeve, the other she threw onto a blacksmith's fire and it melted.

CHAPTER 16

Veranna awoke when she heard the Koosti woman gasp. The morning sun revealed the woman's face full of wonder. She looked at Veranna and asked quietly, "Who are you? Are you trying to get us killed?"

Veranna propped herself up on her right elbow and rubbed her eyes. "I told you last night, I am Veranna, empress of the Seven Lands and ruler of the province of LeAnre y'dob. The Creator is with me and will accomplish His purpose."

The Koosti woman led the other two in bowing to her.

"Your highness, forgive me for doubting. I beg you to let me live. My name is Vikkaya; I will obey your every command."

Veranna sat up and acknowledged their bows. "Doubt is only wrong when it is unjustified, so have no fear for your lives. My pledge to you is that I shall do all I can to win your freedom." She stood and stretched. "For now, let's get washed up and eat breakfast. Remember, in front of others I am simply another slave."

When they went to the mess room for slaves, Veranna noticed a definite change in activity. Guards were posted at the gates and nobles were in a much busier mode than usual. In the mess room, Veranna saw Beneto and sat down next to him.

"What is going on? I have not seen so much activity around here since I arrived."

Beneto glanced around quickly before answering softly, "One of the estates was trespassed last night. Six guards, Leopards, were injured and subdued. There must have been a number of thieves to penetrate the guard force so effectively. Every estate is increasing their domestic and hired guard units."

Veranna smiled to herself. "What were the thieves after?"

Beneto shrugged and kept his voice low. "No one knows. Nothing was stolen; the only damage was bruises on the guards. That is the worst part since their abilities are now in question. Injured pride has made them announce that they will kill first and ask questions later."

Veranna hoped that no innocents would die due to the guards' reckless zeal. It would also allow for opportunities since overreactions would leave gaps in the guards preparations.

"What is on our list of duties for today, Beneto?"

"I have been ordered to take a number of slaves over to the king's estate and help with their chores. They have diverted a number of slaves into guard routines and depleted their house staff. Cleaning and laundry will occupy us all day."

The king's estate was on the northwest side of the city and easily made up half of the entire city area. Located atop a gentle knoll, the main house commanded a panoramic view. Although fifteen feet high, the wall encircling the estate did not interfere with the view of the harbor. Tropical and temperate plants were set out in concentric beds from the house, with wide swaths of lawn in between. The house had been whitewashed recently, allowing roses, daffodils, peonies, lilacs and other exotic flowers a background against which their beauty and variety could shine forth.

Veranna took in both the esthetic and strategic qualities of the landscape. Poplars, palms, oaks and firs would provide excellent hiding places, but they evoked deep emotions. Words rolled through her mind, indistinct but swirling into a pattern like cogs finding their proper mesh in a wheel turning to an ancient flow. She recognized the feeling, for she had experienced it the same day that she and the Genazi first looked down on the plains of

Loreland before engaging the evil duke, Weyland, in battle. The words fell into the flowing rhythm and led her to break out in song.

The breeze blows past willows, oaks and the flowers.
Rain falling down brings life saving powers.
Fowl and the fishes glean both field and sea.
In awe of our Maker shall we all now be.

Beneto stared at her as though he was seeing a ghost. The other slaves wondered how she could seem so happy while on the way to a hard day's work. Veranna ignored their attentions and reveled in the euphoria she felt welling up within. She felt one with the land and sang out again.

The waves keep on rolling and wash clean the shore.
The moons in their courses let us know before;
The will of our Maker and how we should live.
In all things rejoicing, His praise we must give.

Beneto shook her knee to gain her attention. "Veranna, please, you must cease. The guards will hear you and report your singing. It is not allowed for you to sing that song. Only the rulers are permitted."

Veranna felt as though she had just floated gently back to the ground. Seeing the distress on Beneto's face, she knew that he feared for their safety.

"I apologize for alarming you. The land looks so beautiful that I simply had to acknowledge the Creator's wonderful works."

Beneto glanced around to see if anyone was within earshot. "I do not know where you learned that song, but you must be careful. A slave singing it will be accused of blasphemy. The rulers are the only ones considered fit to make statements about the Creator."

Veranna shook her head in disbelief. "Incredible! Here you have an entire kingdom walking around in darkness under the brightness of the sun. If the people would open their eyes they could see and be free. Recognition of our Creator is true freedom.

Nobody taught me the song; it arose within me when I surveyed the land."

Beneto clasped his hands together. "I beg you, do not do that while we are here. It could easily bring our death."

"As you wish. However, the day is coming when all shall be free to marvel at their Creator." She fell silent and put on her broad-brimmed hat. Seeing the gate approaching she noticed that the guards had walked away to instruct slaves new to guard roles. Without knowing why, she looked at the heavy gate and thought, 'Open.' It swung wide and let the wagon drive through.

When Beneto saw no one present to open the gates he became agitated, fearing that the guards would think they had somehow broken through. He halted the wagon and waited for one of them to approach.

Several tense seconds passed and Veranna decided to demonstrate to him that it was she who controlled the gate. She placed her left hand on his shoulder and said, "Watch." She then looked at the gate and said, "Close." It closed smoothly and silently.

Beneto's eyes were saucers and the other three women were confused. Vikkaya became more nervous seeing Beneto so on edge.

"What is going on? Who handled the gate?"

Beneto pointed at Veranna and she used the moment to enforce her authority. "I have told you before that the Creator is with me. You need have no fear before the Seacorrans, for I gave you my word that you will be safe. The Creator will see that my word is true." In a calm tone she said to Beneto, "Please, let's get to the work and get it done. I am anxious to see the layout of the buildings and grounds."

It took a few minutes to arrive at the main house. Beneto drove around to the back and saw a man with gray hair and pockmarked face in reform slave clothing. "Adann, good morning my friend. It has been too long."

Adann smiled briefly and shook Beneto's hand. "Hello; it is good that you have come. With the king and queen here we have been hard pressed to get our work done. I hope you brought some help who can handle the demand." His brown eyes scanned the others and he shrugged his shoulders. "Most of the work is inside, so it is good that you brought the women. The outside work you and I can do together. It will be like many years ago."

Beneto shook his head wistfully. "How true, my friend. Well, let's get it done."

With that, Adann led them into the house and introduced them to the main housekeeper, a woman in reform clothing. Her hair was a mixture of brown and gray, and she stood about five and a half-feet tall. Gray eyes and a solid build complemented her firm manner.

"We have a lot to do. If you desire to be lazy, then you desire the whip. Need I say more?"

No one needed an explanation of her point. She led them to the washroom and directed Veranna and Vikkaya to start washing clothes, then took the other two women to clean in the upper stories of the house.

Lunch was quick and they were back to work. The slave women were each assigned a large hall to dust, sweep and mop, with nobles going about their business as if the workers did not exist. Veranna was surprised when she walked into a large room used for music and saw queen Sreba speaking with an older noblewoman. The queen's face was sad and she resisted crying.

"I tell you, mother, it is more than I can bear. I thought that giving him a son would bring us closer, but he simply goes on his way as if I mean nothing to him. He prefers the company of others."

The older woman, Grand Duchess Waverly, put her arm around Sreba's shoulders.

"My dear, have you spoken to him of your feelings? He may not be aware of how sad you are." She gently moved Sreba to a couch and had her sit down. The duchess was not as tall as her daughter, but she was far sturdier. Age and wisdom lined her face, lending her an authority beyond nobility.

"Oh mother, it is like speaking to a wall."

"What has he said?"

"He says that I am too soft and that I should participate with him when he goes for a hunt or sword practice. He prefers Countess Rosen's company; she takes part in all of those activities."

The mother shook her head in understanding. "You are caught between duties. If you do all he wants, you will neglect your queenly duties. If you do not, he sees it as a sign of rejection. Try to weather this storm as best you can. He is still young and has some maturing to do. Think of yourself as the seawall guarding the harbor. It hinders the ships passing in and out, but it also keeps the waves from pounding the docks. It is said that our noble ancestors could open it. Who knows, it could be all myth grown over in time."

"I will try, mother. Sometimes I cannot even think of anything to say. I wish that I knew a love song that would convey to him the ache I feel inside." She noticed Veranna pause and give the harpsichord a looking over. "You, slave, do you know how to play that instrument?"

Veranna froze for a moment and then gave a short bow, making sure to keep her eyes from being seen. "Yes, your highness, although it has been quite a while since I did so."

Sreba looked at her suspiciously. "You are familiar to me. Are you not the whore I had punished in the city square a week ago?"

"That I am, your highness."

The queen's features turned to amazement. "Most people die from the punishment, yet here you are working. How is this possible?"

Veranna decided to use a touch of boldness. "The Creator healed me, your highness. It seems that He has some use for me yet."

Sreba and her mother were speechless for a moment. The queen then laughed. "Slaves are such fools. With the wounds you received, you will be scarred for life. No man will want a deformed whore; you will have to reform just to survive."

Veranna pulled her shirt up to expose her stomach and back, revealing no trace of scarring. The two women were shocked and eyed her with wonder. Sreba started to say something when a man in noble uniform walked in and gave her and her mother a respectful nod after gazing at Veranna for a few lingering seconds. She quickly pulled down her shirt and blushed while lowering her head.

The man spoke first to Sreba, bringing her to her feet. "I am heading out to the country estates to inspect their security measures. I should be back in about a week." He then turned and addressed the duchess. "I trust that all is well with you, my lady. Is there anything I might bring you from the countryside?"

The duchess inclined her head and bent her knees slightly as she replied, "Thank you, my lord; if it is not too much trouble, a crate of ripe peaches would be wonderful."

"Only the very finest for you, my lady." He bowed to her and then to Sreba. "Goodbye, dear wife; a week shall pass quickly." He straightened, turned and marched out the door, pausing only to turn and look at Veranna once more before proceeding down the hall.

Sreba sniffed and blotted a tear from her eyes. "You see, mother? He is cold to me; I try to act according to my position, but he shows me disdain. What am I to do?"

The duchess answered soothingly, "You will have to act more like what he desires. You cannot act the queen to your husband. Take note of what he praises in the women whom he finds attractive and emulate them."

Sreba scowled and looked at Veranna. "That would make me nearly as much a whore as she."

Veranna could not hold back a glare of anger and resentment. Sreba did not notice, but her mother did. The queen sat down, leaned her head back and closed her eyes. She waved her hand loosely in Veranna's direction and said, "You are used to satisfying men; play me a song about love that will make me imagine being a married woman."

Veranna stifled an urge to reply angrily. She curtsied and bowed before sitting down in front of the harpsichord. Starting in a minor key, she thought about how much she missed Karsten and sang of him longingly.

Raise up your hand and fend off the morrow.
Use your strong arm to hold back the sun.
Let not the stars now fade and bring sorrow.
Let not this night of our love be yet done.
Hold and caress me with kisses unending;
Keep the desires of our passion alight.

Fill all my days with sweetness surrounding;
Give not our love a moment's respite.

Raise up your voice and call to me dearly.
Give now your ear to hear my reply.
Know for a truth my heart pours out purely.
It shall hold fast as time passes by.
Moment by moment I crave your attentions.
Each day in passing brings love vistas new.
Take me to where my words need no mention.
I long to see and embrace you anew.

Raise up your smile and vanquish my sorrows.
Whisper so tenderly all else fades 'way.
Make sure your love fills all my tomorrows.
My very being hold fast in your sway.
Always remember your touch is as nectar.
Keeping my heart in a calm, restful bay.
Come to me, come to me, come now this moment.
Come to me now and steal me away.

Veranna sighed and looked up toward the ceiling, praying that she would find Tyrzah soon and be home in Karsten's arms.

Sreba covered her face with her hands and sobbed as her mother patted her on the shoulder to console her, but the queen got up and walked quickly from the room.

The duchess shook her head and sighed, losing track of the fact that Veranna still sat at the harpsichord. Speaking more to herself than anyone else, she said, "That poor girl wants him to change while she remains the same!"

Veranna said softly, "It is that way for all of us; we become like baked clay that is reformed only when broken. Fortunately, my husband is just the way I want him to be."

As if speaking to a friend, the duchess shook her head in agreement. "Yes, I was fortunate to marry a man who was quite agreeable." She suddenly recalled Veranna's status. "Who are you to speak with me with such familiarity? I could have you flogged again for such a breach."

"I mean no offense, my lady; I hope to be able to help your daughter through this time of upset. We are near to the same age and station."

The duchess's head snapped back and she frowned. "Station? How could my daughter share station with a whore! That is an idea worthy of great punishment."

Veranna's voice now grew angry. "I am not a whore. That was an excuse given by a false belief. Some smuggler, who must have thought I would die from the sting of a spider, took me captive. I was brought here and sold to Lord Knoxun. It was simply assumed that anyone taken as a slave must be under the Creator's punishment, so they branded me a whore to bypass the Creator's laws of justice. I tell you truly that I have only one man and that is my husband."

The duchess gave her a hard look. "I believe you, for your song could only be for one special man. As to the rest of your behavior, you conduct yourself as one of the nobility, and finer than most of them. Who are you?"

Veranna removed her hat and stood up straight. Looking directly at the duchess, she spoke proudly. "I am Veranna, Empress of the Seven Lands and a direct descendant of Ergon, the heir of Dunamays, of the line of Emeraldia."

Duchess Waverly nearly fainted. This young woman exuded royalty with every beat of her pulse, and had the strongest emerald green eyes that she had ever seen. More than that, the name Dunamays was well known from their history. He had been the heir to the ancient throne of Seacorro, but rebelled against the kingdom's doctrine of the Creator. He led a following away north and west into the lands ruled by the fierce Koosti barbarians. It was said that they had all died there as punishment for their rebellion.

"My dear girl, regardless of the truth of your claim, I strongly advise you to say this to no one; you would be tortured and killed. Your ancestors were condemned for heresy, a heresy that threatened the foundations of the nobles' right to rule. One man, a long time ago, questioned the logic of the nobles' rights and was imprisoned. He has been a slave ever since."

"Are you referring to the man named Beneto?"

"Yes. He was young and impulsive, so even though born to a noble line, his doubts about the Creator's willing certain things left him a slave."

Veranna risked a tone of reproach in her reply. "Beneto is a fine man, and being sentenced to a life of slavery for investigating the ways of the Creator, is a total miscarriage of justice. To be consistent you should make a slave of anyone who ever has a doubt about your beliefs. You would find yourselves all to be slaves."

The duchess gazed far back in time and a tear came to her eye. "You sound like me, for I said much the same to the Council of Nobles when Beneto was judged."

Veranna realized that the woman was full of reluctance and sorrow as she recalled days long gone by. "You were in love with Beneto; have you seen him since that time?"

"No, for shame fills me with dread to look upon him. We spoke of marriage but it was not to be. I married another and have been happy. Beneto had no chance."

Veranna felt her sorrow and saw that she was a woman of reason and conscience. "My advice to you, my lady, is to send for him today and set things right. It is the least you can do; he will thank you profusely. He is here with the rest of us workers on your estate."

The duchess fell silent for a few moments as she considered her options. Then, she straightened and gave Veranna a smile. "You have wisdom and boldness; those make for a fine ruler. I assume your realm is one of peace and cooperation."

Veranna returned her smile. "We do have many wonderful people in our realm, but the Koosti have made peace difficult after waging two wars against us. We have a tenuous truce at present; the wife of the Koosti Potentate, DeAndre y'dob, is now my vassal over an entire Koosti province. She is from the Deeri tribes."

"It would seem you come from the legends and bring other legends with you. The Deeri have not been much of a people for ages. It is said that they had a lineage of priests dedicated to the Creator."

"They still do. The chief of them performed my wedding ceremony."

Duchess Waverly shook her head in wonder. "Ancient days are upon us." She gave Veranna a regal nod and spoke respectfully. "Your highness, I am very sorry for the way you have been treated. I ask that you be patient until we can see to your freedom. As a slave, only the Council can declare you free and turned from wicked ways."

"I shall try, my lady. However, I have a duty that requires immediate attention. One of my subjects, a little girl named Tyrzah, was brought here and sold. I must find her and return her safely to her parents. That is why I had to subdue the guards on the Merchani Estate last night; I was looking for this girl."

Eyes wide open with surprise, the duchess exclaimed, "That was you? One woman defeats six Leopard guards and sets the estates in panic! Dear lady, that is enough to prove your claims to me. The line of Dunamays was said to be gifted by the Creator with special powers for battle. It was Beneto who read between the lines of the ancient accounts and saw that the Seacorrans lost a minimum of six men for each of the Emeraldians. It seems that you repeated history last night."

Veranna smiled and looked down. "The Creator does have quite a sense of finesse." She moved away from the harpsichord and continued dusting. "I do not wish to harm anyone, I simply want to find this little girl and get home."

The duchess gave Veranna a slight bow. "My daughter may have been present at this girl's evaluation. I will ask her if she knows who bought her. As for getting home, unless you believe in dragons or command a stout ship, that will be hard to realize. The mountains on the west are impenetrable and the desert to the north is either frying or freezing. The eastern border ends at jungles full of vicious barbarians. The harbor wall controls the passage of ships in and out, while the rest of the coast is impossible to land on. I will try to think of something, but for now, we never had this conversation."

Veranna nodded gratefully. "Thank you, my lady; you fill me with hope"

"Let us pray that it shall not prove vain. Your presence here is a harbinger of doom for the way of life we Seacorrans have known.

I even wish that you could stay for a time and teach Sreba a thing or two. She is far too weak."

Veranna's eyebrows rose as a thought came to her. "I could teach her how to wield a sword. If the king thinks her boring for not enjoying physical sports, she could give him a real surprise by besting him when he least expects it. Even if she did not best him, a good showing would make a great impression on him."

The duchess thought about the proposal for a moment and her face brightened. "That is a wonderful idea. It must, however, all be done secretly to avoid revealing you too soon to the Council. I hope that some of your spirit will rub off onto my daughter. A bit of feistiness would do her well." She turned and headed toward the doorway. "I need to return to my duties and you might get into trouble if one of the staff thinks you are not busy."

Veranna took her dirty cleaning rags to the washroom in the basement and immersed them in a washbasin of soapy water. The room was quiet and her mind turned to thoughts of Karsten. She imagined being in his arms and laying her head on his chest, enjoying the warmth and security of his touch.

A chill suddenly crept up her spine. She looked around the room and saw no one. As if pulled, her head turned to look down at the floor. A rectangular seam, partly covered by dirty laundry, could be made out in the dim light. In her head a faint sound arose, a song borne upon the waves of the sea, or a spring breeze through trees. Curiosity overcame fear. She stepped over to the outline in the floor and moved the dirty laundry away. A pull ring lay on one end of the outline. It was cold and rusty, but as she pulled, a section of the floor lifted easily even though made of old oak. A set of stairs ran down into a storage cellar. It was dark, but her night vision allowed her to see everything. The room was three times the size of the washroom. Barrels and ceramic urns sat in stacks around the stone support columns that rose to the floor above. She turned to look at the southern wall and the song in her head grew stronger.

✲ ✲ ✲

CHAPTER 17

Yanbre awoke from a nap he had drifted into after lunch. Working nights to patrol the streets with his men left him tired during the day, even if he managed to sleep in the morning. He stretched and shook his head, thinking that someone was singing in a nearby hallway. It was a faint, lofty tune that he could not quite grasp. The more he tried to isolate any part of it the more it eluded him.

He walked into the corridor near the mess hall to see if someone was there, although he did not expect to see anyone since they tried to give him quiet times for his naps. He continued down the hallway to see if the volume of the song would change in any given direction. Passing several people who looked at him curiously, he wondered if they heard the singing, yet paid it no mind.

A few minutes later he came upon Karsten in a junction of hallways. A bit embarrassed, he said self-consciously, "Ah, I hope this does not seem an odd question, but do you know where the singing is coming from?"

Karsten stopped and listened for a moment and then shook his head. "I do not hear any singing. Are you sure you are not still half asleep and dreaming?"

Yanbre smiled and gestured in frustration. "I am sure that I am not asleep; however, I am sure that I hear the singing, as well."

Karsten's brow furrowed. "Do you recognize the voice?"

"No. In fact, trying to make sense of it is eluding me."

"Has this ever happened before?"

"Not exactly. When the empress came from the Genazi lands to battle Duke Weyland, I heard your singing while still in my cave hideout. I could understand it clearly."

Karsten took a moment to consider what to make of this phenomenon. His left eyebrow rose as a thought occurred to him. "Let's get to an upper balcony and take a look. If it is what I think it might be, we can then conclude that you are not crazy."

Yanbre chuckled, "That would be a great relief."

They quickly climbed several sets of stairs and passed through an embrasure onto a balcony. The bright sun interfered with spotting anything in the southern sky, but after a few minutes a large, dark cloud moved in front of it. Karsten suddenly pointed up into the sky toward the southeast.

"Look, Yanbre, the moons are aligning! Every time we have seen this before there has been something important happening with Veranna. Wherever she is there is something she must accomplish and see through. The singing you hear is connected with it. Your link to her through your armor must be resonating with that purpose."

The castellan looked down at the ring he wore on his left hand. When Veranna had been revealed to the people of Clarens, it had let him know by emitting a bright flash of light. He nearly jumped when another leaped from it into his eye.

"Karsten, I believe you are right. Veranna has come to the point where she will be revealed to someone. I only wish we knew where."

The young Genazi lord lowered his gaze and said, quietly, "So do I."

The city of Grandshire teamed with people and commerce. Wagon after wagon lumbered through the streets loading and unloading cargos. Barges waited in line at the river docks to deliver their goods from far lands or to carry goods from the empire to other nations and peoples. Swarms of workers hurried to complete their tasks before heading to the banks before closing time.

Duke Russell Heilson looked over the city as he walked along the wall of his castle. Tesra was with him, silently appraising the changes evident since the Koosti war.

"Tesra, it is hard to believe; can this be the same city? I would swear that the population has doubled since the war."

The sturdy Mother of the Academy, and adopted mother of the empress, nodded her agreement. "I believe that we are witnessing a demonstration of one of Emeraldia's main tenets: Respect for life brings life. The Koosti Empire simply survives by sucking the life from others. Emeraldia flourishes by giving people a real opportunity to grow and achieve. They can earn a living and invest in their future without some rampaging lord confiscating their money and land under the guise of 'for the good of the fief.'"

The duke let out a hardy laugh. "Ah, Tesra, you and the empress are good to have around just to rile the prissy nobles who think they are entitled to everything. Those fascists cannot comprehend that anyone might think they should prove worthy of their positions."

Tesra smiled wanly. "Only too true. Veranna has a great advantage in growing up among the people. She learned hard work and humility. Her nobility comes from a mind submissive to the Creator." She paused and then asked, "How many men do you have patrolling the streets for this man named Dag? The note from Tolemera said that it is likely he will head here."

Heilson leaned forward and rested his elbows onto the top of the wall. "Right now I have twenty. They are mostly doing passive work, since we do not know what this Dag looks like, and it will probably be another week before he arrives. Secret travels take more time. In the next few days I will increase the number of men and hope we can net this slippery fish. Karsten will tear his head off if he does not divulge what he knows."

Tesra grunted, "That will happen after I tear a few other parts from him first."

Heilson grinned and shook his head. "The wiles of feminine grace! No wonder it took a dragon to satisfy you." He changed the subject matter and asked, "By the way, how is your son doing?"

Tesra took a deep breath and exhaled slowly. "He is growing quickly and is quite strong. After a few months I swear he is demonstrating cunning and humor. I am sure that he shall grow to be a challenge."

Heilson chuckled and said teasingly, "If anyone should know how to handle such a child, it is you." He paused and saw her eyes anxiously scan the city. "Do not worry, Tesra; we will have this man, Dag, soon enough and squeeze him for every shred of information possible. Veranna will be back before you know it."

Tesra took his hand in hers and patted it softly. "Thank you for easing my heart a bit. It is getting hard for this old she-goat to keep up a good attitude under such circumstances." She stood straight and smiled brightly. "How about we join the soldiers for weapons drills? I need the exercise."

Heilson let out a deep guffaw. "Only if you promise not to injure any of them. The bruises on the last squad are still smarting."

They laughed and headed for the training yard.

✠ ✠ ✠

CHAPTER 18

In the Red Tailor Inn, four days later, Rita Caterman readied for a night out. Not just any night out. This was a first. Her husband, Malcolm, was minding the inn thinking that she was simply needing an evening of relaxation. But that was not her desire at all. Tonight she wanted to try and penetrate the seamier sector of the city to see if she could not get some information on this man who had fled Tolemera. Tesra had mentioned that he might well be in the know as to Veranna's whereabouts. The empress was her friend, and anyone who would harm her was Rita's sworn enemy.

She donned a dress of reds and blues that had a provocative vee-neck design with thin straps over the shoulders. She blushed to see so much cleavage show as she looked into her mirror. She took a swallow of wine and forced herself to ignore the scolding her conscience doled out. She must blend in with the loose women who frequented the alehouses and brothels over toward the northeast section of the city. She just might overhear a helpful bit of information or encounter someone who could lead her to Dag.

After letting down her hair and styling it around her shoulders, she slipped a slender, razor-sharp dagger through a garter on her right thigh, and placed a coil of thin but strong string under each breast where they would not show. She then put on an old coat that could be discarded at need, and covered her head with a dark linen cloth.

A half-hour later she started passing a number of lewd shops and people. Whores and escorts strutted along the streets while others advertised themselves in the doorways of unkempt buildings claiming to be inns. Raucous music and entertainment poured out and helped cover the conversations of its denizens from being overheard. Smoke and dim lighting ensured that those inside could identify those entering such rooms before their eyes adjusted.

Rita headed further east along the street and located a shabby tavern with several side doors, dark corners and windows low to the ground, ideal for quick exits. Some of the words painted on the outside to list food and drink were spelled incorrectly, and the doorman was one of the seediest brutes Rita had ever seen. His face looked to be made more of scar tissue covered by a veneer of hog oil. His beady, blue eyes leered at her as she approached the entryway and his voice sounded more like a talking crocodile's.

"Ain' seen yer face afore missy. You one 'a Sinda's girls?"

Rita recalled some of the times that whores had accompanied men into the Red Tailor. They were sultry and possessive toward their clients while brazen in speech and manner. She tried to emulate their style and wondered what Kreida would do. Caution would reveal her more quickly than a pronouncement.

"Nah, I work independent. Up street mostly, but the constables are bastards these days. Ya' got any worth tendin' inside?"

The man grunted and spat. "That ain't the question. Are ya worth their gold?"

Born and raised in modesty, Rita had no skill in prideful self-promotion. She felt a moment of panic before a thought jumped into her brain. *Think Kreida!* "I am worth every last penny and more, you idiot. If you say otherwise I will make sure you can't even please your pig at home." A menacing glare and fists on hips made her seem like a veteran of the brothels.

The man just smiled lustfully. "Got a little bite in ya, huh? That's good around here. These are the terms if ya wanna work me place. Half 'o what ya gets from the men and I gets ya all night to the mornin'."

Rita sneered and laughed derisively. "You will get a fourth and only five minutes. I am not one of your common pieces of trash, so get one of your own tramps for the night. If any part of your head still works you will let me do my work and make money. You will make more that way, too."

The man gave her a long, hard look before jabbing his thumb toward the inside. "Ya had best back up yer braggin' with some results. And, ye better not try skimpin' on my cut, or I'll do my cut in a way ya won't like."

Rita tossed her head to dismiss him as totally irrelevant, and then proceeded into the room. She suppressed an immediate urge to cough from the smoke, and the cheap ales and wines sent out odors just as sickening. Thinking of what Kreida might do, she walked up to a table where several men sat on sturdy chairs, some of them in the process of being seduced by whores sitting on their laps. Rita grabbed a dull, clag wine mug from one of the men and took a sip. She spewed it out and sneered at the other women.

"Cheap and totally unsatisfying." She looked at the man whose mug she took. "You want better. Don't waste your money on…poor quality." The three whores started to stand and put Rita in her place, but the men laughed and pulled them back.

One of the men, Hugh, said to the rest, "We needs a good whore brawl; its been a long time."

They all laughed and wagged their heads in agreement. Rita gave Hugh a disparaging look. "They would not last a second. An ugly bull like you should know that. Look at how worn out they are already."

The men laughed again and had to restrain the women. Hugh looked Rita in the eye, challenging her bravura.

"True, you ain't as calloused as these wenches." The men laughed again. "But, what makes you think you can do better?"

Rita looked at him as though he was a total idiot. "Have these tramps ever pleased an emporer? Of course not; Dalmar Gelangweil had fine taste in women. If he were still alive I would be ready to serve his every desire. These new-fangled Emeraldians did not have sense enough to stay out of the way."

Hugh gave her a conspiratorial leer. "Yer tongue wags true, but yer likely to get in trouble. A woman thinkin' clear around here ain't common."

Rita snorted haughtily. "I am no common woman, you dolt. If you can't meet my fee just say so and quit wasting my time."

Hugh glanced at the others around the table and then looked Rita up and down. "Bad timin' lovey; we's savin' our gold for the cock fights later. After I triple my money, I'll come get ya. If yer alone, I'll just take ya without payin'."

All of them at the table let out sinister chuckles. The whores urged him to take her right there on the table. Rita raised her left eyebrow in subtle menace as a thin smile came over her mouth.

"Do not do anything stupid that could have lasting consequences. Just point me to someone worthy of my skills."

Hugh eyed her once more as he considered his reply. "Yer got a style likes ya been around high folk. Only one we know yer type is back in the corner by the hallway. Maybe he ain't spent all his gold on the regulars here."

Rita pretended that the man no longer existed and gradually made her way back to the corner where a man sat alone in the shadows. His eyes and teeth gleamed with cold light, but his skin had an oily gleam. She pulled back a chair and sat down, the two of them eyeing each other warily. When he made no attempt at a greeting, she took the initiative. Her heart pounded as she put on a bold front.

"Are you going to offer a lady a drink, or are you as ill-mannered as the rest of these pigs in the room?"

The man raised an eyebrow and waved over one of the wenches. His speech was crisp and direct. "This whore wants a drink. Get her one, cheap."

Rita glared at him. "Cheap is it? I thought a man of your station would have a sense of class; it seems not." She knew from the color and aroma of his drink that he was enjoying one of the more expensive brandies.

"What makes you think I have station?"

"You are drinking Fraleisian brandy. Few but nobles would spend so much on an evening drink. And, since I spent a good deal of time in Imperia, I recognize your accent. It is not a commoners'."

"What were you doing in Imperia, and why did you leave?"

"I often served the emperor's desires. Since he was usurped there has been a downturn in my particular specialty in Neidburg."

"If you served the emperor, what was the name of his favorite woman?"

Rita had to think hard and quickly. She remembered the stories she had heard about Dalmar and his followers. "Her name was Tasha, and she was my chief rival. Her demise was well-earned."

"You two fight like cats?"

"In a manner of speaking. Dalmar would not let us injure one another, so we came up with alternatives."

"Oh, yeah?"

"One time I put special herbs in her vegetable dish that caused her bowels to run for a week. I had Dalmar all to myself. She was furious; the more so since she lost a lot of weight and looked like a skeleton without breasts."

The man nodded and grunted. "I remember that time. It took a few weeks before Dalmar used her again. I was in charge of locating young girls for him and helped plan the sacking of the Academy, in Clarens. Too bad we didn't get this worthless tramp calling herself an empress."

Rita barely controlled herself from slitting the man's throat. She refocused her anger to make it seem as though she was in agreement with him.

"The girl has yet to learn what awaits her. In the meantime I will keep alive the ways of the Gelangweils' as best I can. For now I am simply earning a living."

The man was silent for a moment. After scanning the room once more he quietly said, "If you are as good as you say, I might be inclined to contribute to your cause."

As she leaned forward, Rita made sure that a generous amount of her cleavage showed and that her voice came out in husky sensuality. She was sure that this man was her target from his voice and manner. The fact that he seemed to have recently arrived, and that he had an ample supply of money, convinced her that she was correct.

"I can demonstrate my worth all night long if you wish."

"The emperor was satisfied?"

"Very; he was in a fine mood for days."

"If you can't live up to your brag then I won't pay you a penny."

Rita laughed disdainfully. "You should count yourself fortunate. When the Erains take power once more, I will be back to Neidburg earning a lucrative income. If you perform well, I may even put in a good word for you."

The man downed the rest of his brandy in one gulp and stood up. A slippery smile on his face, he reached down and put his hands around Rita's sides and lifted her up, exposing even more of her breasts. "A little gold should be worth a good night's pleasure. Come on, let's not waste any time."

His left arm around her waist, he pulled her close and led her down the hall and out a side door. The faint light of two of the three moons illuminated their path enough that they did not stumble over obstacles. In a few minutes they were walking along a canal that led to the river. Rita wondered where the man was taking her.

"There are no inns this way; do you have a home near the water?"

"No, but you do."

He grabbed her hair at the back of her head and pulled down hard. The force sent her to her knees and he stepped behind her, holding a slender blade to her throat. The slightest movement on her part could bring that blade through her flesh and end her life. The only thing she could do was try to delay him and see if an opening came for her to escape.

"Ppp...please, I won't fight you. Just let me live."

"You will live or die at my whim. First, you will tell me who you are and how you know so much about Dalmar Gelangweil." He gagged and hog tied her before letting her say anymore. "The water will be your home for good. The critters will feast on your flesh until only your bones are left. Before that I will take my pleasure with you, as will the men I bring from the street who will help you remember things you might otherwise forget."

He threw her over his shoulder and carried her into a rotting building along the bank of the canal. Struggling against her bonds was pointless and the gag muffled her screams. The man laid her onto an old workbench, tied her down, ripped off her blouse and tossed it away after lighting an oil lamp. The floorboards squeaked as he walked around and the shadows swallowed the light.

"Now, my pretty, let me see if some sense has gotten into your head. Tell me your name. You shall never forget mine during the short time I will keep you alive. The name 'Dag' will be one of dread for you." He clamped his right hand onto her throat to stop any attempts at screaming, then undid the gag.

Rita figured that trying to lie to an expert liar would achieve little, so she answered in simple truth. "My name is Rita."

"Ah, that's a good girl." He paused and looked her over lustfully. "Would such a pretty thing as you be working alone or is there someone with you?" He used his left hand to fondle her, sending a shiver of disgust through her whole body.

"I am working with my friend, Jerban."

"And where is this Jerban?"

"Right behind you."

The man frowned and turned to look over his shoulder. Out of the shadows came Jerban's hulking body with a speed and agility unthinkable for someone so large. As his huge ham fist streaked at Dag, time seemed to stand still for the killer. Jerban's fist slammed into his left eye and sent him to the floor. As he fell, his knife slid without pressure across Rita's throat. It was razor sharp and sliced smoothly.

Rita screamed as blood ran down her neck, and an instant later, Jerban pressed a handkerchief over the wound before cutting her bonds.

"Rita, it'll be okay, child; don't go panicking. The cut didn' go deep. Keep the cloth pressed tight. It's just a surface cut. You'll have a scar to tell a tale 'bout."

She broke down and cried with relief. "Oh, Jerban, you wonderful old man! How did you know I was here?"

"I saw you when you strolled into the bad parts o' town. I been lookin' for this guy called Dag and figured, like you, that he'd be in these parts. You took a great risk commin' down here, girl. But it looks like it paid off."

Rita composed herself and nodded agreement as she hugged the lumpy man before her. "Let's get out of here, Jerban. We have to get this man to the duke right away."

He reached down, effortlessly picked Dag up and threw him over his shoulder. Rita found her torn blouse and managed to wrap it around her chest before they headed back to the street. Jerban knew the streets and alleys better in the dark than most people during the day. In minutes they were back to more respectable parts of the city and found a carriage for hire. Soon they stood before Tesra and the duke explaining what was going on.

The duke called for his healer to tend to Rita while Tesra resuscitated Dag. The left side of his head looked as though a blacksmith's hammer had pounded it.

"Jerban, you nearly decapitated him. I suppose it will serve as a good introduction to the real thing. However, first things first; he will have a lovely time with the interrogators."

"Aw, Tes, I was only helpin' out, old friend. I hope he was worth it."

"So do I, my friend. We are going to take him immediately to Tolemera. Lord Karsten will no doubt wish to lead the interrogation."

Duke Heilson, wanting to increase Dag's sense of fear, clasped his hands behind his back and casually walked past him.

"I had thought that hot pokers and removal of body parts would be bad. However, I believe Karsten has far more productive means for getting a man to confess his guilt. I would love to be there and see what awaits our dear Dag. Hopefully his head will heal enough along the way so that he feels every drop of torture."

Tesra's voice was as cold as steel. "Let us hope so." She turned to the duke. "If the squad is ready, I would like to get going, now."

He bowed and waved at the doorway. "It is waiting for you, my lady."

"Thank you, my lord. Please, when this mess is over, come to Tolemera, right away. Bring Rita and Jerban with you, too. In the meantime, ready your forces to depart for whatever location we get from this Dag."

"Yes, Tesra. We will be awaiting your summons." He motioned for the two guards to take Dag to a wagon used for transporting prisoners, and for Tesra he had readied the most comfortable coach he had on hand. Off they sped to the river docks where a swift transport would sail them to the eastern edge of Smooth Lake. Looking at the sails, the anxious Mother of the Academy prayed for the Creator to raise up a strong wind.

CHAPTER 19

Beneto nearly skipped into the slave quarters on the Knoxun estate. Veranna spotted him standing inside the doorway, wondering why he seemed so excited. She walked up to him and did a quick curtsy.

"Good evening, Beneto. You seem as though ready to burst. What is going on?"

He grabbed her arms just above the elbows and a smile beamed across his face.

"Veranna! It is amazing; the queen sent Lord Knoxun a letter saying that, as far as the throne is concerned, I have finished my course of reformation and can be declared a citizen. They left it up to Lord Knoxun to make the final decision, but I am sure he will agree."

Veranna gave him a hug. "Beneto, that is wonderful. Will you be able to return to your academy and teach?"

His face changed to serious contemplation. "I do not know; such posts are assigned by the throne. I may stand a chance if an old friend has any influence."

Veranna gave him a wry, questioning look. "The queen's mother?"

"Yes, she and I once…" He was shocked at her question, a touch of fear entering his eyes. "How do you know that?"

Veranna took his hand in hers and gave him a comradely grin. "I had a little conversation with her the other day. I believe that she still feels a great deal of guilt over how you have been treated."

He looked down at the floor, an elderly sage reflecting on his own deficiencies. "I cannot blame her; she even tried to help me. What happened to me was largely due to my inability to close my mouth at the right time." He paused as a thought struck him. "Of course! It is because of you that I am being set free. You must have impressed the queen's mother greatly. What else did you discuss?"

"I told her about the little girl, Tyrzah, and related my background to her. She seems to think that I am in for a very difficult time."

He turned and paced through the entryway as a distant recollection formed in his mind.

"She is a wise woman and very likely correct, for in you I see the fulfillment of ancient words written down by a seer of the old line."

Veranna rolled her eyes and grimaced humorously. "I have grown accustomed to such things. Even my name was taken from an ancient prophecy."

"I am not surprised since the Creator has such a way of bringing about His desires. His words may be obscure when given, but fulfillment comes in the most surprising and intricate ways."

"True. What is the message you think applies to me?"

"Not long after your ancestors departed this realm a seer, unrecognized for hundreds of years, wrote down what was considered to simply be a poem. Scholars have tried to see if it ever has been fulfilled in the past, but I am one of those who argue that those attempts to match the poem with past events were unsuccessful. Here it is:

Out of the waves the forest shall grow.
After it passes through mountains of snow.
A sapling so fair shall bow down the trees.
The crest of the deeps shall bend to its knees.
The trees shall then blossom and bear worthy fruit.

The Creator of all shall be their pursuit.
The hardness of armor shall crumble as clay.
The deeds done in darkness will be shown in the day."

Veranna's brow crinkled in thought as she examined the words. "A forest passing through mountains of snow? That is obscure to me, just as a sapling bowing down the trees is odd. Have your people thoroughly examined the metaphors?"

"Yes, but there is still disagreement. How does a forest grow out of waves? Is the reference to the waves past, present or future? And what is the crest of the deeps? Consensus on these issues is lacking."

Veranna folded her arms across her chest and leaned back against the wall. "*Crests of the deep,* typically refers to the sea. The empire of the Seven lands has contact with the sea only on its western side. That is opposite from where we are."

Beneto waved his hand toward the north. "Past the border of Faresea lie the forests where the various Arborii tribes roam. I do not recall any reports of a sea in that direction, and the Arborii are cannibalistic savages who avoid everyone else. More than likely we shall not know the explanation until fulfillment."

Veranna nodded agreement and then turned serious. "Tonight I am going to search three or four of the estates to the northeast. The little girl, Tyrzah, is sure to be scared to sickness by now."

Beneto bowed and spoke quietly. "Your highness, you fill me with fear. What you are doing is very dangerous. Many of the estates have hired trainers to increase the effectiveness of their guards. One of these trainers is described as uncanny in his ability to wield a blade. Not only that, but the number of guards has increased. If you are killed or injured, then the little girl's fate is sealed."

Veranna smiled appreciatively. "Thank you, Beneto; I shall be extra careful. All I would like to ask of you is advice on how to get out of the city and on my way home."

He thought about her request for a moment and his eyes seemed to look far away. In a resigned voice he said, "Only if you take me with you. Here, even though a free man, I shall never be rid of the onus of slavery. The academies will be reluctant to hire someone under official scrutiny for so long, and I have no close contact with family. A fresh start would do me good."

She put a hand on his arm. "As you wish. However, it will likely be a perilous course. You will need to help me plan how to get away and have a chance to survive."

He smiled conspiratorially. "I do have many friends and not a few favors to claim. More than likely we will have to sneak aboard a ship heading southwest for other ports of trade."

"I was smuggled into this land, so being smuggled out should not prove too bad. I have never been on a ship on an ocean. I pray that the weather and sailors shall be amenable."

"The hardest part will be getting past the sea wall. Old tales say that it once stood wide open and allowed many ships in and out. As it is now, we shall need to hide very well; the narrow inlet in the wall allows only one ship at a time and can be fully defended by a small contingent of men. They search the ships for anything illegal. The great, floating barriers can hold any ship in the inlet and allow the defenders to fire-bomb it."

"I leave it in your hands." She pulled her sword from its sheath and looked it over. "I must be a hunter tonight. Pray that I do not need to draw blood."

Beneto bowed and headed back to the main house. Veranna waited until dark and changed clothes, the other women knowing better than to ask what she was doing. Out into the black of night she went, a lioness seeking a lost cub.

✶ ✶ ✶

CHAPTER 20

A faint breeze carried the smells of the waterfront up into the regions north of the city of Seacorro. Night had fallen, the stars shimmering through the sky, and the second moon shined with a pale, reddish hue. More lamps flamed on as roving guards patrolled the streets.

Veranna flitted through it all, a ghost passing by. The first estate she searched on the far eastern side of the city was less than average in size, allowing her to quickly determine that Tyrzah was not there. The guards were lax and she left the grounds easily.

The second estate lay north of the first and was three times as large. Guards, many of whom wore leopard skin attire, patrolled regularly. Penetrating the grounds would require precise timing.

She waited for a gap in the patrols' overlapping routine and found a sturdy, elastic tree branch about eight feet long. Getting a running start, she vaulted up and onto the top of the ten-foot high wall. Immediately she dropped to the ground and scanned her surroundings. She saw two sets of three guards approaching cautiously, their weapons drawn. They did not know what they were seeking, but the unfamiliar tap against the wall had them on edge.

Veranna's night vision helped her see the guards' weapons easily. Swords, knives, batons and barbed chains were ready for action.

Employing tactics learned from their recent increase in training, they approached the area of suspicion from opposite directions to limit the number of ways an opponent could maneuver.

It was a perfunctory decision as to how to increase her odds. Stealth and surprise would be maximized to sew confusion among their ranks, and provide a number of openings.

The guards, three to her left and three to her right, closed in on her, not quite sure as to what they were looking for in the dark. Suddenly, the guard third from the left was off his feet and landed hard on his back. The guard second to the left flew back from a foot thrusting powerfully into his stomach. The last guard on the left swung his sword blindly at the dark form in motion. His blade missed easily and a split second later he was tossed into the air toward the three other guards on the right, knocking one of them to the ground. The other two lost their sense of teamwork and started for Veranna.

She grabbed two batons from downed guards and blocked the sword blows, smacked the one on her left side with a sharp strike to his right wrist and heard it break, then hit the guard on her right on his left knee. His leg buckled and he fell back. A second later his comrade joined him on the ground, swift blows to the forehead putting them out cold. Fear gripped the other guard as he tried to crawl away for help. He and two others collided in their desperation, impeding their movements. Perfectly aimed blows sent them all into the realm of unconsciousness.

Veranna held on to the batons, not wanting to cause permanent injury or death if she did not need to. She scouted out her surroundings, tied and gagged the guards, then ran toward the main buildings. Keeping to the shadows, she wondered how soon other guards would find the ones she had downed.

The slave quarters and other outlying buildings held no sign of Tyrzah, but it made sense that such a little girl might be kept in the main house. It was mostly dark, but a few candles and lamps showed where the servants still labored. When an older serving woman opened a back door to remove trash to an outside container, Veranna darted silently up the five steps and into the house. She quickly searched the main floor and headed up the servants' stairway to the second. There were more rooms, even though they were smaller than those on the main floor, but the most difficult aspect was the long, straight hallway. Anyone exiting a room could easily cross her path.

The doors were well maintained and opened silently. The rooms were either empty or had people sound asleep. The next-to-last room on the left opened easily, but the entryway was not as deep as the others. Her shoulder brushed the wall on her right, making a discernable sound. She froze and looked into the room. To her left, about five feet away, was a large bed with a man and girl locked in fervent sexual activity. Veranna's eyes popped open wide and she fought to stifle an embarrassed gasp. Still, the man stopped for a moment to see if he had actually heard something. He looked to be in his early or mid forties and the girl was obviously seventeen at most. Her voice was wispy through heavy breathing.

"Master, why did you stop? Do I displease you?"

His reply was full of contempt. "Shut up, girl; I am not finished with you yet."

Veranna took the opportunity to move closer to the door while he spoke. A moment later he resumed with the girl and Veranna hurriedly slipped back into the hallway. She realized that her face was scarlet and her breathing too quick. She took a minute to calm herself before heading to the third floor.

Tyrzah was not there. A number of young children occupied side rooms, but she was not among them.

Veranna paused to look out a window before heading down the stairway. Dozens of torches lit up the grounds as guards paced back and forth in search of something. She knew that she was their quarry and quickly scanned the landscape for the best way out. The northwest border had some trees and a few buildings along the way that would offer cover, and the neighboring estate could then be searched as well.

Making her way to the back door, she peered out cautiously, then flitted down the steps to the cover of a nearby tree. Lanterns flared at various points on the grounds as the guards spread out to seal off possible escape routes. There were many more guards now, some in set positions and others in roving patrols designed to herd their prey to a given point.

Veranna timed the patrols and waited until the crossover point was at its weakest. She darted for the cover of another tree twenty yards away. Just as she reached it, a Leopard guard sprang from behind it while swinging his sword. His aim was imprecise in the darkness and Veranna instantly closed the gap between them. She swung the baton in her right hand and hit the nerve in his right forearm. He screamed in pain but it ended abruptly when she jabbed her other baton into the hollow of his throat.

A flurry of activity erupted from the other guards when they heard their comrade scream. Their circle of patrols collapsed inward as a strong voice barked orders.

Veranna knew that she had to get serious in the fighting. She dreaded having to kill and said a quick prayer that the Creator would allow her to escape without taking anyone's life. Forty feet away was a long, tall building with many windows. Shadows clung to it despite the torches and lamps so she sprinted for and dove into the foliage beneath a window.

The guards still had no clear idea of who or what they sought. However, their leader knew what he was doing and kept them organized. They surrounded the building and started beating the shrubbery with spears and poles. Some used swords to poke through the bushes.

Veranna forced open a window and in one quick jump was inside the building. As she came down toward the floor she saw a tough, wooden bench running along the wall. She put out her hands and caught the edge of the bench, then flipped onto her feet. The floor was oak and apparently in regular use. Staffs, spears, knives, swords, maces and chains lined the wall on one side while protective practice gear lined the other.

She realized that this was a training room for the martial arts. She did not want to become the practice dummy and ran to the north end. Looking through the door window she saw scores of guards, and through the other windows she saw that the guards were a thick hedge all around the building. An opening in their line would be hard to come by.

Just then the doorway on the other end of the hall opened and guards poured in. A second later the gas-fueled lights flamed on and revealed her foes. A dozen of them had bows and took aim. She fell into her total battle mode. The arrows streamed at her but she deflected them with incredible speed and conservation of motion while keeping her eyes on her opponents. Their arrows spent, the guards drew their swords and spears for a simultaneous attack. They halted when their leader's voice carried through the hall.

"Halt!" A lean man over six feet tall walked in confidently and surveyed the scene, his eyes full of admiration and curiosity at Veranna's skill. "It seems that we have more than a common criminal paying us a visit." He pulled off his hat and gave Veranna a short bow.

Veranna felt her first thrill of genuine fear. The man's dark-blond hair was shorn to the crown of his head and on top it stood up straight about two inches. On the handle of his sword a green 'R' radiated like a small flame. This was neither Leopard Guard nor anyone from the ranks of the Seacorrans. This was a Swordsman of Randal, one of the most deadly fighters in the known world. Their skills surpassed the natural bounds of men, for the House of Randal was rewarded by Veranna's ancestors for their allegiance in ancient days when the Emeraldians departed Seacorro. The Creator endowed them with skills to help them survive and train others to defend themselves against evildoers. A Swordsman of Randal had aided the rebellion in Loreland, led by Yanbre. Emeraldia owed them a great debt, and kings and queens showed them honor. Regardless of rank or station, people would provide room and board to them wherever they roamed. Their homeland, far to the north of the Seven Lands, provided them more than enough opportunity to hone their skills in actual combat. No, getting past this man would not be easy.

Veranna slowly placed her batons onto the bench behind her while keeping her eyes on the swordsman. Her hands and eyes were the only parts of her body not covered by the black outfit she wore, but she reasoned that the swordsman's sharp gaze had seen the shape of her body and knew she was a woman. Calmly, she drew her sword and assumed a fighter's stance.

The swordsman drew his own blade and chuckled as he spoke to the guards. "You feeble oafs! A woman bested you. I am beginning to wonder if all of the training I have given you is a waste." He calmed his mirth and spoke to them like a drill instructor. "Pay attention and learn from how I reduce this thrill seeker to the simple little girl she is. Almost a shame that we shall have to strip her of her clothes and send her to the punishment pole down in the city."

Remembering the terrible scourging she had experienced on the pole, Veranna could feel her anger rise. She forced herself to calmness and her voice came out in a mixture of disgust, sadness and judgment.

"Had you honored House Randal's commission you would not be facing such a quandary."

The man's eyebrows rose and he looked at her intently, clearly intrigued. "You have me at a bit of a disadvantage; no one around this part of the world seems to have ever heard of House Randal, let alone its commission. I wonder how you know about it, and, if I do not kill you, I will enjoy torturing the information out of you. Your being from one of the upper castes here will not spare you my attentions."

"And you, Swordsman, shall not be spared my wrath. As your liege-lady I shall punish you severely for violating your House Oaths."

"My liege-lady, eh? You are having visions of grandeur from a land far away." He fell into his combat stance and barked, "On guard!"

The two circled slowly to the center of the hall, their blades held ready. In a blink, Veranna closed on her opponent, lunging and thrusting in complex angles. All the swordsman could do was fend off the blows and back away. He turned and she drove him back to the center of the hall. He took a deliberate step back and held his blade vertically in front of his face to salute her.

"My apologies for the disdain I showed you. I can definitely say that you are not from these parts."

Her voice grim, Veranna returned his salute. "Accepted. You speak truly that I am not Seacorran."

They resumed circling, watching each other for the slightest hint of intent. The swordsman suddenly pounced, releasing a barrage of blows too quick for the guards to follow. Veranna concentrated on her task and let flow the gifts of the Creator. With one quick flick of her sword she deflected a petite lunge and jabbed the tip into the hollow of his right shoulder. He stepped back and touched the wound with his left hand. It was small and bled little, but the psychological impact was tremendous. His eyes narrowed as he considered her anew.

"Not even an imperial assassin ever achieved so much against me. What a shame to have to kill you!"

Veranna kept her voice neutral and said, "Do you yield?"

He laughed nervously. "I have never been in this position, before. Of course I cannot yield at this point; I am still sizing you up." He nodded and slowly stepped toward her again.

Mixed emotions ran through Veranna. Anger wanted to consume her over the violation of oaths shown by this swordsman, but practicality moved her to hope that he may prove useful. All she could do was generate the right opening in his defenses.

She lunged and feinted straight for his stomach, then swept the tip of her blade down to strike the inside of his right thigh. He nimbly blocked both attempts and darted to his right to get behind her. She barely deflected his strike toward the backside of her arm and was unable to regain her balance quickly enough to adequately defend against his follow-up. His left foot swept her right leg from under her and she fell hard on her stomach and chin to the wood floor. The pain nearly caused her to black out. Instinct took over and she desperately rolled away just in time to avoid a kick to her head. She got to her knees and brought her sword up to block a strike aimed at the tendons of her right elbow, but her position left her vulnerable to a left-handed jab that connected to her eyebrow. The impact blinded her eyes for a moment and also propelled her back far enough that she could roll to her feet. She barely evaded a swinging blow of his sword and jumped back further to take a moment to collect herself.

He pounced, and a flurry of strikes subconsciously fell into a formal routine that neither of them had ever executed at this speed. Anticipating the routine, Veranna appeared to falter at a critical point. The swordsman rushed in to take advantage of the mistake, but at the last split-second Veranna redirected the momentum of her blade and broke the pattern. With preternatural speed she deflected his blow clockwise, which turned his torso slightly in the same direction. Up and around counter-clockwise came her blade. She brought it down flat with a hard snap onto the backside of his upper left arm. The slap echoed through the room but was drowned out by the loud cry of pain from the swordsman. He backed off and glared at her as he held his arm.

"Who are you? I have never seen the like in all of my travels. Surrender now and I can talk the king and queen into sparing you punishment. We could be rich from instructing fighters in this realm alone."

Disappointment and anger again tinged Veranna's voice. "That is the last thing that a true Swordsman of House Randal would seek. Since your honor comes from what you sell, I shall see to it that even then you shall know no profit."

Pain and humility drove him to rashness. "I have had enough of this game. I shall cut you down and not even waste time spitting on your grave. I am the Master of the Sword here and will not tolerate degradation by a commoner such as you."

He leaped at her and struck blow after blow. They were easily deflected but allowed little in the way of countermeasures. Veranna subsumed her emotions and fell into automatic response mode while another part of her mind analyzed his strategy.

From the doorway on the other side of the hall came motion. A quick glance revealed a nobleman in nightclothes, the same one using the slave girl for his pleasure. The guards bowed but he, the duke, simply motioned for them to carry on.

With anger getting the better of him, the swordsman grew more frustrated with every second. Although none of the others could see the minute flaws in his technique, Veranna saw them clearly. Again, she directed his momentum one way and then brought her blade down in a hard slap, connecting with his right, outer thigh. He yelped and staggered back. Rage boiled up as he heard the laughter from both the duke and his guards. Swinging powerfully, he raced at Veranna to take her down with brute force.

She took the maneuver in passing and swung her sword to knock his downward. The point of his sword bit into the wood floor and caused him to stagger. With one lightning-fast blow to the bridge of his nose, Veranna sent him face down to the floor. He hit hard and his sword fell from his hand, but he was too dazed to notice. His head throbbed and fear reduced him to incoherent mumbling as he slowly got to his hands and knees. All he could expect now was to see his opponent's blade ready to slice across his throat. Instead, he heard a royal voice of hot steel burn into his heart and soul.

"Arise, swordsman, and receive your judgment." Holding his blade in her left hand she turned it so that all in the room could see the green 'R' symbol. "This sword has been a badge of honor for House Randal for many generations. Never before have I heard of it being shamed in the ways you have done. You have aided the despotic and sold your honor for gold. Since you saw fit to deny the commission of Randal, it is only fitting that you be denied its blessings. For attacking and seeking the death of your empress, you are forbidden to enter the Seven Lands ever again."

The swordsman looked at her with puzzlement and incredulity. "My empress?"

"Yes! You are exiled from the Seven Lands and no longer share the blessings of House Randal."

Lightning blazed through the ceiling of the hall as a thunder-clap shook the building. The bright light fell upon the swords-man's blade in Veranna's left hand and illuminated the 'R' symbol. It quickly faded and the blade split in two along its length, then shattered as it hit the floor. The guards and duke fell to their hands and knees, stunned by the awesome display of authority accompanying Veranna's words.

She took the opportunity to grab the batons and sprint through the doorway. Archers patrolling the grounds saw a dark blur of motion racing for the gate and fired their arrows desperately. Veranna saw two guards busy untying those she had subdued earlier and headed straight for them. Ten feet away she leaped from the ground and flew through the air to give each of them a swift kick to the forehead. They collapsed instantly and she grabbed a set of keys from the belt of one of them. Frantically she tried several keys until one of them worked on the lock. She threw open the gate and started to run out. Just before she cleared it, an arrow sped by from behind and to the right. It sliced into her flesh just below her right breast and continued on to the ground.

She let out a tight yelp and clinched. It saved her life. In the next half-second a sword blade flew across where her head had been. She swung her batons and struck at the first person in view. A sharp blow to the left shin followed by one to the back of the head knocked him senseless. Three more guards rushed up to engage her. She countered without deliberate thought, a whirlwind in their midst. In one quick moment they writhed on the street in pain from broken arms, legs and battered muscles.

Holding her left hand over the bleeding cut under her breast, she sped back toward Knoxun's estate. The darkness was a cloak and shield.

CHAPTER 21

Soon after lunchtime, the swift boat carrying Tesra to Chenray pulled up to the docks. The tallest building was four stories high, and most of the structures were made of wood and clay. Many of the streets were paved with bricks and stones since the late emperor Dalmar's demise, and trade had increased sharply. The small amount of dockage forced the river vessels to wait in line for moorage and unloading.

Tesra, Mother of the Academy and adopted mother of Veranna, was anxious to get to Tolemera with her prisoner. The delay at the docks irked her to belligerence.

"Get out of the way, you oafs! I am on important business and cannot be delayed. Unload after I am on the way out of this backwater."

The harbormaster, a man in his late fifties with a short beard and fat stomach, paused in his business to see whose voice resounded across the water. When her boat hoisted an imperial flag, he hurried to the docks to get the current cargo skiff out of the way. Fifteen minutes later, Tesra's boat floated in and began unloading. Maneuvering along the dock was tight due to the cargo waiting to be loaded or hauled away, but Tesra's voice drove the men to frantic speed. Ten minutes later her carriage and horses were ready for departure. As she climbed into the carriage she pointed at the harbormaster and barked an order. "You; climb up with the driver and direct him to the nearest place for food, for both people and horses."

The harbormaster was stunned. Nobody addressed him in such a manner, especially on the docks. However, this woman's demeanor conveyed great authority, and her carriage bore the emblems of imperial service. He bowed, climbed onto his own horse and signaled for the driver to follow him. A few minutes later they stopped at an inn near the center of town. It was built of plain wood and had a simple layout, but the aromas from the food were wonderful.

Tesra hurried inside and soon had a large store of food for herself and her guard escort. The horses would later eat oats and other grains. For now, she ordered the driver to head northeast for Tolemera.

They left the smells of the lake behind and soon entered the grassy, rolling mounds of the Gap of Tarlan, between the northern and southern stretches of the Boar's Spine Mountains, as they trailed off into Imperia. They continued on an hour past nightfall, since the road was well-maintained and two of the three moons were half-full. The guards had to search awhile for enough wood for the campfire, and the horses were eager to rest. After walking the prisoner, Dag, around for a little exercise, Tesra instructed the guards to tie his wrists and ankles before chaining him to a wheel of the carriage. The light from the fire in the middle of the camp flickered in his dark grey eyes as Tesra plied him with questions.

"What is your full name?"

His voice came out surly and full of venom, "Dag."

"Do you not have a last name?"

"Likely, but you'd have to find my father to get it. Too many idiots to choose from to know who it is."

"Where were you born?"

He shrugged his shoulders and gave her a greasy smile. "Don't know that neither. The Hankers who took me said my mom was a whore who didn't want no kids."

The Hankers were nomadic people with bad reputations. Nothing was off-limits as long as it brought in some money. Children would be stolen from small towns and transported across the empire to be sold to childless couples. Animals, clothing, tools and everything else were fair game.

Tesra gave him a hard look. Either he was very clever or he was dumb enough to never learn from mistakes. Criminals often used hard luck scenarios to soften their judges, while others tried to divert consideration from their crimes to unrelated matters.

"Your upbringing is irrelevant; all that concerns me is your role in the empress's disappearance. Tell me all you know and I can spare you the grueling interrogations you will suffer."

Dag responded with a low chuckle, "I don't know nothin' old hag. It aint right to torture someone for no cause."

Tesra gave him a menacing chuckle of her own. "There is more than enough cause to hold you in jail for a long time, and witnesses have heard you speak treason against the throne. Yes, you have given us a good deal of cause."

Dag refused to say anymore and looked away to the north. Tesra could see that he would not discuss anything further, so she stood and turned to walk to her tent. She looked down over her shoulder and said to him quietly, "I could have spared you much pain, but you have chosen otherwise. I leave you to contemplate your future."

She sat with the guards and ate some food, pondering the changes in her life since Veranna had rescued her from the fate of being a dragon wife under the Koosti. Her loving, adopted daughter had braved extreme peril to save her, and the young empress's prayer that the Creator would heal her mother had been answered instantly. She looked and felt several years younger and had enhanced hearing and eyesight. Before that horrid ordeal she thought she would need spectacles for reading, but now she could read fine print with ease. Also, her hearing was far more sensitive than she could ever remember. The most unusual enhancement was her ability to see things better in darkness. It was not as powerful as Veranna's night vision, but it was definitely an improvement over the norm.

She bade the guards goodnight and laid down on a cot in her tent. Sleep came to her quickly and a dream arose in her mind. She looked into a clear, sunny sky. Looking down, she saw a harbor on the sea. The harbor was full of ships shaped like dragons. Looking to her right, she saw a forest of tall, green firs marching down from the north to the harbor. The trees climbed aboard the ships and sailed away to the south and out of sight.

She awoke to the sound of strained whispering. The guards were trained to communicate silently at night, so the whispering had to be a dispute. She stepped out of her tent and looked in Dag's direction. A black-clad figure strove to undo the chain securing Dag to the wagon wheel, and Dag was whispering curses for him to hurry.

Tesra grabbed her staff and ran at the man clad in black as she yelled for the guards. The man finally unhooked the chain and drew a short sword just in time to block Tesra's swinging blow. He stepped back and prepared to counter attack, but could not find the opening he needed. The woman was a highly praised fighter and demonstrated why. He had no relief from her onslaught and had to concentrate totally on defense.

Tesra could see Dag striving to move away. She jabbed her staff and struck the bridge of his nose, knocking him back flat on the ground. The other man took this moment to strike back and put her on the defensive. He was amazed at how agile and coordinated her movements were. Blocking flowed to striking to evading to striking again. Her stamina surprised him, too. No sign of exhaustion entered her technique.

Tesra heard the guards running and horses stamping. Torches lit up the night and showed several dark figures on the northern periphery of the camp. When Dag rolled on the ground, Tesra stepped on the chain attached to the bindings on his wrists. Still dazed from the blow to his head, he found it hard to get his bearings. He jerked hard on the chain and pulled Tesra's foot out from under her. She stumbled forward and into her opponents range. A swift jab to her forehead knocked her back. Dazed, she saw a guard rush up to engage her foe. The guard fought bravely but was no match for their enemy. Before Tesra could get her head clear, the guard fell to the ground as blood spewed from his mouth and stomach. When the black clad man helped Dag to his feet, Tesra saw a quick flash of light on a small piece of gold around the third finger of her assailant. Even in her dazed condition she recognized the ring and yelled a warning.

"Raven's Blade! Beware! Raven's Blade!"

Fear and desperation drove her to her feet. Still sluggish, she followed after Dag and the other man to see where they went. Twenty yards away they each mounted a horse and galloped off to the north with six other black clad figures.

The guard captain rushed through the camp barking orders. In his late fifties, he was not as quick or agile anymore, but experienced and efficient. He had been asleep when the attack began, and only had time to don his armored breastplate. It saved his life, protecting him from a hard dagger strike to his heart. He fought off his opponent and wondered why the man quickly ran away. He now understood why. Killing everyone in the camp was not the ambush's goal. They wanted in and out in a hurry, likely to retrieve the prisoner. He took a head count and saw that eight of his men were either severely wounded or dead, leaving twelve able men. After sizing up the situation, he conferred with Tesra.

"My lady, the three wounded men need someone to look after them until we can get some healers here. I am sending a man back to Chenray to fetch some along with more troops. If you wish to pursue the raiders we will be eleven against eight. If they are indeed Raven's Blades, then those are not good odds."

Dawn was not far away, and the shock of the raid still echoed through the camp. Tesra was ready to boil over with rage and had to keep a tight hold on her tongue.

"I would pursue those wretches even if they were a hundred. We need to get Dag and head for Tolemera right away. Get the men and horses ready. We are already liable to lose our prey if we don't move quickly."

"Aye, my lady."

It took nearly a half-hour before they were ready to ride. The raiders had killed two horses and scattered the rest, causing a forty minute delay behind them. The eastern sky brightened considerably, giving Tesra a small morsel of hope that they would be able to travel more quickly and make up some time against their foes.

CHAPTER 22

The sky was gray with early morning clouds as Veranna made her way to the washroom in the servant's quarters. The swelling over her left eye had eased, but the discoloration was noticeable, and the wound under her right breast made itself known with every movement. It had closed and scabbed with a speed unlike any she had ever tended. Still, a snug bandage helped keep it from breaking open. Raising her hands over her head to put on a shirt brought a sharp jab of pain in the wounded muscles, reminding her that even simple chores would be very uncomfortable.

Back in the sleeping room, the other three women sat on their mats and stretched their arms and legs. After a long yawn, the Koosti woman turned to Veranna and frowned in puzzlement.

"What is wrong? Yesterday you hardly worked at all and used your left arm for nearly everything. You wouldn't raise your head and let us see your face, and you hold your right arm close to your body. Are you injured?"

Veranna had hoped to hide the fact of her injuries by pretending as though nothing had happened. The Koosti woman's sharp eyes had become familiar enough with Veranna's mannerisms that a change from the norm was obvious. Lying about her condition was not only uncharacteristic, it would also be pointless. Her reply came out in a bit of self-conscious stammer.

"Well, uh, y-yes...um...but not seriously."

The Koosti woman's eyes grew intense with concern as she reached out a hand, put a finger under Veranna's chin, and gently lifted it up. In a motherly tone she said, "Look at me."

Unable to refuse such compassion, Veranna turned her head for the woman to have a full view. When the woman moved closer and carefully touched the bruised area, her fingers felt cool.

"Ah, dear girl, you have a fine lump over your eye. It is still warm to the touch and soft; I can do nothing for it now but have you put a cold, wet cloth on it. It looks like it has been healing for over a week."

"Uh, actually it was the day before yesterday." She lifted her shirt and showed her the wound in her side, "I was struck by an arrow, too. It still hurts to move my arm or breathe."

Once more, in a motherly way, the Koosti woman frowned and scolded her. "You should be more careful; all it takes is a moment for something to injure you far worse. Come here and I will place some herbs on the wound that will help with the pain."

A half-hour later they headed to the main house to help with breakfast preparation. After eating and cleaning up, Beneto came in to the house, but not through the slave or servant's doors. He entered through the main doors and sat down at Master Knoxun's dining table. His shirt was bright blue and his pants black. The shirt had a feather pen symbol sewn onto the left breast, bringing Veranna to conclude that he had been accepted back into the Academy. She hurriedly prepared a serving of sausage, eggs and fresh-cut fruit for him. She nearly cried seeing the look of joy and dignity on his face.

"Beneto, I..." She stopped as he raised a finger to interrupt her. In a quiet aside he addressed his concern.

"Veranna, I am now a citizen. Remember, as a slave you need to refer to me as 'sir', or 'mister'. We don't want any troubles arising from improper etiquette."

She smiled and gave him a short bow, "Yes sir. Would you like some tea with your breakfast?"

He returned her smile and nodded. While she was in the kitchen, Master Knoxun walked into the dining hall, bringing Beneto to his feet and bowing respectfully.

"Beneto, it is a wonderful day seeing you restored to your proper place. You will always be welcome in my home. If there is anything I can help you with, all you have to do is ask." He reached out his hand for Beneto to shake.

"Thank you, my lord, for your generosity. The letter of recommendation you sent to the Academy convinced them to admit me on a provisional basis. I will have a room, desk, meals and access to research materials enough to keep me satisfied till the end of my days."

Knoxun's eyebrows rose in surprise and admiration. "Beneto, thank the Creator that you have been so blessed. I hope that my grandchildren will have the opportunity to study under your tutelage. Have they assigned you an assistant?"

Assistants aided the scholars in researching topics and writing letters, besides drawing up academic materials used in the lecture hall. They had to show mastery of the language and excellent writing skills.

"Not as yet, my lord. The list of qualified candidates is virtually non-existent."

Veranna set a teapot down on the table and started to pour some tea into his cup. "As a matter of fact, my lord, I was wondering if I might make a request of you in that regard."

"By all means, Beneto."

"This slave, here, would do very well as an assistant."

Veranna's heart pounded and her complexion blushed. Lord Knoxun stared at Beneto, clearly surprised, his face drawing into a silent question of 'why'?

Beneto proceeded quickly to convey a sense of utter confidence in his decision.

"Yes, my lord. She is highly trained and has excellent literary skills. Her mind is sharp, and since she graduated from an academy, she is well-acquainted with the scholastic process." He reached out and lifted Veranna's left hand up for Knoxun to see, "This is her graduation ring. And, as you may have noticed, my lord, she is an excellent worker. Besides, the tax credit you would receive for allowing her to be an assistant in an academy would more than cover your expenses for purchasing her."

Knoxun was silent for a while as he considered Beneto's proposal. "I should never have let you go from my staff, Beneto. Your cleverness has served me well over the years." He gestured toward Veranna, "I agree to your request. However, I am retaining ownership of her. My first wife bore me a daughter and my second has proved barren; I will likely need this slave to bear me a son. She has the royal eyes and excellent build. Keep her healthy for me."

Beneto nodded deeply, "As you wish, my lord."

"Another thing, Beneto. Twice a week, she is to be taken to the king's estate. The queen and her mother are impressed with her and want her back for routine services."

"Yes, my lord. May I take her with me now?"

"Yes, but …" A concerned frown came over his face as he looked at Veranna, "I cannot help but wonder if I should not restrict her to the estate. She arrives here after being bitten by a spider, and lives, then recovers more quickly than anyone I have ever heard of. Then, she has nerve enough to sass the queen, gaining a terrible punishment. We both know those treated this way perish. Yet, she makes a full recovery in a few days, and now has the trust and respect of the queen and her mother. This is all very suspect, Beneto. Who is she? Her eyes are greener than the royal family's. Were you to tell me she opened the seawall, I just might believe you."

Beneto smiled brightly to cover his alarm at Lord Knoxun's shrewd appraisal of Veranna.

"My lord, she is a rare one, indeed. I expect great things from her, and thank you again."

"You are welcome, Beneto, and I thank you for such excellent service through the years. Go in peace."

Beneto and Veranna bowed and went out the back door of the house to quickly get to the slave quarters. Picking up her few things, Veranna felt more unsettled than when she had arrived in this land.

"Beneto, what is going on? We were planning on escaping and now you are back in the academy. And, Lord Knoxun is very suspicious. What are you thinking?"

Beneto held up his hands and kept his voice low, "Veranna, I will explain more when we reach the academy. Suffice it to say that your ability to move about freely will now be greatly expanded. And, in the academy, we will have access to much more information. We may be able to locate this little girl you have been searching for."

Veranna took a deep, calming breath and shook her head in agreement. After a long pause, she stated emphatically, "I am not going to bear Knoxun any children. The only man I will have children with is my husband."

Beneto gave her a fatherly smile, "Of that I have no doubt. However, you and I shall give birth to a different kind of children; the children of ideas."

The academy grounds lay directly east of Seacorro, along an ancient road nearly an hour's quick trot out. Veranna noted well-tilled fields of vegetables, grains, fruit and nut orchards quilted the landscape. She looked around and felt glad to be away from the city, but sad too, since the land reminded her of Loreland. A song, unbidden, rushed from her heart and out through her voice:

I looked out in wonder at what lay 'round me
At fields and forests not far from the sea,
The city behind and the wild lands ahead,
Into them all I am blessedly led.

See all the roses in yellow and pink.
Flowers in blue, reds and gold make me think,
Of the One who sees to it that all are well fed,
Into them all I am blessedly led.

Up in the clouds I watch birds as they fly.
Rivers and streams full of fish pass me by.
Elk, deer and badgers; the One gives their sted.
In view of them all I am blessedly led.

Tall white-capped mountains look down as I pass.
Glittering snakes o'er my path through the grass.
Fair, running rabbits and monsters of dread.
Through this marvelous world I am blessedly led.

Beneto stared at her in wonder. "Either you are one of the greatest tricksters of all time, or you are the Creator's emissary come to shake up our world. I translated that ancient song forty years ago; it is likely still locked away in an academy vault unseen since then."

Veranna shook her head, smiled and held up her hands in a gesture of ignorance. "I do not know, Beneto. It is like the other day when we went to the king's estate. Certain facets of my ancestry seem to well up from within when I encounter them in my life."

Beneto returned his attention to driving the wagon, unable to dismiss the eerie sense of supernatural forces at work in the woman next to him. The song she had just sung had been a favorite among the people at least three hundred years before her ancestors had departed Faresea. Past and present were knitting together into a future of unforeseeable consequences, a wave that would wash the sands clean. Would he remain on the beach, or be swept away with the tide?

CHAPTER 23

The audience hall of the castle swarmed with nobles and their advisors. The buzz of conversation made it difficult for Karsten to hear any particular group of people, but the tension over Veranna's absence was clear.

Karsten knew just how important it was for him to demonstrate confidence that Veranna was still alive. If he could not, the Council of Lords would be required to settle on a new ruling family. He would receive little recognition for his marriage to Veranna since he did not come from a noble lineage. House Erain would regain the throne, then move to eliminate the Genazi altogether. Civil war would erupt and leave them all so weak that virtually any neighboring realm could invade and take over the lands. The Koosti to the east, any of the Nomadic Unions to the north, or the barbarian tribes to the south would see a fruit ripe for plucking. The Erains were too centered on their own ideas of power to see the inevitable.

The chamberlain pounded his staff on the floor and called for the people to come to order. Groupings formed along political lines and according to hierarchy. The Erain houses dominated one side of the hall, with Lady Gelangweil at the front. Beside her sat the Earl of Crellain, a middle-aged, fat man with sandy-white hair close-cropped, and on her left was the archduchess Loray of Provorn. Wavy, dark hair cascaded down to the middle of her back, complementing her dark tan and deep blue eyes. On the tall side, full-bosomed and slender, she was jokingly referred to as the 'mistress' of the Seven Lands. Her mind was keen and her ambitions insatiable. Now in her mid-thirties, she was a well-seasoned political maneuverer. She had married, at age fourteen, the powerful Duke of Provorn, who was then in his mid-forties. She bore him a daughter while fifteen years old, and ten years later he fell dead while dining one evening. It was strongly rumored that the young duchess had added some poison to his food. Investigations led nowhere and she assumed full power over the duchy, reigning as an archduchess after Dalmar Gelangweil raised her status to a princess of the realm. She brokered the promotion by agreeing to serve as Dalmar's mistress, and by giving her thirteen-year old daughter to him as a concubine. While she saw Lady Galengweil as her chief rival, the two of them recognized the necessity to work together to dispose of Veranna.

On the other side of the room sat the non-aligned houses. Duke Roland, of Starhaven, was at the front since he served as Duke Heilson's representative. Amilla, the Marquise of Sudryni, sat next to him. Both of them had matured wonderfully since the war with the Koosti, and no one made the mistake of misjudging their abilities simply because of their youth. They had sharp minds, strength of resolve and were very fair in appearance. Amilla, especially, had blossomed into a lady of fine beauty, leading many noblemen, both young and old, to vie for her hand. So far she had committed to none, but carefully weighed her options.

The chamberlain pounded his staff three times, and called out, "All rise and give homage to his Excellency, Karsten, Prince of the Genazi and Prince-consort to her imperial majesty, Veranna."

Karsten walked in through the tall pavilion doors and headed straight for the dais without looking to either side. He turned and faced the assembly, a stern, commanding look on his face, bringing the others to wonder about his mood.

All in the assembly bowed except for certain Erain nobles who simply inclined their heads slightly. Karsten returned their bow and sat on his throne placed just to the right of Veranna's Emerald Throne. He spoke like a wise father informing his family of decisions he had made.

"My lords and ladies, it is imperative that I keep you informed as to the condition of our beloved empress. Happily, every indication we have is that she is alive. Unfortunately, we do not yet know where she is. We do have one promising lead that we hope will give us a better idea as to how we should proceed. I will try to answer your questions as best I can."

A young nobleman on the Erain side held up his hand. When recognized by Karsten, he bowed quickly and asked, "My lord, I regret having to cause you grief, but why are you confident that her majesty is still alive? Usually a ransom offer accompanies such abductions."

Karsten stood and paced a moment as he considered his answer. "My lord, I appreciate your concern, and your question is a good one. My reasons for believing her to be alive are these: First, if someone simply wanted her dead, they would have killed her and not bothered to go to the trouble of flying in and out on dragons. Second, no sign of either her, or the little girl with her, have been found in the stream or fields where they were last known to be.

"Third, Lord Yanbre and his knights share a mysterious link with the empress. Were she dead that would cease.

"And fourthly, this castle has not transformed into its defensive mode, which it was in before Veranna was revealed as the rightful ruler of the Seven Lands. Remember, until she came here it had been in that mode for hundreds of years. Her death would return it to that mode until a legitimate successor came and opened it again."

Archduchess Loray spoke without being recognized, a note of skeptical disdain evident in her voice.

"These proofs you offer are wholly inadequate; they can be explained by far simpler reasons. It behooves us to proceed to selecting a new ruler for the good of the empire. Failing to install a leader will invite any and all barbarians to sack our Lands. Why have you not addressed this?"

Karsten had to force himself to remain calm. He purposely walked along the dais until he was directly in front of Loray.

"The proofs you call inadequate are wholly adequate for a thinking person. The armor of the knights and the castle's condition were adequate enough to help overthrow a despotic regime. To choose a new ruler while the empress is still alive would be treasonous. In the meantime we are keeping a good eye on all hostile entities."

Lady Gelangweil's face showed anger at Karsten's reference to the Gelangweil regime as despotic. Loray smiled at him as though he were an idiot.

"I realize that you may believe such things, but the rest of us are born and bred to proper leadership. We know the necessity of a strong ruler to give the Lands coherence. The maintenance of a strong empire is far more important than any one ruler, even an empress. To ignore the empire is a greater treason."

Before Karsten could respond, Baron Ciclanno's voice rose up.

"Hear, Hear! The lady speaks sense. Why risk an entire empire when we can move forward with confidence? Surely House Erain and its confederates are more than capable of ruling an empire."

Karsten's voice was hard. "We are not at liberty to simply dismiss our empress while she lives. The empire will remain safe until we have her back. All that is required is for each of us to remain loyal to her and honor our vows."

Loray stood and turned to face the others, making sure that her figure was displayed for maximum effect.

"My lords and ladies, it seems that we have reached an impasse. The empress's consort wants to maintain leadership despite the fact that he holds no hereditary authority. Those of us bred to the demands of leadership recognize the need for stable, inherent authority to guide us through these troubling times."

The room became ominously quiet as each person realized the direction she was going in her argument. Trying to sound like the embodiment of all wisdom and practicality, Loray articulated every syllable precisely as she stepped up onto the dais.

"In light of these facts, we are forced to vote on the proper course for our future."

The room broke out in loud conversations as everyone turned to his or her fellow and voiced an opinion. It took several minutes before the chamberlain could bring them to silence. Karsten's anger got the better of him for a moment.

"I care not for your presumptions of authority; your rightful liege-lady has already determined who shall serve her when in absence."

Lorays eyebrows rose a bit and a smile spread across her face. Karsten had stepped into her trap.

"Is her reign one based on law or not?"

Karsten' voice was a menacing growl. "You know it is."

A note of triumph carried through her words and posture. "Well then, we all know the law well enough to realize that we must vote." Her voice changed to royal command as she said, "Chamberlain, you will now conduct a vote. The issue is this: Shall we proceed to install a new leader according to the ancient laws of hierarchy, or, shall we proceed under the current assumption that the empress is alive and returning soon?"

The chamberlain, an elderly man from a minor noble family, called out for all the rulers of the major houses to raise their hands if they wanted to select a new ruler. Four hands rose. Archduchess Loray turned to Karsten and sneered.

"As you can see, four of the Seven Lands choose to select a new leader. You are dismissed Genazi."

Karsten wanted to slap her silly, but kept his rage in check. A thought suddenly occurred to him.

"Not so fast, my lady; the vote is not yet done."

Loray now grew increasingly hostile. "Of course it is, you fool. You should have learned by now to leave law and ruling to your betters."

Karsten clasped his hands behind his back and stepped back to the center of the dais.

"We shall see how well you know the law." He pointed to the chamberlain and said, "Finish the vote."

The chamberlain bowed and called for all those wishing to maintain the current regime to raise their hands. Three arose: Earl Tomius of Imperia, Marques Amilla of the Sudryni, Lord

Roland, of Starhaven, also representing Duke Heiland's Land of Grandshire.

Before Loray could say anything more, Karsten pointed to Kreida, who stood at the back of the room, and said, "Lady Kreida, you have been named a princess of the Genazi by the empress. How do you vote?"

Kreida thought that she was simply an on-looker in this meeting. Now, she was right in the middle. She yelled for those in front of her to make way as she pressed to the front. With dramatic flare she spun around and glared at the people, finally fixing a feral, angry stare on Loray.

"I, as Princess of the Genazi people, proclaim fealty to our empress, Veranna of the line of Ergon! All who refuse her rule shall be enemies to the Genazi people. Choose wisely."

The chamber was deathly silent, shocked to the core by Kreida's ferocious way. Karsten broke the silence.

"The vote is a tie. According to the law a tie results in no change." He turned to Loray and mimicked her, "Lady Loray, you are dismissed."

Sore consternation wracked her features as she stared daggers at him, "This is not going to end here, commoner. Mark my words: You will regret opposing the will of the lords." She stormed off of the dais and through the doorway.

Karsten and Yanbre exchanged grim smiles, knowing that they had barely escaped disaster. Kreida continued to glare ominously at the members of Erain Households. Baron Ciclanno locked eyes with her and smiled.

"Such primitive passion likely means you would make an excellent bed mate. Come to my chambers later and we can explore your talents further."

Kreida looked at him as though he were a total idiot. "I could go through a dozen like you before breakfast, so don't waste my time. Besides, you wouldn't want to come out sounding like a soprano."

The baron laughed and bowed, then headed out the door. Kreida turned to Karsten and Yanbre, writhing as if in chains.

"Treybal has no idea how much he is demanding of me simply because I said I'd marry him. This Ciclanno moron looks like he could be a real pleasure. Lean, hard muscles and a lot of endurance."

Karsten was not amused with her comments. "You had better pray that we endure until Veranna returns. Those scum have been put off only temporarily by the loophole we found in the law. It is only a matter of time before they gain boldness enough to threaten civil war if their demands are not met. Archduchess Loray will have us roasting over a low fire if we are not careful."

Kreida shrugged and stepped down from the dais. "Don't act so dire; the situation does have its good side. It has been pretty boring without much knife work to do. And, if I capture this Ciclanno thug, I can deal with him in any way I wish."

CHAPTER 24

"One! Two! Three!" Veranna barked out the cadence for Sreba's practice sets. It had been a few weeks since Beneto took her to the academy, and the second training session in that week. Sreba chose days when her husband, the king, was away from the estate so that she could keep the sessions secret, and Veranna arrived dressed as a scribe from the academy. Her friendship with the young queen of Faresea grew quickly, allowing her to speak more candidly each time, and Sreba unconsciously began to emulate some of Veranna's mannerisms. This was noticed by the household staff, who were shocked when Sreba would thank them openly for their work and showed consideration for their hard labors. The queen even displayed more happiness and energy as she went about her duties.

Veranna's crisp voice carried through the long practice room. "Always remember to think of attack and defense like a stick. It has two separate ends, but is one object. Your block of an opponent's blade will provide an opportunity for you to turn the tables on him and attempt your own attack. Tactics begin from the moment you sense the need to enter a contest or battle. Focus your mind and senses to the task at hand, for your whole being is far stronger than any single aspect, no matter how well-trained."

Although glistening with sweat after three hours of rigorous training, Sreba nodded resolutely and raised her sword in readiness. Veranna raised her own sword and made a deliberate, low-speed swing to test Sreba's reaction. Her blade came up with excellent timing and blocked the swing, then flowed naturally into a counter-attack. Veranna commended her good technique.

"Excellent; you are now familiar with a means of defense that is applicable in many situations. A strong foundation in a few things will sustain you in many. Now, we shall increase the speed of our movements. Concentrate on the needs at hand."

Twenty minutes went by as Veranna gradually stepped up the pace. Without realizing it, Sreba fell into a mode of concentration where the rest of the world seemed to fade away and leave only the training room. It was a nexus of mind and body awakened by the grace of training. She felt reborn and marveled at Veranna's powers of instruction, the joy of life flowing from her and igniting the queen's confidence and skill.

Veranna noticed the queen's mother enter the room and brought the practice routine to a halt. She saluted Sreba with her sword and praised her abilities before turning to her mother and bowing.

"Good afternoon, Lady Waverly. I trust that you have observed how splendidly your daughter is doing."

Lady Waverly picked up a towel from a bench and walked over to her daughter. Wiping some of the sweat from her, she gave her a warm smile.

"I have, and it is like a miracle to me. She seems to have awakened from a long slumber. Even the servants are speaking of the change come over her."

Sreba laughed and sheathed her sword. "I feel as though I have been freed from captivity. If it can happen to me, then why not the servants? Hopefully, I can effect some change for the better. It seems that Veranna came along at just the right time."

Veranna smiled and curtsied. "The timing was not my doing; that was the Creator's. I now understand why he had me brought here."

Sreba gave her a puzzled look. "Are you saying that you are not from this city? Which one are you from?"

Veranna looked at Duchess Waverly. The older woman shrugged her shoulders and looked away as Veranna answered, "I am not from any of the cities or towns of this realm. I come from a land far to the north and west."

Sreba was confused; everyone knew that those lands were inhospitable and ravaged by savages. Veranna was obviously not a savage.

"You look and act like one of us. Your eyes are more emerald green than mine. Where else could you possibly come from?"

Veranna chose her words carefully. "We are related, but very distantly. Our forefathers shared this land in ages past."

"So, what land did your ancestors go to?"

Veranna paused in thought and saw the duchess close her eyes. Boldness was now the requirement.

"My ancestors left Faresea because of a difference of opinion over how to regard the will of the Creator in our lives. The leader of the group was named Dunamays."

Sreba's eyes were as large as saucers and her left hand covered her mouth as she gasped. "You come from the ruling house that was condemned for heresy. The law requires the death of all who come from that line. Why did you reveal this to me? I love you as a dear friend."

Veranna's posture and voice became regal, but she strove to reason with Sreba.

"I value your friendship greatly, and ask that I not be condemned because of my ancestry. As the empress of Emeraldia, I must judge many issues in light of the fact that some of them require latitude in definition. To be dogmatic on gray areas is just as bad as indecision on those that are black and white. I ask simply for respect of my views on such difficult questions."

Sreba felt a rush of emotions. The law was absolute regarding those espousing heresy, but Veranna's laws of reason were undeniable. She had come in the condition of a slave and now made claim to being an empress of a land where the ruling House of

Faresea had gone. That could mean she had a claim to the throne of Faresea. But most immediately she had become dear to Sreba, and the queen did not want to lose her to rash laws.

"You are an empress? How did you end up here apart from the Creator's punishment?"

Veranna smiled warmly and answered in a familiar way. "Sreba, if we can make plans of more than one purpose in our limited minds, cannot our awesome Creator do so all the more? I was abducted from my realm by those with evil motives. Can the Creator turn those motives on their heads and work against them by having me accomplish something good? Of course, and to say that cannot be is to impugn the power and character of the Creator. It could very well be that I am here to heal old wounds and bring a fresh perspective."

The queen was silent as she stared at Veranna and considered her words. Her mother put an arm across her shoulders and held her close, speaking words of gentle counsel.

"Sreba, my old friend, Beneto, was right years ago. We have blinded ourselves by thinking that everything we do is justified because we rule. Nobility should drive us to humility and service. Are we beyond criticism?"

Sreba shook her head and gestured toward Veranna. "Mother, this could start civil war just like that of our ancestors. The Council of Nobles will never accept her claims without some irrefutable sign that she is genuine. I do not want to see her bloody corpse hanging dead from the punishment pole."

A thought sprang into Veranna's mind. "The first step will be for you to accept my claim. Do you wish a proof from the Creator?"

Sreba felt shame for showing doubt of her new-found friend, and wondrous fear that the Creator might reveal power right before her eyes. Such a demonstration had not occurred since long ago in the ancient realm. Her voice came out with a touch of trepidation, "I do."

In royal, yet respectful tones, Veranna said, "Please kneel."

Such was the strength of Veranna's character that Sreba complied without a second thought. Veranna rested her sword blade on Sreba's right shoulder and closed her eyes as she lifted her left hand in supplication.

"Oh, most mighty Creator of us all, you have blessed my ancestors and me with gifts to help us survive and defend that which is right and good. I pray that you would grant Sreba, my distant kin, a measure of those gifts to help her guide her people into your truth. Please, oh Creator, let it be so."

Her eyes blazed with emerald green light and an aura of green surrounded her. The aura moved down her sword and onto Sreba, engulfing and permeating her. The light flared and then faded leaving both women feeling a resonance of the divine.

Sreba twirled like a dancer and laughed with joy. "Mother, she is true! In her lives the House of Dunamays returned home. She speaks no evil and is here to aid one of her subjects taken captive. Oh, mother, I feel as though I have seen and experienced another life in mere seconds. Mother, we must aid her."

The duchess had been impressed with Veranna before, but now she was truly amazed. Slowly, purposely she stepped toward Veranna and went down on her knees as she bowed her head and spoke softly.

"Your highness, please forgive all of the weakness I have shown in not doing what is right. Forgive my ever having treated you as a slave. Command me, my liege lady, I pray."

Before Veranna could answer, Sreba fell to her knees and bowed her head onto Veranna's feet, crying out, "Please, my lady, forgive my malice and stupidity. I nearly killed you on the punishment pole and treated you as dirt. I beg you to let me serve you and atone for the evil I have done."

Veranna was overcome with such compassion for the two women that she found it difficult to speak. After a moment she took Sreba's right hand, and the duchess' left, and helped them to their feet.

"All offense against me is forgiven. Any offense against the Creator you must settle between yourselves and Him. I am sure that He will expect you to serve His will with joy and strength.

"I accept your service and ask that you will be my friends and allies in returning Faresea to its nobility of old. We must be a team, a family united for what is right."

The two other women both exclaimed, "Yes, your highness," and they embraced one another with deep joy.

Sreba wiped tears from the corners of her eyes. "What shall be our first step to accomplish the change we desire in Faresea?"

Veranna thought for a moment and then gave them a conspiratorial smile. "Find out when your husband, the king, will enjoy his next time of sporting with horses and troops. Give him a demonstration of the Creator's gifts with the sword. Then," and here Veranna blushed beet red, "give him a demonstration in your chambers such as no other woman has or could. That should help our cause enormously."

The duchess gave her a look of mock indignation and said, "Are you sure you weren't a prostitute before? My poor, innocent daughter might get ideas."

They all laughed, and Sreba smiled lustfully. "Too late, mother."

☆ ☆ ☆

CHAPTER 25

Tesra groaned as she slid down off her horse. They had ridden hard and closed in on their foes, but needed a few minutes rest. Their foes halted and set up a defensive position among the small, knobby mounds near the foothills of the Boar's Spine Mountains, obviously tired as well. With Ravens' Blades among them, they would feel confident that they could easily defend their position even against Tesra's numerically superior force. As dusk was falling, the Blades would be in their element, killing the soldiers in the dark.

The adopted mother of the empress called for tea to be made; it would help keep them awake and aware into the night. Stale bread and beef jerky would be a welcome meal even if uninspiring.

"Commander, get the men to gathering fuel for a fire. When night comes it will draw our enemies toward it. They will think we are hunkered down around it waiting for dawn. Have the men also get out any spare clothing and blankets, then tie up some large bundles of grass."

The commander gave her an odd look, wondering if she hadn't gone funny in the head with all of the pounding of the day's ride. He then recalled the sly tactics she had used to defend Grandshire against the Koosti and realized something similar must be in the works. "Aye, my lady."

An hour later Tesra scanned the area between her camp and the enemy's. Her improved night vision was not strong, but the half-moon behind high clouds helped. She saw four dark forms moving away from the enemy camp. One went north, one south and the other two slowly moved about thirty feet apart and straight for her camp. 'So, there are four Raven's Blades in the group.' She pulled four times on a piece of twine that stretched over to the guard commander, signaling the number of Blades approaching. The commander pulled once to acknowledge her message, and then moved to throw straw and twigs into the fire. It blazed brightly and revealed the shapes of eight soldiers sitting on the periphery of the firelight. One of them arose and walked away, then returned and stayed on his feet as he leaned on a staff.

Tesra knew that the two Blades sent out north and south would circle around and attack the camp from the rear. From the slight rise, about thirty paces north of the fire, she saw them disappear around the rolling mounds in the distance on each side of their camp. They reappeared over a hundred yards to the west behind the camp and carefully crept toward the horses. Tesra quietly grabbed her bow and nocked an arrow, knowing that the Blades were trained to keep their heads at the same level from the ground as they stalked. A bobbing head would be easier to see even in the tall grass.

The Blade, more to the western side behind the camp, scurried forward. He would wait until the attack started from the front side of the camp and then dash in to kill anyone not brought down in the initial assault. Those fleeing he would catch. The horses and other materials could be sold for profit, while the uniforms would be priceless for infiltrating Grandshire's guard ranks.

He rose up to move closer and was suddenly knocked backward onto the ground. An arrow protruded from the hollow of his throat and his vision and strength faded as he tried to lift his arms to pull it out. His arms would not move nor would his legs. Seconds later nothing moved and he was gone.

His colleagues on the north side edged as close as they dared just beyond the firelight. A guard threw more bundled straw and small sticks onto the fire and then spoke to the other forms sitting or standing around it. He commented that he was going to gather more fuel and stepped away.

Tesra searched anxiously for the other blade on the south side. If he knew his comrade was out of action, he would stay as close to the ground as possible, even going on hands and knees to close in on his targets.

The Blade saw a target move away from the fire and toward himself. Counting down silently from ten, he readied his muscles for a quick, silent attack. Forward he sprang and brought his knife up to slice his target's throat. Just before entering the target zone, an arrow penetrated the muscles and ribs of his left side. He had been trained not to cry out with pain, but the surprise element forced a hard grunt from his throat. He clinched and fell short of the guard, then slashed his knife wildly to try and connect with any part of his prey.

The guard instinctively stepped away and spun around as he started to draw his sword. The Raven's Blade gained his feet enough to lunge and try to tackle him, but a second arrow slammed through his left thigh. He fell to the ground just a moment before the guard's sword connected hard across the back of his neck, sending him to the Creator's judgment.

Tesra kept low to the ground as she moved closer to the fire. Her bow was ready as she scanned the terrain. Suddenly eight dark forms dashed toward the camp from about ten yards away from the fire. Screamed battle cries cut through the night, increasing the sense of fear in their opponents. They attacked the forms around the fire, driving their blades deep into the hearts. Tesra had planned this out, but there were twice as many attackers as she had thought. She quickly said a silent prayer that her arrows would find their marks.

The first Raven's Blade to connect with his target felt a moment of fear. The form he'd attacked was not a man; it was a tightly bound figure of straw with clothes wrapped around it. His blade sank into the board at its back that held it up, and it took extra time and effort to pull it out. He had only enough time to yell a warning to his comrades before an arrow penetrated his ribs and sliced through the main artery leading to his heart. Three of his comrades fell to Tesra's arrows, and two more went down from arrows shot from the opposite side of the camp. The three remaining Blades decided to retreat to their own camp and try to escape on their horses.

Tesra could see them well enough and ordered a charge by the soldiers. Horse hooves pounded the ground as the hidden guards galloped forward. One of them brought Tesra's horse and she jumped into the saddle to speed after their foes. As they neared the enemy camp, she understood why there had been more of them in the attack than she had expected. This was a base camp with a number of slaves to serve their desires. Tesra yelled for the guards to beware the slaves and concentrate on the Blades. The three remaining Blades were aided by the man Dag, as well as by two others.

The enemy crouched down behind boulders lined up at the base of the small foothill behind them. The Blades would put up a great struggle even without the other three men, so Tesra ordered the guards to form into three groups. One at the eastern end, one in the middle and one on the western end.

"Keep them pinned down and don't let them sneak out. Save your arrows for good shots, and keep your horses in random motion so that they cannot predict your exact location. We do not know if they have bows of their own, but we will find out once dawn comes."

The eastern sky grew lighter, helping Tesra and the soldiers follow the movements of their enemies. One soldier ventured a little closer to observe their setup and was knocked off his horse when a Blade used a sling and tossed a stone. The soldier's helmet kept the stone from splitting his skull open, but the impact rendered him senseless nonetheless.

Tesra let loose an arrow, but the Blade dropped behind the boulder before it could connect. She cursed the waste of an arrow and ordered the soldiers to slowly move forward and provoke the Blades to attempt stone-slinging. She and the other archer would then have a chance to shoot them.

Sure enough, a Blade skirted around a boulder to sling a stone. Tesra let a shaft fly and it struck him in the upper bicep. He jumped back under cover and hurried to remove the arrow from his flesh.

Both sides in the contest jumped with surprise when the hillside behind the Blades erupted with noise and motion. Tesra tried to yell over the din and get them to halt but it was no use. Arrows poured down from above and felled the Blades along with the three men with them.

Tesra ran forward waving her arms, yelling for them to stop. She knew it was pointless since the attackers of her foes were Genazi, and Genazi reveled in killing Raven's Blades.

"Stop! Stop, I say; we need prisoners." She reached the line of boulders and quickly scanned the bodies lying around with arrows protruding from them. Seeing the body of Dag, she knew that he would give no information. Arrows stuck out from both his heart and throat.

"Blast! Why could you not wait to find out what was going on before jumping to a kill?" She threw her bow to the ground and glared at the leader of the Genazi patrol group. "I needed to take this cur to Tolemera," she yelled as she pointed at Dag. "He was our only source of information for finding out who abducted the empress."

The Genazi man blanched and stepped back as he bowed. "Forgive me, Mother, but we simply saw the opportunity for the kill and took it. We thought you might be in danger."

Tesra snapped back, "Have you ever entertained the notion that there is more to fighting then simply killing an opponent? You have to learn to think, man. Think!" She yelled at him to free the slave captives and to see to their well-being, then yelled to the captain of the soldiers to ready for departure.

A search of the dead bodies revealed nothing. In typical Raven's Blade style they would yield nothing even in death. This made Tesra even more angry. She barely noticed three straight hours of steady riding. When they stopped for rest and food, she looked up and saw two of the moons align north of the sun, but she paid it no mind. She laid herself down under a large tree and immediately fell fast asleep. A dream came to her mind. The two moons were in line and cast a milky light over a large city set on the shore of the sea. A large seawall with tall towers blocked entry to the city's harbor and allowed only one ship to pass after inspections. A forest floated on the water outside the wall, waiting for the opportunity to enter the harbor. Green and gold eagles circled a high, pinnacled tower on the north side of the city. A beam of green light pierced the sky from heaven and down to the pinnacle. The large building on which the tower was built came into view. It's south side wall became transparent, revealing a huge, royal hall. On the dais at the east end stood a bookstand with an old, leather bound book atop it. The book was open. The pages on the left were filled with names and significant events. The pages on the right were blank. An ancient feather pen wafted into the hall on the sea breezes and settled on the book. A fair hand reached out and picked up the pen. In fine, precise strokes a name was written down at the top of the right page.

Tesra awoke as a guard shook her shoulder. "No! Could you not have waited even a minute longer? Blast!" She stood and rubbed her eyes, then looked at the guard. He did not know what to say in the face of her wrath. She realized quickly that he was only following directions. "I am sorry, young man. A dream was playing in my head and I wanted to see the end of it. Please, forgive my foolish words."

The guard bowed and said, "I understand, your highness. I was told to tell you that some hot tea and food are ready."

"Thank you, sir. Do you know how long I slept?"

He glanced at the sun and made a quick estimate. "I would say about six hours, your highness."

"Six hours? That will give us about six hours until sundown. We must hurry; I want to reach Tolemera as quickly as possible."

After packing her few items into saddle bags she sat down to eat. The aroma of fresh mountain bison meat and fried eggs soon had her gobbling down the food. She realized that it must have been supplied by the Genazi, and thanked the Creator for their kindness. Looking down at her academy ring, she noticed a bright flash of light refracted from the red gem shaped like a quill. A word arose in her mind: 'Write!' The vision faded leaving her curious.

After nightfall they crossed into Loreland, but Tesra allowed only an hour's rest. In a small garrison town she bade her guards great thanks and reward for their service, then headed off in a carriage for Tolemera. Imperial soldiers, two in the armor of Yanbre's knights, escorted her along a smooth road. The green feather designs on their breastplates gave her an idea. She ordered the driver to increase their speed and they reached Tolemera two days later.

CHAPTER 26

High clouds diffused the midmorning sun as Veranna sat at a desk near a window in her small room in the academy. It reminded her of the academy in Clarens where she had grown up. A tear wanted to blur her vision as she recalled fond memories from those days. Learning so many things, and growing to love the instructors and students like family, had comforted her in the absence of parents or other relatives. She wished she could simply abandon the role of empress and move back to the academy with Karsten. She would bear them many children and grow old at the venerable institution, serving her family and community by helping to train anyone with the desire to learn.

A light knock on her door breached her daydream. She stepped quickly to the door, knowing it likely that Beneto would be standing there with his arms full of materials for her. Sure enough, several large tomes tested his strength as he walked in and set them down on her bed.

"Well, here are the works most salient to your research on the ancient kingdom. I can tell you now that you will find little direct mention of your ancestors since their existence was not to be recognized after their departure. You will need to infer things from what is left out of an account."

She had him take a seat at the table and poured him a cup of tea. "Thank you for bringing them; I just wish I had more time to go through them thoroughly. After I got back in last night I finished the work you asked me to do." She handed him several pages of stout paper. "I made sure that there were no ink blotches or margin errors. Some of your scribbling took me a while to decipher."

He chuckled softly but gave her a scolding look. "You are taking a great risk with these nocturnal scouting forays to the noble estates. You got an arrow in you almost a month ago; who knows when one will get you for good. You should leave the finding of the little girl to the queen's mother."

Veranna gave his arm a squeeze and smiled warmly. "Yes, father. Do you want me to wash the dishes now?"

He laughed. "Ah, Veranna, if only you were my daughter I would be the proudest man in the world. However, here in Faresea I am taking it upon myself to serve as your patron and guardian since your husband is not here. I will try to watch your back as much as I can."

"Thank you, kind sir. I am already so much in your debt that I can never repay you adequately." She paused and turned back to the day's business. "I found your paper on the poetics of the ancient realm to be excellent. I am sure that it will help me understand the documents of my Emeraldian ancestors . A grammar and lexicon would be a tremendous help. Do you know of any?"

"The last works along those lines were produced close to two-hundred years ago and are quite rare. If I got my hands on any they would have to be copied quickly and returned. The academy archivist would know whether they are available." He turned toward the door and a look of tension came over him. "Veranna, you must be very careful. You are still classified as a slave in Faresea and are subject to corrective abuse."

Veranna frowned and moved a step closer. "Beneto, is something wrong?"

He looked away, his hands fidgeting nervously. "It is the President of the Academy; he has seen you and desires to further your rehabilitation by taking you to his bed. Under the law you could not refuse him. One of the reasons that I have insisted that you work in your room is to make you less noticeable. I'm hoping that he will be too busy to send for you."

She tried to reassure him that he need not worry. "My dear guardian, with the Creator behind me and you watching out for me, there is nothing to fear. Besides, if he tries to rape me I can always break his nose or... er, other parts." She smiled and patted him on the back before he left the room.

Three hours later she was in a large room shaped like a half-circle, with rows of seats set on a gentle slope as in a theater. Even though she was Beneto's assistant she had to sit off stage behind the curtain, since she was a slave. Six other slaves, two older women, two older men and one young man and woman sat on a bench beside her and waited for commands. Beneto finished the reading of his paper and fielded a number of questions before bowing and taking a seat in the third row.

Another man stood, walked up onto the stage and arranged his papers on the podium. He looked to be in his early forties and of average height, but his voice was mumbly at times. Snapping his fingers, the six slaves sitting off-stage quickly hurried into a pre-planned formation on the stage to his left. He launched into a lecture about anatomy and how various traits were affected by parentage. At another snap of his fingers the slaves removed their clothes and stood with their feet shoulder-width apart and their arms straight out to their sides. Veranna gasped, but the audience took it as normal. The lecturer used a pointer to illustrate his remarks by pointing at parts of the slaves' anatomies. They stood in groups of three with an older man and woman paired off and one of the younger ones between them. The older ones were the parents of the younger and were used to demonstrate how their traits melded into the child. The lecturer then discussed his plans to mate the couples again to see how the traits might differ in the next offspring. He then asked if anyone had questions.

One young man, after several older members queried the lecturer, asked if the presenter could gauge the appearance of parents from a child's traits, and with what level of success. The lecturer nodded and confidently said, "Yes, to a good degree of probability." He then snapped his fingers at Veranna and commanded her to come onto the stage. She arose and warily walked over, then did a respectful curtsy. The lecturer ordered her to remove her clothes and assume the stand of the other slaves.

Veranna's crisp reply whiplashed through the room, "I will not."

The lecturer slapped her and repeated his command, but Veranna did not comply. With a voice full of threat she glared at him.

"I will give you only this one warning: Do not ever attempt that again with me, or any other, or I will break your arm."

The man stepped back in shock and the audience was stunned. Loud murmuring edged the room toward chaos when Veranna's regal voice brought them all to silence.

"Listen to me you pack of jackals!" Her eyes glowed green and brought many to bow before sitting. Only the high, ruling caste had eyes anything like hers. "These are your fellow human beings who deserve respect and dignity. You do not mistreat someone under the guise of a science that is simply a veneer for cruel despotism. Shame upon you! Shame upon you all!"

The lecturer burned with resentment. "How dare you tell us what we should do with our own property! This has been decreed by the Creator and is not subject to your whims."

Hotter by far was Veranna's temper, but she tried to keep her reason to guide her. "I dare because I am a person with a mind of my own, and can respond to the Creator's will intelligently. You, as a teacher here, should value rational decision making."

The President of the Academy arose from his seat in the first row and held up his hands for silence. "Come to order, everyone, order, please." After a moment they all calmed down and sat. "It seems that we have been given an opportunity to debate an age-old question: Are one's circumstances necessarily so, or could they have been otherwise? Our colleague, Beneto, was punished with slavery for questioning the official doctrine. Our entire system of government is based upon it. What we take as obvious may not seem so to others." He looked at the lecturer and motioned with his right hand. "Professor Lecreach, you shall disregard for the debate the fact that this woman is a slave." He then motioned toward Veranna. "And you, although a slave, shall proceed as though a full member of the academy. I do hope that you have more to offer than simply the same tired arguments used by those in the streets."

Veranna eyed him with a touch of disdain. "Perhaps you might advance a bit of your understanding were you to get your feet back onto the street and your head out of the clouds. If you did so you would notice that the official doctrine is seriously flawed. Have you never noticed that your argument is circular? You know it is true because you know it is true. That proves nothing and is no basis for law and punishment. It leads to anarchy or to the despotism of Faresea." She looked at the professor and said, "Suppose I were to take you captive and make you my slave. Would you resign yourself to that life because you believed it was the Creator's will?"

The professor's answer came out like a tooth being pulled. "Of course not. But this is not a question for me since I come from a noble house and have already had the Creator's will shown for my life."

Veranna smiled knowingly and turned to the audience. "Thank you, professor, for demonstrating my point. You based your claim on the assumption that your claim is true. You did not demonstrate the validity of your claim. Your argument is purely circular and therefore invalid. Only brute force and coercion can maintain such an idea for very long. If you give yourself to such a philosophy then you have ceased to be a true member of the academy who seeks to discover the truths of the Creator. Beneto demonstrated integrity and scholarship in trying to get you out of such error, but you could not accept it and only saw your own selfish interests being challenged."

The professor puffed himself up and tried to intimidate her by seeming above her petty contentions.

"Such an argument may appeal to those limited to seeing things only from the vantage point of this world, but to those of us familiar with higher thought it is inadequate. Let me demonstrate why I say this. Do you believe that the Creator is sovereign?"

"Yes, I do."

"Is it possible that His sovereign will can be denied?

"No."

"So, are we subject to his sovereign will?"

"Yes."

"Does He know all things past, present and future?"

"Yes."

"Well then, you have a serious dilemma on your hands. If He is sovereign and His will cannot be denied, then whatever comes to pass must be due to His will. You are a slave because He willed it, and I am a lord due to the same. For you to deny this is to blaspheme and be punished even unto death."

Veranna had heard the same manner of argument discussed in the Academy of Clarens many times. "It seems that your circular reasoning has you captive. You are arguing that how events come to be is simply due to the direct decree of the Creator. You assumed what you are trying to prove. Also your argument requires the belief that the Creator's will can only be accomplished in one particular way. Even we limited humans are not so bound. In effect, you are saying that the Creator is lesser in attributes than we. That truly is blasphemy."

The professor fumed but did not know what to say in response. He walked to the front of the stage and ignored Veranna as he spoke to the president. "My lord, I resent being lectured by a commoner spouting simplistic ideas. Our ancestors settled this question hundreds of years ago and I do not wish to waste my time bandying words over it again."

The president's face was impassive as he asked the professor to be seated. He then turned to Veranna and an oily smile came over his features. "That was quite impressive for someone of such a lowly background. After you reach the rank of reform servant I shall have to request that you be assigned here for further training. As to the issues of the debate, we are compelled by law to reject your position. Our ancestors drove out those who promulgated your views, and they are no more."

Veranna looked him over and knew that sensual desire took precedence in his life. "You abandon truth and reason at great cost, and end up suffering the Creator's judgment."

"That may be, but for now you are required to suffer mine. In my room; I will continue your training and help you conform to the law."

Veranna gave him a look of disgust and waved her right hand across the audience. "Do you see what your law encourages? It is nothing more than an excuse to practice evil and exploit others."

Many in the audience looked down in shame while others responded with hostile comments due to the impact of her words.

The president walked up the steps of the stage, reached out and grabbed her right wrist. "Yes, well, it is not my doing; I just obey the law."

Veranna did not raise her voice, but it penetrated the entire room with its dire tone of threat. "Let go of my arm."

"Oh no; I must take you to my bed and train you to submit."

In one simple blur of motion she twisted her arm free and fixed him in an arm lock that sent him to his knees. It was hard to tell if the pain or audacity of her actions surprised him more.

"I can have you executed for treating me this way! Who do you think you are to rebel against the law?"

Her voice was hard in reply. "By law I am your ruler." She noticed the question and denial in his eyes, as well as in the faces of the audience. "I am the lone survivor to the ancient ruling House of Faresea, led by Dunamays, the king of Faresea and founding emperor of the Seven Lands. You thought he and his fellows were gone, but here I am. I will not treat you with the same contempt you show me and others by forcing them to believe something irrational. But you shall now receive confirmation that my claims are true."

She lifted her left hand high and looked up. "Dear Creator, hear me, I pray, and deliver these people from the darkness in which they live. Let this man be rid of the lusts that control him, and let him serve truly as a leader in this academy. Please, oh Creator, let it be so."

A nimbus of emerald green surrounded her and her eyes glowed like gems. A second later a shaft of light blazed down on the president and illuminated his terrored face. Veranna released his arm and he slowly rose to his feet as though lifted by the light.

A soft voice with the power of an earthquake resonated through the room.

"Speak no more foolishness, and submit to the one I have chosen to rule. For your evil desires I shall punish you now. For your penance you shall advance the study of truth for the rest of your days."

The beam of light flared with a pulse and a crack like thunder, then went out. The president fell to the floor, let out a high-pitched shriek and grabbed his groin protectively.

The audience was frozen with shock at the signs revealed before their very eyes. Only the ancient tales mentioned anything like them. A few of the young men fled the room, but the rest of the men and women made their way to the stage to kneel before Veranna and swear allegiance to her. The professor with whom Veranna debated gave the president a looking over before turning to the others. His face and voice were full of fear and astonishment.

"He...has been...castrated. No blood, no scars; it is as though he was born with no sign of manhood."

Veranna looked at them and took a deep, calming breath. "Are any of you in doubt about the Creator's will?" When none of them spoke up, she asked if anyone knew what had become of the little girl, Tyrzah, whom she sought.

An older dumpling of a woman bowed and said, "Your highness, if the girl has not been located on any of the noble estates, it is quite possible she may have been sent to the copper mines far to the north of here. The children are used as errand runners for the miners." She looked down and wagged her head in shame. "They suffer much abuse."

Veranna's eyes blazed with rage, and a rumbling of the building shook the others to terror. "You craven brood of vile sensualists! How could you, the thinkers obligated to promote justice, allow such heinous treatment of children and others. I am amazed that the Creator has not destroyed you from the face of the world. You are no better than the barbarians you demean." She pointed at a man near one of the exits. "You, I want you to leave immediately for the mines and bring the little girl back to me."

The man bowed and hurried out the door while others helped the president to his feet. He cringed as Veranna stepped toward him and eyed him coldly. Her voice came out like a Mother of the Academy scolding a willful child.

"I warned you, but you would not listen. I pray that you now recognize the error of your ways, and that your books will give you solace now that your primary means of enjoyment is gone." She ordered him taken to his room and given rest.

The others in the room plied her with many questions, curious as to how her ancestors survived after leaving Faresea. Many wanted to know the style of government in The Seven Lands, and how the caste system operated. A number of them asked about the educational system and if the level of technology was different from that in Faresea.

Beneto urged her to leave the academy right away and get to the queen's estate before soldiers arrived and carried her off to some gruesome prison.

"Your highness, the academy cannot change or void the law; only the Council of Nobles can do that. We can only advise, and even then we must be careful not to step on anyone's toes. The nobles love their positions of power and will seek to destroy you. The queen will, hopefully, be of some aid."

Veranna agreed with his counsel and the two of them hurried into a carriage and sped to the queen's estate. Veranna marveled once more at the way in which the Creator operated. Who could have caused so much upheaval in a society in such a short time and with so few people?

They were startled when they saw the queen directing them to the back of the house with no guards present. She stood atop the gate watch and apologized for not being strong enough to open it.

Veranna simply said, "Open," and the gates swung wide. Sreba was amazed but hurried down and climbed into the carriage. She quickly led Beneto and Veranna in through the back door of the huge estate house, and showed them to a room in the basement.

"I am sorry for the crude accommodations, but we should keep your presence here secret for as long as possible. A messenger reached us from the academy about an hour before your arrival.

He claimed that a ruler from the ancient line had demonstrated great signs of authority, so I knew it had to be you. My husband has begun sending out dispatches to the nobles requesting a full counsel meeting. They will want to stamp out any indication of your existence."

Veranna felt totally calm. "It is good that they shall meet. The Creator will, no doubt, give them something to think about. Thank you, Sreba, for being our friend and risking your own life for our sake."

The queen bowed and said, "Your highness, it is the least I can do for all of your help. Since last we met my husband has found fresh appreciation for me." She smiled coyly and blushed.

Veranna returned Sreba's smile. "It seems that you are already enjoying changes. Let us hope that the whole realm shall be... uh...so pleased."

CHAPTER 27

Tesra arrived at the castle just after noon and nearly flew inside. On her way to the meeting chamber near the heart of the keep she barked orders at the guards to fetch Karsten, Kreida, Yanbre, Treybal, Raeki and LeAnre to the room. She attended to only the barest of greetings as she paced impatiently at the head of the table. Kreida was the last to arrive.

"Girl, I thought you would know better than to keep me waiting. Be quiet and do not interrupt." She looked at all of them before continuing.

"I have news both good and bad. First, the bad news is that we gained nothing from the criminal called Dag. He was captured in Grandshire, and we were bringing him here when we were ambushed at night by a unit of Ravens' Blades. They freed our prisoner and headed north to the foothills of the Boar's Spine Mountains. We caught up with them there but failed to capture Dag. Genazi patrolmen filled him with arrows before we could grab him. Another instance of Genazi impulse overruling clear thinking.

"However, I believe that the Creator sent me a vision as a clue to Veranna's whereabouts."

Karsten frowned in thought as he recalled similar events. "There have been dreams of forests on water in a closed harbor, and Yanbre claims to have heard a song with the word 'Seacorro.'"

Tesra stared at him for a moment. "Two moons have aligned more than once in the last few weeks. That is nearly always a sign regarding Veranna. The word 'Seacorro' is a tease in my mind, but I cannot place it."

LeAnre said quietly, "I can place it for you." She waited until all eyes were on her. "Seacorro is the chief city of the kingdom called 'Faresea', which lies far to the south and east of the furthest border of my province. Between my province and that land is a horrible desert. Our contact with Seacorro has been through dragon-riding traders. We would exchange goods and potions for slaves from there. The female slaves are especially good since they tend to be taller and accepting of their fate. They make good breeders for our men and we traded them to the Arbori for rare herbs and minerals that we use in special elixirs. My province has a harbor on the south sea but our people do not travel to Seacorro. Their harbor is impenetrable."

Tesra considered her words and then looked at Karsten. "We must get to this place she speaks of. Veranna is likely a slave and could be in very dire straits."

Karsten agreed but threw in a note of caution. "If their harbor is as secure as LeAnre says, we may need a good-sized attack force to break through their defenses. That could leave us dangerously vulnerable to an uprising by the Erain Houses. We kept them from taking over the empire by only one shaky vote. If Veranna were dead they could rescind Kreida's status as Princess of the Genazi and remove that vote."

Raeki, the daughter of the Ruling Pride of the Felinii, hurried with a suggestion. Her command of the common language had increased since coming to Tolemera, and her exotic appearance brought her a great deal of attention. Flaxen-blonde hair and vertical pupils in her yellow eyes combined with a slender, feline form that all found a delight to behold.

"My lords, go Seacorro and get empress. Keep here nine hundred knights; take with one hundred with more soldiers. Lord Yanbre more than whole Erain army."

Yanbre bowed his head and smiled. "Thank you, my lady. I believe you have a good idea. Speed will be a necessity and a lighter force can move more quickly. I can get the supply wagons moving in half of an hour, but the one hundred knights will take two or three hours to be rounded up and readied."

Tesra did not hesitate. "Get to it. Karsten, ask Lord Roland and Marques Amilla if they would not mind delaying their return to their lands, and call a meeting of the nobles immediately. We need to put some of them in their place before we depart." She then turned to Kreida and Raeki, "The two of you shall accompany us. I want you to pack formal wear since you shall be serving as ambassadors." She looked around the room and was puzzled. "Where is Lord Forrest?"

Kreida just shrugged. "Don't know; he wandered off a few months ago saying that he wanted to see how the Lands had changed since his time. What that is supposed to mean is beyond me. He's not much older than you, Mother. Well, I guess he could be senile."

Tesra gave her a hard look and growled, "Your condition is explainable in different terms. Get moving, and do not get into any childish squabbles."

Raeki gave Kreida a reproving look and headed out the door. "Come, dog breath; Mother give command."

Kreida shook with frustration and yelled, "I have told you a thousand times not to call me that. When we get back from this little trip I am going to rub your nose in horse dung."

Tesra could not help chuckling silently. It was good to see that some things had not changed. She headed up to the mess chamber for some hot food and conferred with Karsten about the strategy they would use in the Council of Nobles.

An hour later she sat in her chair on the dais in the council chamber. Her seat was just to the left of Veranna's emerald throne chair while Karsten's was just to the right. The chamberlain called those assembled to order, and when all was quiet, he bowed to Tesra and Karsten and then stepped to the side of the chamber. The two rulers looked at each other and nodded, then Karsten stood and addressed them.

"I thank you all for coming on such short notice. The reason I summoned you is that we have new information regarding our empress. We received this information from the empress's mother, Mother of the Academy, Tesra. She shall relate her findings to you." He bowed to Tesra and held out his hand for her to take.

She put on an air of mature authority as she took his hand and stood. "Thank you, my lord." Moving to the front of the dais, she swept her gaze over the people. "As some of you may know, we were in hot pursuit of a criminal who had information regarding the empress's abduction. We captured the man in Grandshire and were transporting him back here when we were ambushed by a unit of Ravens' Blades."

Lady Gelangweil and Archduchess Loray said nothing, but their faces turned red with suppressed anger and frustration.

"We recaptured the man and destroyed the Ravens' Blades, but the criminal, named Dag, was killed in the process. However that was after we managed to get the necessary information from him. It seems that a clever conspiracy involved Koosti dragon riders to remove our empress to a land far away. We are readying a force to retrieve her. In our absence Lord Roland and Lady Amilla shall lead the empire."

Archduchess Loray stood and protested immediately, the curves of her figure outlined with tension.

"That is unacceptable. It shall be Lady Gelangweil or I in that role. If you breach the law you are disqualified from ruling."

Tesra's left eyebrow rose and she gave the lady a slight smile. "I agree; a breach of the law is a disqualification. That is why the two of you are not to rule, for this man, Dag, named the two of you as part of the conspiracy."

The room erupted in accusations and arguments. The chamberlain called in more guards to bring the meeting under control. Tesra motioned for Yanbre to come to the front of the dais before she continued.

"Lord Yanbre, arrest these two on the charge of conspiracy to overthrow the crown. They are to be held without bail until the empress returns and judges their cases."

Both cursing and clapping rang through the room as Yanbre led four guards and arrested the two women. They protested and had to be apprehended, yelling threats all the way to the holding room on the second level underground.

Back in the council chamber, Baron Ciclanno pushed to the front and pointed at Tesra. "This is outrageous. You have no cause to hold these noblewomen; if they are not released immediately and reparations made, you will have vengeance demanded to the full."

Tesra's voice was flat and unequivocal. "You will mind your tongue and gestures or I will exact a sentence against you now. These matters will be handled according to the law; we have remedies at hand should you desire to disobey it."

The baron glowered but knew better than to say anymore. The leaders of the Erain Houses were in custody; stirring up trouble might make things worse for them. They would have to wait and challenge the case in the High Court, where the empress would receive a staggering blow to her power. He turned and stomped out of the chamber with his allies close behind.

"Putting those two women in custody is a great gamble, Karsten. We may live to rue that decision."

Karsten put his hand on her shoulder and spoke firmly. "Mother, if it helps us to reach Veranna sooner, I am willing to risk everything. At least we won't have to worry about them usurping the throne while we are away. Our allies can now out-vote them if a challenge is put forward. And, a bit of humility will possibly set some healthy fear of Veranna in them. Our spies are still active in digging up any clues linking the Erains to this man Dag, and the Raven's Blades, so we may end up in a stronger position than we are now."

Tesra smiled and laughed as she put her arm around his waist. "You Genazi are such daredevils! I thank the Creator for you everyday, my son." After a quick peck on his cheek they arrived at her chamber. "Please rouse me when all is ready to go."

Karsten nodded and proceeded to his and Veranna's chamber. He changed into his traveling clothes and hitched his knives and sword to his belt. Looking around the room he imagined Veranna sitting next to him by the fireplace, the firelight dancing on her long, lustrous dark hair. After a few moments he shook his head. An odd feeling came over him and he noticed a book lying open on Veranna's nightstand. He was sure that it was not open a few minutes ago and knew that he had not touched it.

Moving closer he saw that the pages were written in an ancient script. Only those pages to the left were written on, and those to the right lay ready for use. He picked up the book and looked at the title page. In bold, archaic script were the words, *Mysterium Konsequenter Ergonum*, and he remembered having seen the book the day he and Veranna were married. They had hurried away to their honeymoon and forgotten it. A strange foreboding came over him as he looked at the last paragraph, reading slowly due to the amount of deciphering required of the old language.

Not all trees bear fruit, and a graft often brings out favorable qualities. Snow chills the bones but stores water in the mountains that quenches the land's thirst in the hot summer. Rain muds the streets but softens the soil for the farm. Food brings joy, although too much brings fat and lethargy. The Creator's servants must always remember that they serve a calling that brings joy and sadness, hot and cold, peace and conflict. Those knowing not their Creator must be brought into the fold, and this often takes hard ways to break the will and open the mind. Be ready to surrender all, for consequences unknown are to be left to the Creator's wisdom.

Karsten closed the book and set it back on the nightstand, then turned and headed out the door. An hour later and he was off with the others for Zishiye, formally known as Neidberg, down south in Imperia. They would visit his father, Tomius, the Earl of Imperia, and be re-supplied before heading into LeAnre's province in the Koosti Empire. They would then head south to the port city at the extreme end of her province and take ships to this place called Faresea.

One phrase in his mind haunted him as he rode: 'Be ready to surrender all, for consequences unknown are to be left to the Creator's wisdom.'

He could not wait to deliver consequences to those keeping his Veranna from him.

CHAPTER 28

Bright sunlight spilled in through the windows and door-ways of Chief Sarim'tay's palace. Located in his capital city, Dagaran, it was a complex of massive proportions. The front had been formed through hundreds of years of work to accommodate soldiers and slaves. Positioned about a half-mile above sea level, it took advantage of the breezes that blew from the west and east to keep it warm in the cooler months and cool in the summer. To the east lay the vast jungle where dwelt the Arbori. They were relatively few in number and contact with them was seldom. The main difficulty with them came when they dared to hunt and kill a Koosti. The Arbori were cannibals and made no distinction between killing animals and humans for food. In their minds, anyone not Arbori was an animal by definition.

Sarim'tay strode in to his throne room without looking right or left. Guards in red-orange leather shorts and straps criss-crossing their chests preceded and followed him in, their bronzed skin reflecting the sunlight. After the guards came four-scores of slave women to serve the men assembled in the room. They wore silk wraps around their hips, and had hairdos of various types. Bronz-ing of their skin obscured their various ethnic backgrounds, but height, build, bone structure, hair color and eye color revealed an assortment of features. Seacorran, Koosti, Deeri, Felinii and others from corners of the world unknown, went about their duties with fearful, meticulous efficiency. Food, drink and any request from the men was immediately satisfied.

As Sarim'tay walked down the center aisle toward his throne, his masters went to their knees and placed their faces on the floor. The masters were the leaders of the lesser tribes under Sarim'tay's suzerainty. They were absolutely loyal to him and saw death in his service as the ultimate honor. Killing someone at his command brought them joy like no other they could imagine. He had chosen these two hundred from the day of their birth and set them in rigorous physical and mental training regimens. They eagerly examined his every breath for the slightest hint of command. He gave one; a sharp, guttural grunt telling them to sit and relax. They did so, but kept their eyes and ears fixed on him. They gave the serving women, chosen for their great beauty, not a thought as they anticipated their lord's words.

"My sons, I have called you here to tell you that our present plan to destroy the Emeraldian Empress has not yet been realized. Somehow she managed to escape the burial pit in which I placed her. She survived the poison of the spider and lives in the realm of Faresea. Our spies there report that she has caused great turmoil and may end up executed as a heretic. The only disappointment with that would be that it did not occur by my own hand.

"For now we will bide our time and let the next phase of our plan take place. It will delay our goal by a few years, but a fine plan brings its own pleasures as it unfolds. To see the Emeraldian tramp wasting away into the crude form she truly is will be a delight to behold. I shall enjoy her demise as she serves me with great fear and delight. She thinks she is strong and upright, but I shall show her just how mistaken she truly is. First, her character and mind will go, then her life shall be surrendered to me and I shall make her an example to the entire world that they cannot even dream of opposing my will."

The serving women nearly spilled their wares as the two hundred masters shouted as one, "It shall be so for our great lord, Sarim'tay!"

The chief's face remained inscrutable, but inside he smiled as he looked at his sons. "You, the result of my will with the finest of women, shall all sit on thrones and govern the world for my empire. The word 'Koosti' shall be synonymous with mastery over all realms. They shall live and die at your command as you reduce them to their proper place beneath us. We must never forget that the Dark One has ordained that we are to rule this world and subdue it to serve him.

"Our foe is to think that the current Great One, DeAndre y'dob, has all things under his control in the Koosti Empire. She is to believe that the Koosti are accepting of her culture and simply want peace with her. Once this is done, her fall shall be swift and unavoidable. As in desperation on the chess board of life, she shall have no good move to make. Her idealism will deliver her into our hands.

"In a month, summer will begin and I shall go far to the east through the jungle and turn the Arbori to my will. They come together once a year for a week to trade news, women and slaves and to compete for dominance. By the powers the Dark One has given me I shall have them bowing down in awe and serving me with unquestioned devotion. I shall be as a god to them. They shall see me as the source and provider of life."

Outside, in a high watchtower, a caller yelled out the change of the hours. Sarim'tay's eyeballs rolled back leaving only the whites showing. A mass of colorful light appeared in the center of the room and stretched out across its diameter just above and behind Sarim'tay. It coalesced into a moving picture of Tolemera and had sounds with it. The ancient castle of the Emeraldians was occupied by Koosti, and Sarim'tay sat on the throne. Serving him were girls and women of the Genazi, their backs showing old scars and fresh wounds from beatings. They were silent and broken, their tongues having been cut out and their ankles hobbled. Erain nobles were allowed to wear loincloths, but could only speak when commanded. They bowed down at Sarim'tay's feet and obeyed his sons in all of the cities of the Seven Lands. The tall double-doors of the room opened and two guards led Veranna into Sarim'tay's presence. Unclothed to display all of the marks of torture and training she had undergone, her glazed eyes quivered in fear and anticipation of the terrible Koosti lord. The set of her jaw and her cowed posture conveyed madness. Before the steps of the throne dais she fell prostrate on the floor and awaited a command. Her muscles tensed with readiness to obey.

Sarim'tay said simply, "Turn over,' and Veranna obeyed so quickly that she almost spun around in midair before landing flat on her back. The Koosti lord looked at Lady Gelangweil and Archduchess Loray, just an eyebrow showing any evidence that he considered them almost equal to cockroaches. As before, his voice was calm but pregnant with menace as he addressed them. "Do you see this woman?"

They both pressed their faces to the floor as they answered, "Yes, great master!"

"She once sought to resist my will. I have taught her the futility of doing so." He cast his voice in a slightly different pitch so that Veranna would recognize that he spoke to her. "Is that not correct, dung heap?"

Veranna's body quivered again as she cried out, "Yes, great master!"

Speaking to the other two women again he kept his commands simple. "Since you aided me in subduing this stupid girl I will show you great mercy and let you live. You, Gelangweil, will from this day forward, walk through the public areas from morning till noon and proclaim my sovereignty and greatness. You will wear only your loincloth and obey any command of my lowliest servants.

"You, Loray, shall constantly travel to the cities of the Seven Lands and see to it that all the people know of their total subjection to me. Wearing only your loincloth you will demonstrate to the people your absolute submission to me by obeying anything one of my servants tells you to do.

"The both of you will make yourselves available to my soldiers for pregnancy. You will bear sons to serve in my army and daughters to be sold to other lands as slaves.

"Do not make the mistake of thinking that I show you mercy due to some favor I have for you. Here is what you will experience should I ever be displeased with you." He snapped his fingers and

Veranna sprang to her feet and faced him. His voice was direct and plain as he said to her, "You will not move or make any noise."

A crazed smile came over her face as she responded, "Yes, master!"

He reached out with this right hand and grabbed her left eyeball. Her body tensed as hard as steel but she did not flinch or make a sound. In one quick motion he snatched her eye out and held it up for the other two women to see. Deliberately he placed it in his mouth and swallowed. "Turn and face them, dung heap, and tell them how you feel."

Parts of her body spasmed as she turned to the other two women and fought to control her pain. "I serve the Great One, Sarim'tay." Blood drained from her empty eye socket, adding to the look of total madness in her. She smiled and danced as she said, "He has shown me wonderful things in letting me serve him. Let all people give themselves to pleasing his will!" She went to her knees and kissed his feet.

Sarim'tay smiled at the other two and asked , "Do you have any difficulty with understanding my words?"

Both hurried to cry out, "No, great master!"

He then put a hand on Veranna's head as he spoke kindly. "Dung heap, take these two and give them each a good whipping before sending them out to do my will. After that, use the rest of the day to see to the satisfaction of my soldiers in their barracks."

Totally insane, she cried out with joy, "Yes, great master!" Leaping through the air she went for the other two and slapped each hard across the cheek. She grabbed them by their hair and dragged them from the room to the whipping yard, their cries for mercy spurring her to laughter.

The vision faded and Sarim'tay smiled at his sons. "Ah, that day is not far off, my sons."

The men grinned greedily and rubbed their hands in anticipation.

"We will spend the rest of this week in celebration to this wonderful future that awaits us. Remember, only you, my sons, shall know of this plan. Any other must die."

In a minute the serving girls were strangled and thrown over the balcony into wagons that hauled the bodies to the feed lots. Sarim'tay smiled and thought, 'What a fine number of sons I have.' He clapped his hands once and the door opened, a servant awaiting his command. "Bring in the servers; my sons need refreshment." Two hundred beautiful women entered and cast themselves at the feet of the men, begging to serve.

CHAPTER 29

Sreba, the queen of Faresea, moved through the halls of her estate house experiencing both confidence and fear. Since getting to know Veranna, and following her advice, she made great strides in solving the difficulties in her marriage. Now, Veranna was in hiding on the estate after revealing her true status. She would be taken into custody by the authorities, and even the queen could not abrogate the law. Her husband was a stickler for maintaining the status quo, and Veranna was a huge threat to their entire social and political system. How she had survived so long in Seacorro was explainable only by the intervention of the divine. It was still likely that Veranna would be captured and used as a breeder for some nobleman wanting to increase his status. Veranna's intensely emerald green eyes and regal bearing would be passed on to children who would be acceptable in the highest echelons of Faresean aristocracy.

Another complication was the fact that the queen, and her mother, had sworn fealty to Veranna, and were honor-bound to defend her. Now that her husband, the king, had heard of Veranna and sent out summons for the nobles to convene on the estate, keeping Veranna safe was going to be an increasingly difficult task. She would need a miracle to make any progress against the current system.

The queen came to a junction of hallways and, without thinking, stopped. It proved fortunate since a servant came from the hallway on the right pushing a cart laden with dirty dishes. It would have struck her squarely and splashed drink and sauces on her had she continued. The servant bowed her head and begged pardon from the queen. Sreba, again without deliberate thought, told the woman not to worry and that she was just as much at fault for not paying attention as she walked. The servant blinked, smiled and continued on her way.

Sreba reflected on the incident and realized that a month ago she would have been angry at the servant and totally ignored her existence. Her ways of seeing the world and her place in it were changing since Veranna's arrival.

Also strange and interesting was her mood in this ancient house. She felt trapped and bored before, but now the very structure of the building seemed to pulse with a life force all its own. This definitely occurred after Veranna had blessed her with a share of the divine gift. It was uncanny how she knew to stop before the serving woman ran into her. She also knew when Veranna was experiencing emotional distress. A whole new world was opened to her. *How could the ancients have been so foolish as to want to destroy Veranna's ancestors!? We Fareseans are a hard-hearted, foolish lot!*

It had been two weeks since Veranna sought refuge with the queen. Hiding her among the servants had worked so far, but if the king spotted her it would be a terrible situation. Veranna would have to resort to violence to avoid being abused by him. Seeing how she had handled fierce guards and the premier swordsman in the land on other estates, she would have piles of wounded or dead men around her. But could she escape hundreds of guards and soldiers? No, discretion would definitely serve better for now.

She continued her walk and found Veranna in a private room two levels underground. Usually, only servants went down this far. The empress had two of the female servants with her as she played a lute and sang songs. When she saw Sreba enter she stood and nodded as she greeted her.

"Good morning, my lady. You look very fair, but a dark mood seems to be weighing you down."

The servants fell to their knees and bowed to the queen, but one was amazed when she bowed to Veranna.

"Good morning, your highness. I am well, however, I still have worries about your future." She stopped abruptly, realizing that the servants were hearing this exchange. Veranna set her at ease.

"Do not worry, my lady; one of your servants here, Doris, is from the Seven Lands, and told the others about me. She was captured by the Koosti during our last war with them, then sold to Faresea by dragon riding traders. It is wonderful to have someone else around who knows some of the same songs and lore. I have promised her that when I leave she shall also."

Sreba nodded and said, "As you wish, your highness. I must say that I envy your ability to remain joyful even in captivity with doom ready to fall."

Veranna smiled and held Sreba's hands in her own. "It is not because of anything in me; I just know that whatever takes place does so for the Creator's glory. I trust his judgment."

A bit surprised and chagrined by Veranna's faith, Sreba smiled self-consciously and did a quick curtsy. "As you say, your highness. Such an attitude takes some getting used to. Fatalism is like plain rice compared to the rich banquet of the truth about our Creator. However, my appetite is growing!"

They all laughed and encouraged one another. It was cut short when both Veranna and Sreba suddenly tensed with apprehension. They looked at each other and knew that the nobles were starting to arrive for the emergency council that the king had summoned. The queen felt a shiver of fear.

"Your highness, you need to stay down here. The rest of us must be about our duties. We will have to find a way to sneak you off the grounds while the nobles convene."

"True. No doubt you will be expected to greet all of them and see to their needs. I will be fine down here." After they left, Veranna sat in a dark corner, closed her eyes, wrapped a wool blanket around herself and soon fell into a dream.

She flew in bright sunlight above the clouds, over a great sea, in the form of an eagle. Clouds obscured her view, but out of the sun flew a large gathering of eagles, the same that she had seen in a dream far away in Tesra's home. Their leader beckoned her to come near, a sober light in his eyes.

"Your highness, you have risen above the mean things of the earth and been faithful in much. Your subjects love you, although your opponents are nasty curs. They will think that they have defeated you, but you shall soar to greater heights. Time will not be an issue; the only thing that will matter is faithfulness. Do not think to conclude before all is done, and do not presume to know the end. You shall mend that which has been riven, and outlast that which is to pass. Your heart shall break and be knit; your spirit dampened and then fired. You serve not your own will, but shall be blessed by Him you serve. Preserved you shall be for the day when your Creator brings you forth to draw the strands of his designs into a tight knit cloth. Until that day you shall be seen by those from kingdoms at the ends of the earth. Some shall think your outcome just; some shall be indifferent while others shall see themselves in you. Be not afraid nor show remorse; neither bitter nor anxious. You shall serve as a testimony to all."

Veranna frowned at the majestic bird. "Your words are full of foreboding; am I to know no peace and joy in this life? I can stand only so much pain and sadness!"

The eagle eyed her for a moment, both sympathy and reproof showing.

"Have no doubt that your Creator holds you in His hands. All things in this life shall pass as they give witness to His power and will. You do not know how much you can bear, even if He does. We shall aid you still.

"Now, look down and see that He moves the world."

Veranna circled down below the clouds and was amazed at the sight before her. A forest of evergreen trees made its way along the surface of the sea and connected two far-flung pieces of land. The trees rooted and dry land appeared on the causeway. New plants sprang up lush in the midst of the forest, thriving on their renewal.

The empress spread her wings and set down on a mighty branch to enjoy the sun's bounty.

She awoke to the sound of a song ringing in her head. The words were strange, allowing no interpretation. High and lilting, it brought a freshness and liveliness into the recesses of her mind. She remembered her experience in the washroom and decided to make her way there. It was on the other side of the huge building, and getting there undetected could be dangerous. More guards would be posted and roving teams of soldiers would be looking for her. She kept her head down and tried to melt into the surroundings.

More and more people crowded the halls as both servants and nobles headed for work and rooms.

The headmistress of the women servants spotted Veranna and called out, "You, come here and pay attention."

Veranna now felt very conspicuous, but tried to make everything seem as normal as possible. "Yes, ma'am?"

"Help Count Graf get his things to his room and then prepare his bath for him. See to his needs and help him prepare for the evening meal. Here are the rest of his bags." She pointed at four stuffed, leather bags with carrying straps.

Veranna hung a bag on each shoulder and grabbed the other two. They were heavy and clumsy in design. She gritted her teeth and concentrated on the task so that pain or weakness would not show. "Which room, ma'am?"

"Eighth room on the north side." She turned and bowed to a man dressed in fine black and gold clothing. Tall, with light brown hair and a short trimmed beard, his taut waistline and rippling muscles evidenced someone in good physical condition. His expression and manner indicated that he expected, and was used to getting, total obedience from slaves. "This slave will show you to your room, my lord. If she fails to please you in any way be sure to notify me immediately. Her punishment will be swift and severe."

The count simply nodded and followed Veranna as she headed for the north wing. The bag straps dug into her shoulders, and sweat made her blouse stick to her skin. The distance seemed endless due to the slow-downs in clogged hallways and the waiting for higher ranked nobles to be shown preference. Finally, they reached his quarters, which had three rooms inside. One for the bed, a receiving room and a bathroom. She lugged the bags into the bedroom and placed them on the bed, then started opening them for unpacking. She yelped with shock as the count's hand impacted her bottom. She shot up straight and stiff, but just before turning to slap him hard she got control of herself. His voice was jaunty as he looked into the bathroom.

"Hard butt; that is good. You won't be one of the weaklings with no stamina. Hmmm. Good size breasts, too. You will do well while I am here. I want you here after I finish my meetings with the other lords. Make sure that wine and cigars are plentiful, as well as food for any guests. You will always be ready to help any woman I take to my bed. They will need bathing and help with their clothes. Now, get my bath ready."

Veranna was red from her bosom to the top of her head. Embarrassment stifled her tongue and all she could do was hurry to prepare his bath. Pipes ran from cisterns on the roof and down to the tubs. She filled it quickly and poured in most of a large, copper pot of hot water that simmered on a cast iron stove. Keeping her gaze down she returned to the bedroom and said, "My lord, your bath is ready."

"Good. Help me get these boots off." He sat on the bed and raised his left leg.

Veranna had to pull hard to get the boots off, then placed them in the closet and hoped that he would tell her to leave. Her heart sank as he stood and held his arms out to the side.

"Quit dawdling and get me out of these clothes before the bath goes cold, you idiot. And make sure those boots shine like mirrors for my ride tomorrow."

She carefully removed his diamond cuff links and laid them on the cherry wood dresser, but hesitated to turn back to the count. His anger rose with every delay.

"Hurry up, girl, I do not have all day!"

Reluctantly she turned and started unbuttoning his shirt. Her only other experience with handling men had been Karsten, and while serving as a nurse in infirmaries. The count was clearly used to having women tend to his desires. She stopped after removing his shirt and took a step back. He was not pleased.

"Foolish girl! Get on with it or I shall give you a beating such as you have never heard." He tensed to slap her but paused as the door swung open. His face lit up and he sounded like a little boy happy to see his mother. "Patreya! Thank goodness you are here. This idiot whore is so slow that I will never get my bath."

The woman walked in with a sure sense of command. Bright blonde hair cascaded down over her shoulders and bosom. The low-cut style of her pale-blue, silk gown left little to the imagination, and her light-blue eyes gave Veranna a quick glance as she moved to tend to the count. In one quick flick her right hand swung up and slapped Veranna crisply across her left cheek. It was not a powerful slap, but it stung anyway.

"How dare you not serve my master's every wish! You will be punished and taught obedience."

Veranna had been looking away and missed evading the slap. However, she realized that the woman had referred to the count as 'my master'. She was a slave, too! The count obviously had developed a desire for her.

"Excuse me, please ma'am; I am new to this."

Patreya sneered at her. "Then watch and learn. Tonight you shall be instructed in how to please him in his bed. If you do not, you will receive a painful beating. Get into the bathroom."

Veranna was glad to be out of the bedroom. When the other two walked in, she gasped. They were both naked and went straight to the bathtub. Patreya did not even look at her as she gave commands.

"Get over here and wash us down; then, since you are so unused to doing your duties in the room, go to the kitchen and fetch us a meal. Do not be slow!"

Seeing her opportunity to leave without raising any alarm, Veranna hurried to wash them. She closed her eyes and recited a song in her head to block the sounds of the two groping one another. Either the two had no sense of shame or Patreya was eager to maintain a noble lifestyle while still a slave. Maybe both.

She sped out the door before another command could be voiced and headed for the washroom. Passing Sreba in the hallway, the queen asked her why she was running through the halls and risking exposure. Veranna related the song running through her head after the dream and how it had come to her before, in the washroom. As other servants and nobles passed them, the queen purposefully gave her a command to go there. Understanding her intent, Veranna bowed and quickened her pace.

The song increased in intensity as she went down the stairs into the room. Looking at the wall where the focus of the song was clearest, she could finally make out the words.

Years have no meaning; time passes by.
The sun keeps arising, a bright morning sky.
The schemes of the crafty all fail to succeed.
The Creator has spoken; His word guaranteed.

The link He has chosen has not been delayed.
The name He has honored shall not be dismayed.
A servant so faithful, a leader so true.
The one called to power again to imbue.

Veranna's head was filled with the song and a rush of emotions. It was like being swept into a swift river rushing over a roaring waterfall. Pain throbbed through her skull and she fell to her knees. In her mind flashed the memory of when she first came to the castle in Tolemera. Tesra reminded her of who she was and Veranna's power extended through Yanbre to open the gate. Here she understood that she had to exude power or be lost to her people all the rest of her days. The words finally formed in her mind as she started slipping into unconsciousness.

"I am Veranna, the heiress to Dunamays of Faresea. Open!"

The painful throbbing ceased and the song was no greater than a breeze through trees. In the middle of the wall before her was a wide slab of rock sinking down below the floor level revealing a huge darkness beyond. She stood and trembled as she took a fearful step forward. Amazed and curious, the darkness engulfed her.

✵ ✵ ✵

CHAPTER 30

Karsten looked out from the crow's nest of the ship, its middle mast the tallest of the three. He and a hundred imperial knights were augmented by a thousand Genazi warriors from Zishiye. Having taken sail a week ago, Lord Tomius had exhausted any and every logistic he could to see them on their journey with all speed. They reached the southernmost tip of the Koosti province belonging to LeAnre a day sooner than they had expected. The only real difficulty had been commandeering the necessary number of ships to take them to the land called Faresea. Not a few of the ship captains resisted being forced into sailing somewhere not of their own choosing. Only Karsten's vow that they would be well recompensed by the Emerald Throne kept them pacified.

Sailing south for close to two weeks, they swung north in the night after passing a corner of the continent. The conflicting currents made for choppy waters and caused sea sickness in many of the troops. Most had never been on a ship before. As they entered the calmer waters the moons came into clear view. Karsten estimated that they would align later in the morning. This always accompanied significant events involving Veranna.

The wind was with them, but Karsten was anxious to find the northern edge of the sea. The ship's captain said that Faresea bordered the water, and that the chief city, Seacorro, lay right next to the bay protected by a mighty seawall. The shoreline was unapproachable on both the eastern and western sides for many miles, and inland it was virtually impassable. A small Seacorran force would be able to hold off a huge armada with such a set-up.

Tesra's voice cut through the wind. "You men make sure to get your breakfast. We need you ready and able. Kreida, start herding them through the galley."

The crew and soldiers numbered a hundred and twenty men. Kreida reduced the crewmen to puppies eager to serve her every desire. Her rascally manner and sense of humor infatuated them with longing, but all it took was one stern look from Treybal to stay their desires.

"C'mon, you minnows! Get in and get out. Don't let your mouths hang open as you lust after me; close 'em up and get to chewing." She went along the line like a drill instructor. "You tars sitting down, pretend that your meal is your favorite whore in the city. Get your enthusiasm up, and only your enthusiasm. Move; move; move!"

Karsten could not help but laugh at Kreida's antics. The men moved along at high speed just to make sure that they did not suffer her ire. A number of them brought sausages to her as they exited the galley. One was bold enough to leer and tell her to consider it an appetizer. Kreida gulped it down and gave him a savage glare as she told him that it was far too small to satisfy her. She gave him a playful slap and told him to work off his impulses on the masts. The man cackled and went right to work.

A half-hour later and a faint, dark line formed on the northern horizon. Karsten paused to make sure that his eyes were not failing him, and called out, "Land ho, to the north!"

Sailors hurried to their stations and the captains barked orders to send a signal flag up the mast to alert the other ships that land had been sighted. Sounders began scanning the ships' paths to warn where shoals and shallows lay. Gulls flew out to the ships and looked for anything thrown over that they could eat. Karsten hurried down the mast and went below deck for a few moments. When he came back up he had a folded piece of forest-green cloth in his hands and approached the captain.

"I need you to raise this flag to the highest place on the mast. The other ships will know to raise theirs as well."

The captain, a deeply tanned, oily looking fellow, frowned as he stared at him for a moment, but reluctantly submitted to the request. Soon the flag of forest green was billowing in the wind atop the mast. On it was an emerald-green and gold eagle with a feather pen in one claw and a sword like Veranna's in the other. In ancient script under the eagle were the words, 'Honor and Glory to our Creator.' The knights, soldiers and Genazi cheered as the flags sailed proudly above. Lord Tomius had commissioned their production after conferring with Karsten, who studied the ancient works mentioning them.

The ships could not move quickly enough for the husband of Veranna. He longed to hold her in his arms. When at last the sea-wall was in clear view he grew more anxious. It was nearly as high as the mast of the ship, with archers and catapults ready to fire. On its signal pole rose a flag with a black square surrounded by a red border. Karsten asked the captain what it meant.

"It means that they are refusing us entry to the harbor, and that they are ready to fight if we try to push our way through."

The young Genazi lord fumed but kept his head. After a few moments he told the captain to raise a flag signaling parley. It was not very long before a small, two-mast ship came out of the harbor. Coming alongside, the captain ordered a gang plank to be placed between them.

Four rugged-looking marines preceded a tall, slender man in his mid-thirties, who made his way across. He looked on Karsten and the ships as though trying to determine the breed of a dog. Peering down his nose he barely acknowledged them with the briefest of nods.

"What is it you do not understand? You are not being allowed into the harbor. You can sit out here until your ships rot away for all I care. Any attempts to enter shall end in your death. If you are merchants you should obey the protocols and ask for inspection."

Karsten was in no mood for wasting time with the man. His voice came out in a threatening deadpan that made the man's face burn red.

"I do not care one whit for your ideas of protocol. My wife, the empress of the Seven Lands, is being held here and I want her back. If you or this city want to remain standing at the end of the day you will release her. Failure to do so will result in your total destruction."

It had been a long time since the Seacorrans had faced assault. The harbormaster was not used to dealing with invaders. He took a step back and drew himself up haughtily.

"This is the sovereign realm of Faresea; the king shall determine whether anyone is free or not. I have no idea of whom you refer to as an empress, and I do not take orders from anyone save the king and queen. Any aggression on your part, and you die."

Karsten took a step closer to him, and his body looked more like a lion's, ready to pounce. "You can save us both a lot of time and trouble by inquiring about my wife's presence and getting her to me. If you do not, then you are doomed."

The man sneered and spat. "I will save us both a lot of time by removing your pigeon-brained head. Be gone or be dead. You can see for yourself the results of trying to break through the wall if you look into the water in front of it. You will see the remains of ships now covered in coral."

Karsten's face drew into a feral, battle-lust smile, his Genazi upbringing urging him to cut the man's tongue out. "You have one hour to bring my wife to me or be destroyed. That is all there is to say."

"So be it. You idiots shall die on the rocks."

The man stomped back to his small ship and ordered it into the harbor. Soon a red flag appeared on the signal pole of the seawall fort and a bell sounded across the water. The guard towers in the city picked up the signal and responded with a warning to the city.

Karsten said to Treybal, "Find us a way to neutralize the seawall defenses. We can't afford to have any ships sunk and blocking the entry to the harbor."

Treybal's eyebrows rose as he considered the command. "That will be hard. We could lose as many men by drowning as by their arrows. We will have to risk getting close enough for our own archers to keep theirs from firing while we try to get some tar and oil thrown on the upper openings in the fort. That still will leave us vulnerable to small ships attacking us as we try to get into the harbor."

"Seems we have few options. Get the men ready."

Treybal bowed and passed his orders on to his subordinates. Karsten donned an emerald-green tunic and readied his bow. Nothing would get in his way. The rest of the men followed his example and donned the green. Archers took to the masts like branches on trees. They rose into the burning sun.

CHAPTER 31

eranna called out but no one answered. Her voice echoed back from the depths. The temperature in the room was normal, as were the odors, and there was a familiarity about the area that she could not pinpoint. The castle in Tolemera had marvelous properties that she stumbled over at times, and even the palace of DeAndre in Banaipal, responded to her will. All of them were places where her ancestors had dwelt for some period of time. This room must go back all the way to the time of Dunamays.

"Alight!" The very air seemed to quiver for a moment before dozens of gas lamps flared to life. She gasped as the room was revealed. A set of green, marble steps led down to a wide central aisle of blue marble measuring at least a hundred feet long. At the other end stood a throne nearly identical to the one in the castle in Tolemera. Alternating pillars of obsidian and granite stood at twenty-foot intervals along the aisle, with gold and silver lines a half-inch in width spiraling around them to the ceiling of embedded crystals. A huge flag of forest-green lined the wall behind the throne. Veranna gasped once again as she recognized the very design that Karsten had thought of. An emerald and gold eagle with a feather pen in one claw, and a sword in the other was eerily like the one he had drawn. Under the eagle, written in gold letters were the words, 'Honor and Glory to our Creator.' Karsten's vision had been prophetic.

Approaching the throne, she saw a sword identical to the one she had inherited from her mother. It looked new and unused as it shined in the light. Next to the throne was a short stand with a book opened to the middle. Words on the facing page glowed as if with a light of their own. As she sat down on the throne, a connection with the book arose in her mind. The glowing text shivered and went out of focus, then fell into place. She could read the text and hear the voice of the author.

You have come to the throne of your ancestors. Always remember that this is due neither to chance nor to any virtue of your own. It is the Creator's will that you satisfy, and that will shall prevail over all attempts to thwart it. Time is not counted, but fidelity is. Set aside all heartache and disappointment. The Emerald Throne serves to spread the knowledge of the Creator throughout the world. He will use you to accomplish this goal in ways you cannot imagine, nor would you desire them.

Our House is divided on this cause. Persecution by those desiring power has increased. I loathe spilling the blood of my kin. My family and I shall depart and seek a new land where we can have fresh ground on which to build the Creator's glory. Those staying behind shall be left to their own designs. They shall rot from within until the Creator's chosen one comes to call them back to their oaths. Dignity, knowledge and power will accompany you as the throne arises in their very midst. Be not afraid; your Creator is with you.

The words went out of focus and no longer glowed. Veranna felt a moment of dizziness and closed her eyes. When she opened them she saw that the book was closed. However, she knew that the words would be with her all of her days.

Another voice suddenly came into her mind. It was an imperial knight calling out to her!

Your highness, if you can hear me, know that we come to your defense.

The knight on board the ship with Karsten was surprised and cried out with joy when he heard her voice in his mind.

My lord knight, I am here in the king's residence on the north side of the city. I am unhurt and face a call to duty by the Creator. Be ready for my call.

The knight nearly shook with joy. *Yes, your majesty. We are ready. Please pardon me, your highness, for speaking personally, but your husband, Lord Karsten, is leading us and is very anxious to see you.*

Veranna's heart leapt. *And I him! I must now concentrate on my task. It shall not be long.*

She stood and walked around the dais, examining objects as she considered her course, then closed her eyes and looked up as she raised her hands in supplication. "Dear Creator, I am here to do your will. I am weak and full of flaws. Keep me from error and give me strength. Let me not be ashamed in your sight nor in the eyes of my ancestors. I am your servant. Command me, my Creator."

Only the lamps placed around the dais remained lit. The others faded and failed while the emerald throne glowed with a light all its own. In back of the throne a tall, oak cabinet appeared. The doors opened and revealed a gown truly fit for a queen. Purple velvet with golden thread with embroidery, a brocade of silver flame, and bright white ermine around the collar stunned the eyes with beauty. She was even more amazed as she tried it on and found it a perfect fit. Looking in the mirror mounted on the inside of the cabinet door, she could hardly believe how much she resembled the paintings of her ancestors mounted on the walls of the castle in Tolemera.

A square box made of wood attached to the back panel of the cabinet caught her eye. She felt around its exterior until she located a subtle latch. Pressing the latch, the top of the box opened. Inside was a wondrous tiara of emeralds, diamonds, rubies, gold and silver. Matching earrings and a finger ring lay beneath it as she lifted it to test its weight. It caught the rays of the lamps, creating a dazzling refraction of colors that penetrated to the furthest corners of the dark room. She donned the jewelry and sat down on the throne. The emerald-green light emanated more powerfully from it and a large shaft could now be seen above. As it detached from the floor and started to rise into the shaft, all Veranna could think was, 'I am a servant, and always shall be.'

CHAPTER 32

The lords and ladies of the Kingdom of Faresea milled around the great room of the king's estate house, waiting for the council meeting to begin. The north wall ran straight and held a small dais where the king and queen had their royal chairs. The dais was a half-circle shape, the front radius measuring close to twenty feet. It's age was a guess, but it had to be on the order of hundreds of years old. The north wall ran true east and west for a hundred and twenty-feet. The south wall was curved in a half-circle shape that paralleled the front of the dais, and had tall windows giving a full view of the city and harbor. The ceiling was rich oak and mahogany, contrasting with the main floor of light maple, and dais floor of bronze colored ceramic tiles.

The king and queen entered and everyone fell silent as they bowed. Sreba's eyes darted around the royal room showing tension in her neck and shoulders. Her light-brown hair was styled up and allowed a silver tiara to fit around the crown of her head. Walking to her chair she prayed that Veranna had found a safe place to hide.

The chamberlain pounded his staff on the floor three times and called for all to give homage to the king and queen. The men knelt and bowed their heads while the women curtsied and bowed.

The king and queen sat down, then the king signaled the chamberlain to call all to arise, after which he addressed them directly.

"I have called you to council on short notice to relate a matter that has not been a concern for the throne for hundreds of years. I speak of the Great Heresy that the ancient ruling House of Dunamays promulgated before departing the realm and being destroyed. We now have one among us, a slave, who claims to be of that line, and empress of an empire called the 'Seven Lands.' According to witnesses, she has demonstrated the gifts of the ancient rulers and bears them great resemblance. Have any of you witnessed such signs?"

The duke of the estate where Veranna fought the swordsman of Randal arose and said, "Aye, my lord; she put on an impressive display, indeed."

"Duke Geldon, did you witness this directly, or did you only hear the rantings of crazed slaves?"

"My lord, I witnessed the events myself. She put down a number of my guards and defeated my sword master in a duel. After defeating him she held up his sword and lightning came through the room and destroyed the blade. His gifts for combat have vanished. She claimed to be his liege-lady and denied him the blessings of his House. As you know, my lord, this man was the best fighter we have ever seen."

Shocked murmuring broke out as the nobles speculated about the rumors spreading of a fearsome warrior on the loose. Those not believing the stories regarding the ancient rulers, now entertained doubts. Could it be true? Obviously someone of power was shaking things up.

The chamberlain called for order and the king continued his questioning.

"Is the swordsman with you?"

"Yes, your highness."

"Bring him in."

"Yes, your highness."

After several minutes the swordsman entered and stood before the king and queen. After he bowed, the king resumed his questioning.

"You, sir, are known to us as an amazingly skilled Master of the sword. Is this true or not?"

The swordsman found it hard to look up, and his posture was more like that of a man caught red-handed in a crime. The conceited humor in his voice was now replaced by a sullen humility.

"The answer to your questions, your highness, is both yes and no. I retain skills achieved by training and experience, but the gift bestowed upon House Randal by the Creator is gone from me."

"How did this happen? And why does this House Randal have such a gift in the first place?"

"House Randal was rewarded by those known as Emeraldians." Another round of murmuring swept through the room. "We, of Randal, helped them fight their way through the enormous opposition they faced after leaving Faresea, and were blessed with enhanced fighting skills after swearing allegiance to the Emerald Throne. The Emeraldians continued west and established a new empire which is now known as the Seven Lands.

"The blessings of the Creator were revoked for me when I demonstrated infidelity to my sworn duty. The one I fought enjoys the favor of the Creator and punished me according to my error. I know of no one, other than the empress of the Seven Lands, who could have done this."

Tongues wagged when he fell silent. All in the hall were forced to consider the possibility of the rightful heir coming to the throne of Faresea. The king tried to restore calm and reason to the meeting.

"My lords and ladies, nothing is established in this matter yet; we might easily have a trickster trying to deceive us. Also, we will need a demonstration of such claims before our very eyes, and not from the stories of others. Is there anyone else who has witnessed the powers ascribed to this woman?"

After a long, silent moment, Beneto walked up and bowed before the king. Fear made his body shake, but Veranna deserved his loyalty and the truth was the only way to avoid shame.

"Your highness, I witnessed the power of the Creator at work in her. After her majesty, the queen, had sent her for punishment on the pole, her body was healed in a moment when a green aura surrounded her. No sign of damage could be seen on her. Where the muscles and bones were plain to see through the torn flesh, there is now no trace of injury."

The king looked at him as though he thought him mad. "Are you sure that you simply are not imagining things? Stories tend to get muddled over time."

Before Beneto could answer, Sreba stood and bowed to the king.

"My lord, he speaks truly. I sent the woman to the pole and ordered five full lashes be given her. I saw her about a week later and could not believe my eyes. She even had a greater demonstration; she forgave my horrible mistreatment of her and helped me in ways to be happier. She blessed me, my love, and only the Creator deals in such mercy and kindness."

The king did not know what to say for a moment. He could not call his own wife, queen of the land, a liar or fool in front of the nobles. And her voice and countenance held no hint of deception.

"She blessed you? In any tangible manner, or are you simply being poetic, my dear?"

Sreba stepped down to the floor and asked for a large clearing in the center. She then turned to her husband and requested that he join her. "My love, have you ever seen me train with the sword or be athletic?"

"Not at all."

"Then let me give you a demonstration of the blessing given by Veranna, Empress of the Seven Lands and heiress to the throne of Dunamays."

When she saw his eyes light up with fear and shock at how easy she was with that information, she went to a nobleman and requested use of his sword. She then ordered the Swordsman of Randal to do his best against her in a sparring match.

The king started to laugh but was cut short when he saw the serious concern on the swordsman's face. The man even looked scared!

Sreba saluted with her sword and assumed a fighting stance. The swordsman responded in kind and the two of them each waited for the other to make the first move. The queen struck first, springing forward in a blurring lunge. The swordsman blocked but was forced to retreat to evade her swift follow-up swing. He circled to his left and Sreba kept after him, not allowing any counter-attacks.

The king, as well as the nobles, were amazed at her skill. Attack and defense melded into a flurry of motion in which it was hard to separate one from the other.

Sreba stepped back to the center of the floor and waited for the swordsman to come to her. His face showed beads of sweat and his eyes did not stray from watching her every move. He pounced. Planning to force her back and overwhelm her with complicated technique, he was rebuffed when she easily turned the tables on him and forced him into a desperate defense. After a maze of swift exchanges he suddenly found the tip of her blade pressed lightly against his throat. All he could do was freeze and hope she did not follow through.

Sreba stepped back and held up her blade in salute to signal the end of the match. After returning the sword to the nobleman, she looked at her husband while speaking to the swordsman.

"Tell me, swordsman, is my skill level that of an untrained woman?"

He bowed and sheathed his sword. "No, my lady, it is not. You have no equal among your people, and in those of House Randal you would place among the higher skill levels. You have, indeed, been blessed by my liege-lady, the Empress of Emeraldia."

All eyes turned to the king to see his reaction, and no one dared to speak. The king thought that he must be dreaming, but there was his wife before him, resplendent with life and skill.

"My love, you are truly transformed. I have considered you weak, but now you radiate vitality and skill."

He would have continued but a warning bell's peal wafted up from the city and was reinforced by others relaying the alarm. The nobles rushed to the windows to see if they could spot the reason for the disturbance. Their concern drove the reason for the meeting from their minds, but it was not long before a messenger arrived and they found out that it was closely connected to the meeting's agenda.

The messenger bowed and reported, "Your majesty, the harbor master says that a large fleet of ships bearing soldiers is threatening the city. They say we have one hour to surrender up someone named Veranna, their empress, who is being held captive here, or they shall destroy the city."

The king fumed as he stared out the windows to try and see who threatened them. However, it was too far away. He spoke to the messenger after a quick scan of the nobles' faces.

"Has this rabble fleet raised a flag showing allegiance?"

"Yes, my lord. The flag is forest green with an eagle in the center. It is emerald green and gold, with a sword in one claw and a quill pen in the other."

The king looked puzzled, for he had encountered that symbol somewhere before. He called for Beneto to help him remember when he had seen it. Beneto bowed and spoke confidently.

"My lord, you saw it in books and paintings about the ancient realm. If you look up you will see it painted in the upper walls of this very room. It is the emblem of House Dunamays; it has returned to Faresea."

Rage overtook the king. "Even if this woman is of that line, she is still a slave here. She will bear me an heir who will hold both lines of power in this kingdom, and then be of no concern to us. As to these scum in the sea, they will never get into the harbor. Let them rot where they are!"

Several voices sounded in the crowd, showing support for their king. Sreba, the swordsman and Beneto objected to his remarks, the queen feeling a pang of jealous anger. Her voice held condemnation as she spoke.

"My lord husband, I shall be the only one to bear you an heir. And, Veranna of Emeraldia is now our rightful ruler according to all of the signs we have been given. To speak such words against her is treason."

The king laughed at her. "Foolish woman! I hold the power here, and she is a slave. She shall do me whatever service I command. Only her rising on the lost, ancient throne before my very eyes could persuade me otherwise."

As the words left his lips the building vibrated with a low rumble. The people wondered if the ceiling and walls were about to fall and kill them. The dais slid away and a moment later another rose in its place. At the front and center was a strikingly beautiful woman sitting on a throne of gleaming emerald. Her eyes glowed with emerald fire and her countenance smote fear and respect into the hearts of all in the room. Sreba, Beneto and the swordsman fell to their knees, as did a good portion of those in the room. She arose and spoke, her voice piercing into even the stubborn ears of the king.

"I am Veranna, descendant of Dunamays, and I come to call this land back to the rightful worship of the Creator. It is He who chose my ancestors to ensure faithfulness to Him. As He commands, so shall I obey."

The king stood staring at her agape, thinking that his mind must be fooling him. "This is not possible. Who put you up to this sham? Faresea is my realm and will remain that way. I will find out who has perpetrated this hoax, and have them hanging by their toes and eaten by flies."

Veranna looked down on him in stern warning. "When you find the one who made all of these things take place, you will be before your Creator. You have had ample demonstration that I am who I say. Any refusal on your part shall result in your being deposed."

The king's face was red with rage. "You are nothing here; unless you have something more persuasive than dressing in fine clothes and climbing through holes in the floor, I command you to my chambers. I will teach you the meaning of submission and service."

Before Veranna replied, a vision came to her. It was from a vantage point in the sky, looking down upon a ship in the harbor. Her heart skipped a beat when she saw Karsten. The view in her mind followed a circular pattern showing all of the ships outside the harbor, and each flew the flag of ancient Emeraldia. She realized that she must be seeing things through the eyes of a green and gold eagle. In her mind she called out to it, 'Come!' She then spoke to the king again.

"I understand your confusion and reluctance, for in your place I might well do the same. However, to crave the satisfaction of your lusts with the wife of another is inexcusable. It matters not that you have been doing so for years. Evil is still evil, and your pursuit of it marks you as an enemy of the Creator."

"You speak foolishness, girl; it is the Creator who gives me the power to use you as I please. You may be an excellent fighter, but you cannot defeat all my forces. The imbeciles on the ships will not be able to help you, for they will never pass the seawall." He turned and spoke to the others in the room. "Have any of you witnessed that which cannot be explained by other means than what the girl claims? If she were really good in her trickery she would have scrounged up a green eagle or two just like the myths say of our ancestors." He turned back to Veranna and gave her a smug smile. "Oh, but providing the non-existent would be expecting too much now, wouldn't it?"

Veranna just looked down at him and stretched out her left arm to the side. A moment later a large, green eagle with gold on the fringes of it's feathers flew in through an opening in the ceiling. It landed on Veranna's arm and bowed to her before turning to the assembly and letting out a loud scream.

The king, as well as all the other Fareseans, were stunned. Here was a green eagle, a creature of ancient lore and myth, right before their eyes! A sentry ran into the room and reported that a whole swarm of them was circling over the estate. All but a handful of the nobles went to their knees and bowed their heads in homage to Veranna. The king, however, was not yet convinced.

"I do not care if you are from the body of Dunamays, himself; I rule in Faresea, and my troops shall enforce my will."

Veranna shook her head and sighed. "Pride and stubbornness are keeping you from making sound judgments. Since you need to be forced into reason I shall loose my troops on the city and let them fight all opposition until they reach us here. You shall be guilty of the blood of all those slain." She lifted her right arm and pointed toward the harbor. "You have taken great confidence in the protection provided by the seawall. Watch and know terror as you are relieved of that delusion." She said clearly and forcefully to the distance, "Open," and the ground began to tremble.

Some of the noblewomen fainted as the seawall fortifications toppled down into the sea. The wall itself pivoted from where it was attached to the mainland and swung counter-clockwise until what was its outer face now paralleled the coastline. The harbor was fully open for the first time in hundreds of years.

Veranna said to the knights aboard the ships, 'Come! Fight your way to me on the north side of the city. Slay only those necessary to advance.'

The ships hurriedly pulled up their anchors and caught a brisk south wind to speed them into the harbor. Karsten was the first to jump into the shallow water and set foot on the beach. Arrows flew around him until his own archers felled the Seacorrans. The ships with the horses breezed over to the piers and rushed to unload. Soon, a strong strike force of cavalry pounded along the stout wood and made land. The masts of the incoming ships held soldiers armed with bows. In their green tunics, they made the masts look like fir trees sending out deadly needles. Jumping to shore or piers, the Emeraldians quickly made a beachhead and methodically pounded their way into the city. The Seacorran guards were no match for Veranna's men, and Karsten organized his forces into a fighting machine that threw back all opposition.

The Seacorrans were unused to fighting in their sheltered realm near the sea. Many of the guards and soldiers realized that they were not of the same caliber as the invaders and threw down their arms. Treybal assigned a squad to escort the captives to holding points until peace was restored. The civilians screamed and sued for mercy, but were gratefully confused when the Emeraldians simply passed them by and left them unharmed. In no time the Emeraldians took control of the city and made their way to the king's estate, as the green eagles guided them directly to the main house. The gate opened on Veranna's silent command and Karsten led a hundred knights and troops onto the grounds. The guards were pushed aside without bloodshed and commanded to await new orders.

As Karsten entered the assembly chamber, he caught sight of Veranna upon the dais. He wanted to run and embrace her but noticed that she led a formal meeting, and that he should follow protocol. Seeing his dour face, they hurried out of his way as he marched to the dais. He stopped and bowed before jumping up the steps to embrace and kiss Veranna. They lingered a moment in each other's arms before he stepped back and reported.

"Your majesty, the city is secured and we await your command."

She nodded regally and said, "Thank you, my lord." As she turned to the assembly, she gestured toward Karsten. "My lords and ladies, allow me to introduce to you the Prince Consort of the Seven Lands, heir to the Earl of Zishiye and a leader of the people known as Genazi. He is my husband and chief chronicler of my court. He shall see to the transition of Faresea to a realm based on justice and the Creator's laws. Such was the basis of the ancient realm, and it is so for the Seven Lands. The first change that I command is the end of slavery."

The room erupted into a hundred conversations. Karsten signaled the chamberlain to bring the meeting back to order. Veranna continued as though only a minor interruption had occurred.

"You have exploited slaves for your own vile desires under the idea that you functioned in a reformatory role. You violated the specific will of the Creator and tried to cover your evil by saying that you were upholding the law. Punishment must fit the crime. Your life-long sentences of slavery have made a mockery of justice."

A man to her left, heatedly asked, "So what are we to do for servants, and are we not to be served according to our stations?"

Veranna kept her voice level, "You will need to start hiring workers. It is not such an expense when you consider the amount of money you spend on feeding, clothing and tending to them. They will be free, and you shall be able to ensure quality work by hiring those with real skills. Your economy will boom due to the number of households that will result.

"As to your stations, you are born to serve your fellow man for the Creator's glory and the goodness of society. Your ancestry does not make you master of anyone, however, it does make you responsible. Heritage is not a guarantee that you shall have noble ranking; character and skill are the requirements. I shall remove from power any lord or lady whose conduct is unbecoming for their office."

A deafening silence came over the crowd as each turned to the other to see if they had heard her correctly. She was mandating a total rethinking of the Faresean system. Just as several of them were about to speak, another person entered the room. The foot-falls were confident and an eerie chill crept up Veranna's spine.

CHAPTER 33

Chief Sarim'tay sat on a silk cushion and stared inscrutably at nothing as the serving girls exited his royal chamber. His sons sat on the floor before him, making no sounds or movements as they awaited what their father, and master, had to say. The chief's red robes contrasted with their red-orange ones even as a dark, unfathomable void formed around him. His voice seemed to come from within that bottomless rending of reality.

"My sons, you shall witness that my plan for conquering this world in the name of the Dark One, is coming to pass. His will determines the destinies of all. Watch how the various parts of this grand design are set in motion."

He closed his eyes and chanted silently. A miasma of colors formed deep inside the void, and then streamed into the chamber up to the ceiling and as wide as the room. In the display marched two armies the Koosti had rarely encountered. These were from a land to the furthest eastern edge of the continent. Civil war racked that land and brother killed brother on the battlefield. The victor killed many captives and then castrated and hobbled the rest.

Another land, to the far southeast, appeared. Intrigue and despotism ruled and reduced the people to abject slavery. The king of the land beheaded his wife before taking the wife of one of his lords. Poverty and starvation was the way for many.

Another scene arose. It showed a gathering of the people called Arbori, who lived in the vast jungle to the southeast of the Koosti Empire. They emerged once a year in late summer from their tribal areas for a gathering where they held contests for dominance. The males wrestled and the victor could choose any ten females he wished, unless they were evidently already pregnant. Sarim'tay appeared before them in the large clearing and they all fell to the ground, prostrating themselves before him.

The picture shifted and another scene unfolded. The savage tribes to the north of the Seven Lands formed tenuous alliances and set their sights on it, desiring its wealth and the potential slave supply.

Another display formed. In the castle, in Tolemera, LeAnre y'dob went into labor and gave birth. Great was her pain as the midwives helped her with the delivery. She lay exhausted on her bed, but smiled warmly as her son was brought to her. She cried with joy and lifted the child up, proclaiming him to be the future of the Koosti Empire and the ruler of her province.

The scene changed to that of Veranna addressing the nobles of Faresea. They bowed down to her and pledged fealty, although several of them obviously held sinister motives behind their apparent submission.

Sarim'tay was startled when the display left his control, flowing into scenes he could not stop. There came a view of Veranna holding her sword in warning and looking directly at him. Her eyes were keen and her voice as hard as stone. As she spoke, a shiver of fear ran along his spine, and also frightened his sons.

"Do not suppose that any victory will prove final. The Creator uses you to accomplish His purposes no matter what your putrid mind imagines. Even were I to die, you shall not succeed, for greater is His praise in using your designs against you. Conform to Him or be destroyed. You are duly warned."

The image changed to that of Sarim'tay being judged before the Creator and cast into punishment. Blinding white light then consumed the room and the image disappeared with a peal of thunder, shaking the building.

Sarim'tay shook his head and blinked to try and clear the spots lingering in his eyes. Enraged, he let out a war cry and fumbled around the room. A serving girl entered to see if service was required. He grabbed her by her hair and pulled out his knife, then cut off her head and held it up as he yelled, "This shall be the end of that Emeraldian whore. And mercy it will be if this end comes before any other of my attentions."

☆ ☆ ☆

The castle in Tolemera felt the warm rays of the late morning sun. In and outside its walls was a tense situation. LeAnre was in labor, and ladies Gelangweil and Loray were still under arrest and detained in well-attended rooms in the lower levels. They were allowed three visits per day and granted most everything they requested.

Yanbre strode along the wall and scanned the field between the castle gate and the line of woods that separated the castle grounds from the city of Tolemera. Stationed on both sides of the road leading to the city were a legion of soldiers from the houses of each of the arrested ladies. They wanted to intimidate the imperials, and threatened a siege if their ladies were not freed soon. It had not come to blows, but tensions were building.

In the infirmary, LeAnre struggled with the birth of her child. The midwives gave her medicinal herbs to help with her pain, and were surprised at how long it took for the baby to be delivered. She lost a lot of blood but did not pass out, and exulted that her shame before her brother and the Koosti people was now past. She had borne a child who would lead the Koosti to greatness.

When Yanbre heard that LeAnre had given birth, he sat on a stone bench on the balcony in the main tower and looked down. This child would need constant protection from assassins and kidnappers, for he represented a great power struggle among the Koosti. When he inherited his mother's province it would, technically, revert to Koosti leadership. However, would the people of that province have grown so used to Veranna's style of leadership that they would not wish to be ruled by a Koosti? Civil war could break out. If the child grew to love power in the Koosti way, then he might turn against the Seven Lands and renew hostilities. So much would depend on his upbringing and essential character.

He shook his head and decided to head to the mess for some food and song. It was too easy to get mired in dark thoughts about the future. Looking up, he was shocked when he saw the Curtain of Power. Only Veranna had the ability to see the curtain since it was related to her unusual powers and heritage. Something strange was going on. It turned stranger when the curtain seemed to split in two, resulting in an exact copy. Two curtains! He saw this through the connection he had with Veranna because of the armor he wore, but did not understand the significance of what he saw. Nothing had changed around the castle and no one else seemed affected. He hoped it was a good omen.

In the mess he sat back in a cushioned chair and sipped from a tankard of ale. Both tasty and potent, he soon drifted into a state of semi-consciousness. A vision arose in his mind as he contemplated what he had seen earlier. Veranna appeared wearing her royal crown and raiment. She sat on her throne and decided issues. Another woman approached the throne and walked up the three dais steps without bowing or asking permission. She grabbed Veranna's crown and tried to throw her from the throne. Veranna resisted and the two of them fought for the crown and throne. Back and forth they punched, kicked and wrestled.

He awoke when a serving girl tapped his shoulder and asked if he wanted some food. For a moment he was disoriented as he was torn from the vision.

"Wha...? Oh, uh, yes please. Some bread and stew would be appreciated. Thank you." The vision had him preoccupied. Was it a literal depiction or a metaphor? How was he to best serve Veranna should this vision come to pass?

He hardly noticed when the girl set his food down on the table. Munching bread without thought, he stared at nothing and imagined a book with an entry being written down in it. Without reading the words, he knew that they were trivial in themselves, but the consequences were mysterious and powerful.

Events were moving like threads on a loom. Just what the final patterns would be was not at all clear. He wondered how he would be woven into the fabric.

CHAPTER 34

The imperial knights sensed Veranna's foreboding and formed a protective barrier around her. The other people in the room saw her looking at the doorway and wondered what had caused her to fall silent. A reform slave, Iyan, walked in. Although he had cleaned himself, and put on freshly washed clothes, he still could not shed the oily, deceptive look that permeated his features. His voice came out in mockery of respectful address.

"My lords and ladies, please forgive this interruption. Allow me to present to you a solution to the problem you face. You want a ruler who respects what you have achieved, yet you also recognize the Creator's backing of the House of Dunamays. It is not an either-or decision. We can have both and avoid unnecessary complications."

Veranna wanted to strike the man down where he stood but wondered what he had up his sleeve. Her voice held a strong edge of warning.

"You are an evil man and seek only the satisfaction of your lusts. Any who know you will discount your words, for they are from the pit of the Dark One. You tried to abuse me when I was disabled, and would take not a care in molesting anyone else. Be done with your lies and remove yourself from this chamber before my husband seeks to avenge the dishonor you showed me."

Iyan looked at Karsten and saw the fierce gleam in his eye. He hurried to present his plan.

"My lady, I meant no harm; I simply followed the law of the land." He swept his arm to indicate all of the Fareseans. "That is all we ever wanted, a rule of law according to our own ways. We still have the opportunity to do so, and that way is with me." He looked out through the doorway and signaled for someone to enter.

Veranna watched as the reason for her foreboding entered the room. A woman walked in. Regal and possessing a strong air of self-importance, she strode in and stood before Veranna. In her sea-blue gown she looked like a shorter and younger version of her. Her voice had an unmistakable eastern accent to it as she eyed the Emeraldian empress.

"Hello, sister; I wondered when we would finally meet."

Veranna's mouth hung open as she frowned in surprise. The face and body of this woman were very much like her own. A line across her forehead that did not parallel the others was obviously an old scar, and the hardness of her expression indicated someone who had suffered great pain. A thousand questions ran through her mind.

"Who are you, and why do you call me 'sister?'"

The woman looked at Veranna as though she were a dunce. "Because *I am* your sister. Carole and Davind were my parents just as they were yours. But I grew up in the east and had to find this out later. My name is Jantay, and it means something like 'revealed in the day.'"

Veranna still could not bring herself to take Jantay's claim seriously. "I am an only child and was present when my mother was tortured and killed by assassins. It is not possible that you are my sister."

Jantay snorted, "Oh, of course, under normal circumstances that may be true. But you and I are not destined for normalcy. You did not notice or remember that our mother was pregnant with me when she was killed. One of yen-Kragar's priests of the darkness noticed as his servant was taking part in our mother's torture.

They paralyzed her and started her dismemberment before throwing her onto the fire. All she could do was scream. One of the stabs into her belly cut my forehead and the servant carved me out of her womb. The priest had black arts at his disposal to keep me alive at such a young age.

"From there I was taken into the east and raised among Koosti. I did not have life as easy as you. I was a slave born to punishment and misuse. I cannot tell you how many men have used me for their pleasure, or how many times I have been traded or sold like dirt. But at least I managed to end up here. We do share the blood of these miserable Fareseans."

Veranna could not take her eyes off of Jantay. Was this a cruel hoax, or was she truly going to have a chance to know this woman as a real sister? Doubt, hope and fear took their turn assailing her heart and mind.

Kreida and Tesra, who heard Jantay's words, entered the room. They followed protocol as they came before Veranna, but the empress gave them both hugs and kisses. Kreida realized Veranna's struggle and decided to help her dear friend and adopted sister in her own way. She turned and faced Jantay, with her hands on her hips and a hard look.

"Ya' just about had me in tears with your little sob-story. I hope its your last because this woman is not just my empress, she is closer to me than a sister ever could be. I'm warning you now that if there are any evil ideas running around in that brain of yours, I will slap them out before they get going."

Jantay was not intimidated in the least. A light, vicious grin on a hard jaw line punctuated her reply. Emerald eyes gleaming, she said, "If you ever want your tongue ripped out and fed to you, then keep up the attitude. I did not come through terror and agony to listen to your idiocy. Shut up, and don't impose upon your superiors."

Kreida's hand started up in an arc to slap Jantay, but Veranna's sharp command penetrated her anger.

"Stop!" The empress gave them both a reproving glare. "This is no time for childish antics. Jantay, how is that you are involved with such a reprehensible lout as Iyan?"

As if speaking about vegetables in a market she said, "As a slave I had no say about my own life. Iyan's master bought me from my previous master with the idea of breeding children with greener eyes. However, I have not been able to conceive after several years of their trying. Iyan told me that he could help me rise out of slavery if I followed his advice. He asked only that I raise him out of the ranks of servants and into the nobility. At the time I laughed at him, but now I see that he was onto something. Having a sister as an empress could help free me from slavery, too."

"That is now true for all; slavery is abolished in this land. Nobility, however, is more than a factor of one's birth; it is a mindset that involves serving the Creator and your fellow man. Let that mind be in you and we are sisters in more than just flesh."

Tesra gave Jantay a looking over and added to Veranna's words. "Even if not a sister, you would at least be a very close cousin. It will avail you nothing, though, if your heart is full of greed and malice. Hard times only make for hard people if they do not use wisdom to see their lives in the right way."

Jantay was tired of what she saw as lecturing. "I can keep control of myself well-enough, thank you. Now, what place do you have for me in this new order that you have in mind? I am through with being bought and sold like a cow, or used only as a body for some man's pleasure."

Veranna saw the underlying pain in Jantay's words and felt her own heart giving way to sympathy. She and this woman claiming to be her sister shared a loneliness of not being raised in a close family. Both had suffered from despotic rulers. And now the time had come to try and make things better. Her heart and mind had to come to an agreement.

"Assuming the validity of your claims, I shall render my judgment. Since slavery is no longer a legal practice, you are no longer a slave. You have the right to decide your own life.

"As to ruling a land because of a claim on your ancestry, I say, no. Ruling is more than your bloodlines. I had the advantage of an excellent education and mentors to guide me. Before I agree to your ruling anywhere, I would require you to undergo training.

The way you have been raised will affect the way you think. Koosti and Faresea have far different cultures than the Seven Lands.

"Also, I want to get to know you as a person. I've never had a literal sister in my life, nor aunts, uncles or cousins. From what you say, it has been the same for you. I do not want to just leave you after meeting you once. I want you to join me when we return to the Seven Lands."

"Is that a command?"

"No; it is a desire of my heart, and the course that my head says is best."

A wry smile followed by an amused grunt preceded her reply. "You are either very naïve or supremely confident in your judgments." Her face went flat in its expression as she bowed. "I shall do as you ask, your highness, although I cannot guarantee that I shall be satisfied."

Veranna smiled. "We have that in common as well." She turned to Sreba and Nicore, then motioned for them to stand before the dais, directly in front of her. "This land has survived in spite of a long litany of evil before the Creator. The two of you shall continue as king and queen of Faresea, and you shall be my regents. For the next three days we will work to produce revisions of the law codes in this land. Then, my husband and I shall return to the Seven Lands while leaving a score of knights to ensure that you remain true to the ideals of our Creator. King Nicore, your wife has already sworn fealty to me. For you to remain as king I will require the same from you."

A long pause elapsed as he considered his options. Fighting would be futile, as would trying to sway all the others against this woman. Too many signs had been given that this empress was genuine. He glanced at Sreba, who gave him a look and nod telling him that taking the oath was a good thing. Kneeling slowly, he lowered his head and raised his right hand in pledge, swearing fealty to the Emerald Throne and the laws of the Creator.

Veranna bowed and swore fealty to the Creator, pledging true and just service to all of the people of Faresea. "I will warn you now that we have many enemies. Various Koosti provinces still see our destruction as their primary goal. We have defeated them twice and they feel a need to avenge their shame. Their leader is a man of great character. However, his position is precarious. Many of his chieftains oppose the peace he made with the Seven Lands, and they object to his Deeri wife being made a ruler of a province. In Koosti culture, women are seen mostly as slaves. My ruling an empire is cause enough for them wanting to destroy me.

"King Nicore?"

"Yes, your highness?"

"I apologize for this imposition, however, I wish to see to the feeding and comfort of my knights and other troops. Also, we should use our time wisely and attend to matters at hand even as we dine. Is this possible with the stores you have available?"

He bowed as he answered, "Yes, your highness; I shall see to it immediately." He strode out of the room barking orders, then notified his commanders to stand down against the newcomers.

In the assembly room, Veranna dismissed the rest of the nobles to tend to their duties, then took Sreba aside to thank her for her support. She kept her voice low as she said into her ear, "Sreba, please, help me with judging whether Jantay is true or false. My own mind is too easily swayed by emotions on this matter."

The queen patted her shoulder reassuringly, "Of course." Her face then drew into a curious scowl as she nodded toward Kreida. "Is that vulgar woman really your friend? She sounds like a street hussy."

Veranna laughed. "Yes, she is my friend, and a good one, too. She comes from those called Genazi, as does my husband, Karsten. Genazi are well-known for skill and ferocity in battle. Karsten is a bit of an exception. He is as adept with the mind as he is with the sword." She took Karsten's hand in hers and kissed him again. "My Karsten is a wonder."

They both laughed, and Sreba excused herself to go looking for her own husband. She wanted to give Veranna and Karsten some time alone. Crossing the room she noticed the academician, Beneto, involved in a deep discussion with Tesra. Alliances old and new seemed to spring forth wherever Veranna went.

The empress introduced Karsten to Jantay, and the three of them spoke for a while as they examined the ancient room that had displaced the house's assembly room. Documents and artifacts were so well preserved from the old realm that Karsten felt he could spend a lifetime studying them. Kreida overheard him and gave him a punch on his shoulder. Pointing to Veranna, she cocked her head and looked exasperated.

"You are supposed to be using your time studying her!"

The atmosphere turned tense as Jantay, not yet familiar enough with Kreida's sense of humor, thought it necessary to defend her sister and brother-in-law.

"That is no way to speak to your empress' husband, be you friend or not. She will decide your ways, not you hers. If you cannot find a way to subdue yourself, then I will find it for you."

Kreida's face went from shocked to ferocious. "Listen here, youngster, I will pin your ears to the wall if…"

Veranna's voice struck them like a slap. "Stop!" She motioned for Kreida to move away a bit, then took Jantay's arm in her own as she walked gently in the other direction, explaining to her Kreida's style and passions.

Tesra, noticing the incident, asked Kreida if everything was alright.

"Oh yeah; no problem. Little sister is trying to insure the family ties. I might have to slap her around a bit for her own good." She paused and then said matter-of-factly, "Actually, I like her already. She has a lot of nerve and fighting spirit. Veranna needs more of her type to watch her back."

Tesra grunted affirmatively, then added, "Do not be too quick in your acceptance of her. We only met her today and have little idea of her background. Remember, if we have agendas, so do others."

The day proceeded with meetings, introductions and proclamations. All of the Fareseans wondered how they would function under the new system, but those freed from slavery were especially nervous since they were now responsible for their own support. Many struck deals with their former masters, and those women slaves who had borne children from masters hurried to file claims of paternity and support for their children.

Three days later and Veranna was ready to set sail for home. As she had said, she left a score of knights to monitor the changes she set in place, and found as many Koosti, Deeri and other foreign slaves as she could to return to their lands. The ship captains had little room for complaint since Veranna promised more than fair compensation for their labors. Sreba, Nicore and all of the leading nobles gathered at the dock to bid her farewell. They bowed and assured her that they would be true to their word.

She curtsied and bowed her head in return, then said, "I trust you to do so and remind you that I shall return. The Creator watches over you for your safety, and for your judgment as well. Goodbye, for now."

She stepped onto the ship and Karsten ordered the captain to set sail. Out of the harbor they went and the sails were raised to the full.

Two weeks later they landed at the Koosti harbor. Ghijhay, the wife of DeAndre, the Great One of the Koosti, greeted them with lavish welcome. Food, lodging, baths and any other service they might want were theirs for the asking. Veranna feared that it was too much for Ghijhay's treasury to put out, but the Deeri woman dismissed her concerns.

"Veranna, you are just as generous, or more, in the ways that you provide for people. Besides, the income in this province has grown at least twelve times what it used to be. Koosti may be used to slavery, but they readily take to earning a better living when they are free. Has your finance minister not reported to you the payments made to your widows and orphans since the end of the war?"

"Well, er, yes, but I had not formed a good idea of just what these changes would accomplish, and those monies were not to be taxed. Now that you mention it, I have noticed that quite a few businesses run by women have sprung up."

"That is true here, too, and I will sa..." She stopped as Jantay appeared and approached Veranna. Ghijhay calmly touched her hand and the amber stones in her necklace flared. She turned to Veranna and looked at her in surprise. "You never told me you had a sister. Why?"

Veranna held out her hand for Jantay to take. "Neither did I know either until over two weeks ago. She was brought forward as a candidate for leading the realm of Faresea in my stead." Tears formed in the corners of her eyes. "I wondered about the truth of her claim to be my sister. Now that the Creator has confirmed it through you, I am so happy that I do not know what to say." She paused a moment and then introduced the two women. "Ghijhay, this is Jantay, my sister. Jantay, this is Ghijhay, from the Deeri tribes, and the wife of the Great One of the Koosti, DeAndre y'dob."

Without thinking, Jantay fell to her knees and put her face to the ground. "Command me, Great Mistress; I am your slave!"

Veranna's eyes went big with surprise, and Ghijhay smiled with understanding.

"Arise, daughter of the empire, and know that you should not humble yourself to me in this way. The only one in this world you might call your master is your sister, the empress." She took Jantay's hand and helped her to her feet. "You and I are peers. Koosti customs are those you should leave behind."

Jantay was flummoxed as never before. "Mistress, I have lived my life under the Koosti. What you say is hard to understand." She looked down and away, expecting some form of punishment.

Ghijhay felt Jantay stiffen with fear as she put her arm across her shoulder. "It will take time for you to adjust, so do not be overly concerned. It has taken quite a while for me to get used to being the Great Mistress of the Koosti." She looked at them both and glanced to her right. "Come with me; I'll show you what kind of meal can be had in these parts."

The three headed off surrounded by Koosti and Emeraldian guards. Tesra and Kreida joined them, but Karsten understood that this was a women's meeting, so he would occupy himself with something else. A few hours later he found them still deep in conversation. He politely interjected himself and requested that they not be offended at his wanting to take his wife away from them. They all laughed and humorously berated Veranna for not tending to her husband. Her face blushed scarlet and she hurriedly curtsied and excused herself. Off they went to the finest inn for the best room reserved for them.

The next morning, after an excellent breakfast, Veranna and her forces headed north for Zishyi. Ghijhay wanted to accompany them and the Koosti marveled once more at the dignity and grace shown by the empress and Ghijhay. They developed a grudging respect for Kreida, due to her randy sense of humor and skill with knives, even though she was Genazi. Tesra was shown great respect since it was widely known that she was admired by Chief Gohie, and his tribe was sworn to her defense.

North and west they rode making good time. Veranna looked up and noticed red rings swirling around the sun.

CHAPTER 35

The imperial company reached Zishiye and enjoyed the hospitality of Earl Tomius and his wife, Learha. While there, they received a note from Yanbre by pigeon. It urged Tomius to send the company with haste to Tolemera. The Erains, and their allies, were mounting an offensive against the castle, since ladies Gelangweil and Loray were still imprisoned. Yanbre hoped that the presence of Veranna would bring tensions to a halt. Otherwise, many lives might be lost.

Veranna and Karsten decided to depart the next morning at dawn. Tomius ordered two-thousand Genazi warriors to bolster those already with her, and a week's hard ride brought them to Tolemera.

Erain forces formed a thick hedge along the road to the castle. Karsten had to work hard and sternly to keep Genazi from striking out and starting a battle, since they felt that anyone opposing Veranna had a death warrant tattooed on his forehead. She was more than an empress to them; she was the Great Mother, whom some considered semi-divine. To die fighting for her was seen as part of the paradise of the Creator.

The imperials formed up in front of the castle wall, facing the Erains, who were positioned about eighty yards away. As she passed them, Veranna commanded their leaders to the throne room within an hour, hoping that reason would prevail.

Arriving home after so long, Veranna just wanted to lie down on her bed and rest. However, duty called; she would think of relaxation after tending to the present crisis. Moving over to her nightstand to find a particular necklace, she noticed an open book. The facing page on the right was three-quarters full with fine, superbly written characters. She lifted it up and saw the title on the spine. '*Mysterium Consequentor*' stood out in bright gold. Looking back at the written page she carefully read it. What struck her odd was that when she had looked at this book several months ago it was written through all of its pages. Now it was only half-full. Intrigued by this discrepancy she focused on her reading.

Victories great or small mean nothing apart from the roles they play in moving all things according to the Creator's will. Have you gained through some struggle? Take it with wisdom, for it may be that it tosses you into a stream of consequences you cannot foresee. Blessings can dull our minds to necessities, and a lapse before the One who judges will increase the difficulties of life ten-fold. The road to triumph becomes the path of sadness and despair.

The battle shall be won, but the conflict will be ongoing. Your House will prevail only through great strife. All sanity shall depart from your mind and prepare you for the years to come. Accept this now and spare yourself much grief, knowing that in the end you shall see the Creator's great blessings. Always remember that the seed you sow will be choked and hindered by the weeds that remain.

She closed the book and placed it back on the stand, then sat on the edge of the bed. A sense of angst filled her as she pondered the words. What did the Creator have in mind for her? Was she to know no respite in this life? Had she not gone through enough already?

Karsten walked in and saw her staring at something not in the room. She was startled when he spoke and placed his hand on her shoulder.

"Are you alright, my love? You look as though something has disturbed you deeply."

She stood and hugged him tightly. "Oh, Karsten, I cannot help but think that I am doomed to a life of terrible events. I feel like running and hiding in some far away land. Take me there and I'll give you all of the children you want and be the best of wives. I want some rest." Tears threatened to pour from her eyes as she buried her face in his shoulder.

He wished that her desire was just that simple: Take her in his arms and ride off and away from all of the responsibilities of this life. He also knew that such a choice would condemn her to a life of guilt and shame. Tending to responsibility and completing hard tasks was as much a part of her nature as breathing. No, a job well done before the Creator, and her fellow man safe and happy, were her greatest joy and satisfaction. The pains and troubles she suffered were only for a season. Faith in the Creator's promises would see her through.

"My love, do not despair. You have my heart and devotion, as well as those of your friends and loving servants. Trouble is part of this life, but we shall fight on together." She pulled him tighter against herself and rubbed her hands along his back. "My love, what started you thinking about these things? Did someone make a remark that made you sad?"

Her face still pressed into his neck and shoulder, she pointed at the nightstand with her right hand, and said, "That book, there, had words which seemed aimed right at me. You can read them if you open it to the middle where the writing ends."

He looked where she pointed and saw no book on the stand. "Which book are you referring to, Veranna?"

She looked up at him and frowned. "The one on my nightstand next to…" She stopped as she looked but saw no book. "This is impossible; I just set it here a moment ago." She searched the drawers of the stand, the floor around it and under the pillows and blankets of the bed. It was not there. "How could it just disappear?"

Karsten looked around the room and spotted the book on top of a dresser against a far wall. He walked over and picked it up. "This is the one I have seen several times lying around. Just before

I left to get you out of Seacorro, I saw it open at the middle where you said was the last written page."

She examined it and said, "Yes, this is the one." She gasped when she opened it and found all of the pages filled with writing. Try as she might she could not find the passage she had read only minutes ago. "This is eerie, Karsten; it must be some type of portent from the Creator. But why the strange circumstances?"

All he could do was shrug his shoulders and shake his head. Just as he was about to speak, a knock sounded on the door. "Come."

Reiki entered and bowed. "Highness, nobles in royal chamber for meeting. Waiting your presence."

Karsten nodded and thanked her, then held out his arm for Veranna to take.

A score of people milled around the royal chamber, waiting for the empress. They bowed, even if ever so slightly, and waited for her to sit. Baron Ciclanno was their appointed representative. He tried to stand tall and imposing to influence Veranna's decisions.

The empress took the initiative and put the baron, along with his comrades, on the defensive.

"My lord baron, I have been informed that you represent the Erains and their allies. I require an explanation as to why you acted seditiously toward the throne. Any act of aggression against your sovereign is treason. Do you seek to cast me down?"

The baron gave a short, quick bow and smiled as though frustrated. "Assuredly not, your highness. It would seem that you have been misinformed. My allies and I are outraged at the unjust treatment of our liege ladies; we must demand their immediate release and recompense. None of our people have displayed treasonous words or deeds; the only reason that our ladies were imprisoned was the claim that some man was said to have uttered lies whilst in the throes of death. Are you willing to judge this matter according to the law, and dispassionately?"

Tesra and Karsten gave her cautious looks. Something was going on in this exchange that she was not grasping. The Erains seemed to be holding their breath and Ciclanno's eyes bored into her. All she could do was perform her duty.

"I shall judge this matter fairly and without prejudice."

Tesra and Karsten twitched and looked down at the floor, while Ciclanno and the Erains had sly grins on their faces. Veranna was at a loss to interpret their reactions, but knew that she had erred in some way. Ciclanno nodded and continued.

"As you will, your highness. My first request is that you free our ladies on the grounds that no real evidence against them exists. The words of a disoriented, lying criminal are not enough to bring about the execution of anyone, let alone the ruler of one of the empire's leading houses."

Veranna's mouth was dry and she felt her pulse pound through her limbs. The request of the baron was easy to decide; however, the consequences were not so clear.

"My lord baron, your request is granted; the noblewomen are to be released immediately." She looked at Yanbre and raised her eyebrows, signaling him to see to their release. A few minutes later and both ladies, Gelangweil and Loray, stood before Veranna. Their hair and clothing were immaculate since their imprisonment actually took place in very nice rooms with servants and supplies. Lady Gelangweil's dress was studded with pearls and silver, and Loray's gown had such a plunging neckline that Veranna mused to herself that going topless would have been no different. The woman was a true beauty, but it would avail her nothing in this hearing. Veranna hoped that this would be the end of the matter and tried to close on a positive note.

"You ladies appear unharmed and none the less healthy in spite of your confinement. As there was cause, initially, for your being held while an investigation was conducted, it is recognized that no more is to be required of you at this time. You may go in peace."

Loray looked at her disdainfully. "I am sorry…your highness… but that shall not be enough. Accordingly, we have the right to demand recompense for the defamation we have suffered. We require satisfaction by contest, and that must be with one from your house… your highness."

Gasps came from several people while Veranna's face flushed red. Her eyes narrowed and her pulse throbbed in her neck.

"You are speaking like barbarians. In the Seven Lands we decide legal issues by reason and principle. If you think you are maintaining your honor by dueling, then think again. You will only show yourselves beholden to base lusts."

Loray smiled placidly as if tutoring an incompetent student. "Not all subscribe to your notions of jurisprudence…your highness. If you fail to meet our demand you shall forfeit your right to rule. The Erain and Gelangweil Houses will have a very clear majority and be required to cast you down; you and all that is yours would belong to House Erain. The same will hold true should your House lose the contest. We will have our satisfaction."

Her jaw hard, Veranna's voice came out ice-cold with fury. "Since you are intent upon showing yourselves in the lowliest of character, I shall agree to your terms. Should you lose, Houses Erain and Gelangweil shall forfeit one-third of their estates to the crown. I warn you now; I will defeat anyone you send against me."

Now it was the Erains and Gelangweils turn to be angry. They huddled together for a few minutes before responding, arguing whether the risk factor was acceptable. Loray composed herself, and a strange sense of diabolical humor shone in her voice, face and posture.

"We find these terms acceptable, and are ready to proceed immediately."

Veranna stood and belted her sword to her hip. "Good. Let us be done with this nonsense and move on to worthy uses of our time." She stepped down quickly from the dais and headed toward the doors. Loray's voice rose above the noise in the room.

"Excuse me, your highness, but you have not designated anyone from your house to represent you in the contest."

The empress spun around crisply and faced Loray. "I will fight my own contest."

The duchess felt her heart miss a beat and her lungs failed to draw a breath. Veranna was taller than she and had fought many battles. Her skills were so far beyond anyone else's that she could strike her down with one simple blow. Fear clutched her so strongly that she could not speak. She had to force herself to calm down and proceed with the plan she had devised for the Erains.

"Your majesty knows the law; you are not able to enter the contest since you designated yourself as the judge of the issue. This is an issue between your house and ours. We do not resign this feud."

At first, Veranna did not grasp the implication of Loray's point. After a moment it all became clear. The duchess was correct about the law; a judge had to remain neutral in a dispute and could not be a participant for either side. That being the case, she could not represent House Dunamays and fight in the contest. But if she could not fight she would forfeit her claim and become the slave of the Erains. The empire would pass to them and suffer the cruel despotism shown by the Gelangweils. She put as much menace into her glare as she could to hide her own desperate fear.

"Assemble for the contest outside the gate; I shall be with you shortly." She turned and headed out of the room to her chambers.

Karsten, Tesra, Kreida, Yanbre and Reiki filed into the chamber behind her. Knowing that Veranna would likely be berating herself for falling into the Erain trap, they made sure to avoid critical comments and centered in on a solution. Karsten tried to help her by assuming some of the blame.

"I should have thought through more clearly the implications of arresting the two women. It is hard to believe that the noble houses would pursue such a Genazi-like tradition."

His attempt to relieve her feelings of incompetence and guilt backfired.

"Oh, Karsten, stop talking nonsense. You did what you had to do. Now we have another horrible choice before us. Do we try to barter for lesser consequences? I could offer myself as their slave in exchange for them not taking over the empire. The people would not be subject to tyranny."

All of the others immediately rejected such a notion, leaving Veranna exasperated.

"Then what am I to do!? I cannot simply sweep aside laws set down for hundreds of years. Everyone would take that as a precedent and chaos would result."

Kreida shrugged non-chalantly and said, "So, fight."

"Have you not been listening, Kreida? I cannot be a participant. A judge cannot serve as the executioner and exploit his position."

"Then get a family member to fight for you."

"You know as well as I that there are no m..." She stopped as the import of Kreida's words struck her. "You cannot be serious! Jantay is not a warrior, nor has she been trained. It would be like sending an animal to the butcher."

Reiki bowed her head and then looked Veranna intently in the eye. "Highness, Kreida sometime get sense. This one. If sister no fight, you lose and she killed by them. If sister fight and lose, she dead and you lose. Only chance is her win, then you win. Creator give you promise; Creator keep. Trust from head and heart."

Veranna felt like bursting into tears. Her throne was at stake and she faced being a slave for the rest of her life. That all paled in comparison to the thought of her sister, whom she had just come to know, being cut down before her. Tesra placed a motherly kiss on her cheek and held her close.

"My dear, Kreida and Reiki are correct. The Creator would not place you in this situation without giving you a means to get through it. Was it mere coincidence that you happened to meet Jantay only so recently? I think not. Besides, the Erains do not know about her; they will be shocked when you put her forward. They think that you will have no recourse but to surrender when, poof, here comes the total refutation of their plans."

Veranna thanked Tesra and looked at Karsten. He gave her a grim nod. "My love, if there is even a remote chance to keep you safe, I will take it. Listen to the others and take comfort in their wisdom. All is not as dark as you imagine."

She placed her head on his shoulder, then opened her eyes and saw the strange book on her nightstand. It was open to the middle and had one sentence written in bold characters on the right-hand page.

Do you curse the sun when you stand bare in its rays too long?

All of the pages following this sentence were blank. Veranna's eyes went wide as she asked Karsten to look at the strange tome. Lifting it up he read the words and examined it again.

"Veranna, this book was written throughout when last we saw it. We are being given a sign."

Tesra peered at it and shook her head. "I was filled with dread when I saw that book here for the first time. No other copy of it survived from the days of the ancient kingdom. Now I understand why. It is an ongoing record that changes according to the choices you make. The old rulers used to consider it an ill-omen, especially when they did evil. It is an enigma and difficult to put any trust in."

The young empress looked down, closed her eyes and put her fingers to her temples. After a silent moment she straightened and resignedly said, "Reiki, please ask Jantay to come here."

The Felinii woman bowed and exited, the door closing ominously behind her.

CHAPTER 36

Windows set high in the southwest wall of Veranna's room let in an abundance of light, but she could remember no darker day in her life. She could survive as a slave and still try to help others, but losing her recently found sister would be unbearable. And what would be the way of life for the people of the realm? Dalmar Gelangweil, for all of his terrible deeds, had been justly deposed, but he at least had sense enough to not crush the common man. Better to hamstring people and still have them be useful. The Erains would likely be far worse, especially if the suspicions of ties with eastern despots were true. After laying out the situation, she turned to Jantay and sat next to her on the bed.

"I am so sorry to have to ask you for this, but I can think of no other way to stop the Erain's from taking control of the empire. It would be like living under the Koosti."

Jantay felt like spitting. "For that reason alone I want to fight. Living Koosti-style is a living death. My mind and body were totally controlled by them, and any chance to resist them is greater than any amount of gold." She paused and looked her sister in the eye. "I will not lie; your death or enslavement would simply be another phase in the torture I have experienced in my life. My heart is hard and will not easily feel pity or love. I work on the calculation that I can make my life less painful living with you. I cannot help not feeling great pangs of sympathy."

Veranna felt so much pain for Jantay, knowing how true her words were. It was hard for the empress, beloved by so many, to imagine the gruesome life that her sister had endured.

"We both bear the scars of our past. All I can hope for is that time will help you heal, to know love and hope once more. For now, I hope that you are very knowledgeable about the knife. The Erains will likely have a top expert ready to fight."

Jantay smiled grimly. "Slavery and chess are not the only things I learned from the Koosti."

The field outside the castle gate held several thousand people. The Erains and their associates, the Gelangweil's , had pressed in on the north side of the road leading from the city to the gate, while Yanbre directed the imperial army to form a cordon along the southern side. The imperial knights rode their war horses in a regular pattern between the wall and the field, while Treybal positioned archers along the wall to shoot down anyone who made a threatening move toward Veranna. She rode out through the gate on a tall horse as horns sounded to announce her presence.

A circular area about thirty feet in diameter was cleared on the south side of the road. Veranna rode to the center and halted, staring at Archduchess Loray as she moved her own horse into the circle. Veranna wanted to slap the smug, gloating smile from the woman's face. The condescending tone in her voice added to Veranna's ire.

"I see that you have decided to act reasonably and surrender without incident. It does you credit, but surely you realize now that ruling an empire was a foolish undertaking on your part. It is better left to those whose stations grant them that place."

Veranna kept her voice as level as she could. "It is the Creator who decides who shall rule. If He chooses the lowliest of peasants, then that is the rightful ruler. He chose my ancestors and pledged His fidelity many long years ago. You would be wise to follow His example."

Loray smiled and shook her head dismissively. "It would seem that you have not faced the reality of your situation. The Creator has decided by leaving you no one to fight for your honor. You shall now dismount and take your place among the slaves. Reality shall be a bitter reminder of just how deluded you have been."

Now it was Veranna's turn to smile. "Reality is a strange thing; it reveals us without prejudice. You show yourself to be in error by assuming that no one else of my house survives. The contest is not done."

Loray frowned and scoffed, "You are the last, girl, so do not waste our time with trivial stalling."

Veranna, without looking away from the woman, signaled for Jantay to ride forward. "Allow me to introduce you to my sister, Lady Jantay. She shall represent House Dunamays in this contest."

Loray, and the other Erains and Gelangweils, were taken aback. It was common knowledge that the empress was an only child. The archduchess's eyes narrowed suspiciously.

"I do not know what kind of chicanery you have in mind; it will do you no good. It will only make your first beating worse."

Lady Gelangweil rode forward and sneered at Veranna. "Get into rank with the servants; I will not look kindly on any more delay."

Veranna said flatly, "You are the ones causing delay by not getting on with the contest. If you doubt that this lady is my sister, then bring forth your pharmakai and have him verify our kinship. Either that or forfeit."

Lady Gelangweil's face flushed with anger. "Very well; we shall settle this quickly." She turned and yelled an order for her pharmakai to come forward. A darkly tanned, bandy-legged man with a bald head came out of the Erain ranks and bowed. Lady Gelangweil spoke with blunt rudeness even though pharmakai enjoyed high regard in all social circles for their knowledge and unselfish service.

"Do you have a test to determine if these two are sisters?"

The elderly man bowed as he said, "Yes, my lady. It will require only a few drops of blood from those involved. Two non-related individuals will be needed to demonstrate the veracity of the test."

Her anger and frustration showed in her response. "Get on with it, man, before this day wastes away!"

The man took out a polished, white ceramic plate from his satchel, and a glass vial holding a clear fluid. From a coat pocket he removed four super-sharp needles. He then approached Veranna and bowed.

"Your highness, may I take a tiny sample of your blood?"

She nodded and held out her left arm. He took four large drops of blood and placed them on the plate. He did the same with Jantay, then from two Erain soldiers. From the clear vial he dribbled three drops of fluid onto Veranna's blood, then addressed the people.

"As you will see, if I now mix the blood from either of the two soldiers with the empress's there is no reaction." He swabbed a few drops of each onto Veranna's blood and nothing happened. "Now, when I put some of Lady Jantay's blood onto her highnesse's, there should be a noticeable reaction if they are close kin." He mixed two drops of Jantay's blood onto Veranna's and it foamed like a boiling cauldron. The pharmakai announced matter-of-factly, "They are very likely sisters or, at least, first cousins."

Lady Gelangweil spat and rode out of the circle, but Loray gathered her wits and tried to sound as though nothing had changed.

"This makes no difference; our fighter will strike down your sister with ease. You shall rue the day that you ever thought of ruling an empire." She motioned toward her comrades and a tall, well-muscled man with close-cropped blonde hair stepped into the ring. Loray smirked as she introduced him. "This is Squire Weston, of House Erain. He shall represent us in this contest."

Veranna looked him over and instinctively gauged his abilities. His build and gait were very similar to those of the Raven's Blades, and he favored his right arm. Obviously he had been trained by the assassins for just such a moment as this. She had a sinking feeling in her stomach as she realized that he was a highly-skilled killer. Even she would have to be very cautious against such an opponent. She nearly jumped when Jantay's voice cut through the charged atmosphere.

"Is this the best you have to offer? I thought you Erains were serious about this challenge. You!" She pointed to Loray, a hard, vengeful look in her eye. "When I am through with this little darling of yours, I will give your soft, little ass a whipping that is long overdue."

Loray looked on her with contempt and then laughed. "I see that your crude nature cannot be hidden. I will make you a deal: If you lose, then your sister gets a public whipping. Agreed?"

"Let it be so."

Veranna, Karsten and Tesra glared at her and ground their teeth. But Kreida laughed and clapped her hands as she spoke to her.

"I am liking you more and more, girl. Are you sure you are not from the Genazi?"

Tesra scolded her and spoke quickly to Jantay as they huddled together.

"This man is a Ravens' Blade in all but name. He is trained to fight with, or without, a knife, and he will show no mercy for the fact that you are a woman. Be alert for hidden barbs that are poisoned."

All Veranna could do was give her a hug and say a quick prayer over her. She was surprised when she opened her eyes and saw the castle gleaming with an emerald-green sheen. Yanbre and the other armored knights also glowed with the same hue and looked ready to destroy any foe. It seemed odd in the midst of such dire circumstances. One thought struck in her mind. She looked Jantay in the eye and said, "Remember your limits."

The younger sister was puzzled by the comment, but the blast of a horn caught her attention. Yanbre, as castellan, had to officiate the contest.

"The combatants will take their positions in the middle of the circle, ten feet apart, and may be armed with only a knife. They shall fight until one of them is dead. Any attempt by any other person to interfere with the contest, will result in forfeiture for their side." He paused until only the fighters were left in the circle. His voice was grim as he called, "Begin!"

Weston crouched down and then sprang at Jantay. Veranna nearly fainted as she saw his blade streak at her sister with deadly precison. She nearly burst into tears as Jantay evaded the strike and watched him pass by. Veranna screamed, "Now, Jantay, strike," but her words were drowned out by the roar of the crowd.

Jantay saw the look in Weston's eye; it was one she had seen many times among the Koosti. The lust to kill was all that mattered. He pounced again, and, just as before, she stepped out and away from the strike but failed to follow up with a counter-strike. Watching Koosti fight had left a stylized imprint on her technique. Weston realized that her speed was greater than anyone else he had fought, and that he would have to limit her maneuverability. He moved closer and feigned a strike in one direction, then kicked where he figured she would jump. Sure enough, his foot connected with her abdomen. She flew back and landed hard on the ground, out of breath. Weston went after her thinking that she was disabled and an easy kill. He was taken totally off-guard when she twisted faster than a mongoose and snapped a kick of her own into the inside if his right thigh. The pain was not as great as the shock. He stumbled back and fell, allowing Jantay a moment to regain her feet.

Veranna could hardly breathe. She saw the flaws in Jantay's style and recognized the Koosti element, but was surprised at her sister's speed and toughness. Maybe the blessings of Emeraldia extended to her. Looking at the castle, she thought that it gleamed all the brighter. Her attention snapped back to the fight as she heard her sister shout.

"Weston, you fight like a little girl. Do you think you will ever become a man?"

Weston's jaw clinched tighter and sweat started to show on his brow. Veranna realized that Jantay was taunting the man to make him overly aggressive and reckless. It paid off. He leaped and swung to connect his knife with any part of her. Warming to her task, Jantay blocked his strikes and turned him around. She had a clear shot at his back, but hesitated. Her knife made only a superficial wound across his hips as he pulled out of range. Psychologically the blow was tremendous. Weston had to readjust his strategy or lose since it was now obvious that Jantay was no simple pushover. Confusion and doubt edged their way into his performance.

Veranna looked at her sister and noticed that she had a faint, emerald-green aura about her. It was a sign of the Creator's blessing, which gave her hope in the midst of the contest.

The combatants circled for a bit as they considered their next moves. Weston wanted to get close enough to give Jantay a nick on a bloodline that would spew enough to fatigue her. Jantay wanted opportunities to counter-strike and dismay her foe. One of Kreida's brash comments sounded in her mind. 'If a man won't come after you, then you'll have to get aggressive.' Jantay saw that his technique had turned passive and decided to take the initiative. With no sign of forewarning, she sprang within striking range faster than Weston could believe. Her blade cut into the inside of his left elbow and severed some tendons while also causing a good deal of blood loss. The butt of the palm of her other hand struck upward and knocked him backward and out of range. The force of the blow was beyond anything he expected from a woman of her size. Her lack of technique was more than compensated for by speed and power.

Weston had to keep his left arm pulled tightly against his body to reduce the loss of blood. His breathing was quick and rough as he strove to regain his composure. A quick glance at ladies Gelangweil and Loray caused him more agitation. Their faces were hard with fear and reproach. He looked at the empress and reminded himself that when he won this contest his reward was to have her as his personal slave to do with as he pleased. Her great beauty of face and form sparked his lust and inspired him to fight harder.

Tesra gripped Veranna's hand and spoke while watching the fight. "Your sister has the blessings of your line, but her lack of training leads her into many mistakes. This contest will end with one of them making a serious blunder."

Veranna nodded but could not take her eyes off of the fight. It was like a game of chess when you have a winning advantage and risk throwing it away with faulty technique. She did not realize how tense she was until Tesra complained that her grip was hurting her hand.

Jantay saw the look in Weston's eyes and knew he was planning something. The slightest flex of his leg muscles and she sprang inside his defenses. The timing was bad for both of them. Her knife passed by his ribs and his knife did not have enough clearance. They slammed into one another and his forehead impacted squarely on her left eyebrow. They both fell back dazed, but as he fell, Weston turned his knife enough that the sharp edge sliced across her right breast to under the left. She screamed and fell to the ground, her blade flying several feet away. She did not hear Veranna's horrified scream.

They both experienced a moment of disorientation from the head butt. Weston vaguely heard Jantay's agonized moan and saw his chance. Seeing her collapsed form, his legs wobbled as he stepped toward her. Down came his knife in a wide arc aiming for the back of her neck. It seemed to happen in slow motion as she rolled onto her right side and kicked up with her left leg. Her foot drove with desperate force precisely into his groin and he felt mind-numbing pain explode through his body. His knife fell to the ground beside her head and his body hit the ground so hard he lost consciousness.

Jantay crawled onto his back, grabbed his hair and pulled backward to expose his throat, then grabbed his knife with her right hand and placed it over his windpipe. She looked at Veranna with a question: 'Should I kill him?'

Seeing the bloody wound over Jantay's eyes and across her chest, Veranna was filled with horror. It transformed into rage at the Gelangweils and Erains. Her right hand clenched into a hard fist as she made a striking motion with it.

Too late, Tesra saw the exchange between the sisters and yelled, "Nooooo!" Jantay sliced across Weston's throat and his blood gushed out.

Veranna screamed in vengeance and relief at her sister's victory. Rushing forward, as Yanbre signaled the end to the fight, she lifted Jantay to her feet and frantically embraced her. Jantay's wounds closed as Veranna absentmindedly exuded power. The large bump over her eye did not go away immediately, but no more blood oozed out.

Jantay was soaked crimson on her front and arms. Her face was also splattered with blood and gave her a terrible, deadly appearance. Her face twisted into surprise at the unbridled affection her sister showed her. A part of her mind softened as she returned the joyful hugs. Over her sister's shoulder she saw the ladies Gelangweil and Loray dismount and kneel down in submission. She turned Veranna toward them and told her to acknowledge their compliance.

Seeing them kneeling, Veranna felt not a shred of sympathy for them.

"You gang of evil, power-hungry brutes! I hope that you are happy with all of your scheming. If you spent as much time planning how to make life better, you would not be seeing so many die just to feed your carnal cravings. I hope that shame will finally lead you to wisdom. Now, get out of my sight!"

They got to their feet when Jantay stepped forward and yelled, "Stop!" All eyes fixed on her as she pointed at Loray and said, "You and I have a bargain to fulfill. Get over here, right now."

Loray began to twitch as terror took over her features, and pleaded to be excused from the deal she had made with Jantay. But the younger woman would have none of it. As Loray screamed and tried to back away, Jantay stepped forward and grabbed her by the hair, yanking her into the circle. When some of the Erain guards tried to interfere, Lady Gelangweil ordered them to back off and obey the bargain their lady had made.

Having received many beatings from Koosti and Faresean masters, Jantay knew exactly how she wanted to proceed. She ordered two of Loray's guards to hold her arms, and then she shoved her to her knees. Retrieving a short rider's whip from a saddle, she grabbed her knife and cut away Loray's clothing from the middle of her back and down to her feet. She took the whip and swung it hard. It whistled through the air and gave a sharp snap as it connected with Loray's bare bottom. The woman let out a wretched, high-pitched wail that pierced all the way into the city streets. Her body spasmed so hard that the guards could barely keep hold of her. After four more blows, Loray passed out and had to be carried away by her people.

With the taste of victory and revenge fresh in her mouth, Jantay walked over to Lady Gelangweil and spoke hotly, "Bargain fulfilled." She threw down the whip and took Veranna's hand in hers. "Let's get back inside and dismiss these vermin from our minds."

Before she turned to go back to the castle, Veranna said to Lady Gelangweil, "Do not think me so stupid as to believe that you did not conspire in some way in my abduction. I will be watching, and I will not be gentle in my responses to your foul ways." Surrounded by her loved ones she strode into the castle and asked a servant to have a hearty dinner prepared for them. Celebrating her homecoming and newfound sister, she took any and every opportunity to introduce Jantay to all they encountered.

Kreida, feeling her wine, loudly declared Jantay an honorary Genazi. "But that means you will have to attend regular weapons training. A few changes in your technique and you will be able to handle any man." A sly look on her face emphasized the double meaning of her words. When Veranna scolded her for such impropriety, Kreida rolled her eyes and said to Jantay, "It may be sad, but true; your sister has not learned how to have any real fun."

Jantay just shrugged and shook her head. "While still a slave to the Koosti I heard rumors of the barbarian empress who was a virgin. We found it hard to believe. All of the women felt a strong pang of envy since the joy of being with a man had been crushed by overuse. It will be quite a while before my desires take hold of me that way."

Kreida's face turned sickly as she lamented, "Ugh! It must run in the family!"

Veranna laughed and said, "Kreida, you are surrounded!" She then turned more business-like. "That reminds me; you and Treybal have been putting off your wedding day far too long." She turned to the hardy Rockhound and raised her eyebrows as she smiled. "Would a week from today be acceptable to you?"

His response was quick and definite. "Yes, your highness. It's best we leash the wildcat as soon as possible."

The whole room broke into laughter when Kreida let out a frustrated groan. She sat and downed a full flagon of wine as the women surrounded her to plan the wedding.

The sun set in a glorious blaze of colors. Tesra looked out her bedroom window and noticed one of those colors before the sun set behind the western mountains. Red; not just any red, but a shade that filled her with an ill omen. Blood-red.

CHAPTER 37

Chief Sarim'tay sat on his silk cushions, contemplating how much infrastructure would be needed to effectively rule his empire when it extended from the eastern to the western shore of the continent. All of his many sons and grandsons would be required for the task. The whole world would look upon him as a god and beg to die in his service. He and his sons would be busy impregnating the women of the other lands in order to gradually replace the inferior peoples with superior Koosti stock.

A knock on the door interrupted his musings.

"Come."

The door opened and one of his sons entered, fell to his knees and bowed his head to the floor.

"Great Master, the one you sent for has arrived."

"Bring him to me."

"As you command, Great Master." He swiftly rose and went out the door, then reappeared with another man following him. They both fell to their knees and bowed their heads to the floor.

Sarim'tay remained inscrutable as he said to the man, "Sit up and give me your report."

"Yes, Great Master." He looked disheveled after a long and hard journey, but expectatious of a sizeable reward for completing his task. "I was successful, Great Master, with getting the Emeraldian Empress to accept the woman, Jantay, as her sister. Your servant among the Erains reports that Jantay fought and won a duel with a Gelangweil assassin. The level of training given her was perfectly done; she just barely won the contest. Her sister is said to have been very upset during the entire event."

In a totally level, impassable voice, Sarim'tay asked, "What of the girl, Jantay? Is her other training holding?"

"Yes, Great Master; every indication is that she has no awareness of the ways in which you have molded her. She shall be your tool to take the Seven Lands under your rightful rule."

"Are the Fareseans now loyal to their new, long-lost empress? Is it probable that they will follow her younger sister? Invasion of that land would be too costly for what it's worth; I need it open for occupation without battle. I want as many of their women alive and able to bear Koosti children as possible."

"Yes, Great Master, the Fareseans are already very loyal. They hold the Emeraldians in high esteem even after all these centuries. She is seen as a renewal for their stultified culture. I am very confident that Jantay will be readily acceptable to them once her sister is no more."

Sarim'tay smiled to himself as he saw his plans taking shape. The years of patience and planning were coming together into a sweet net of total conquest. He smiled outwardly at the man giving the report and spoke gently.

"You have done your task very well, Iyan. Know that your Great Master is pleased. Your service is to be rewarded."

Iyan grinned greedily as he imagined the chests of gold he would cart away as his payment. He would never have to work again and could buy whatever slaves he desired. The vision was short lived. Simultaneous chops hit precisely on each side of his neck severing his spine. His eyes popped wide as he fell forward, dead. Sarim'tay's son picked him up, carried him to the balcony and threw him over the rail into a wagon below.

Sarim'tay smiled at his son. "Very well done; an axe man could not have done better. No mess to clean up either. Come, we shall dine and enjoy entertainment. After that we shall tend the latest captive women from the eastern realms. A number of them are said to be strong and beautiful. We must impregnate them and increase the number of our off-spring."

"Yes, father; I shall make you proud in that way, too." He clapped his hands and summoned the serving girls.

CHAPTER 38

Trumpets blared as Treybal escorted Kreida down the aisle and into the pavilion. The ceremony was short and sweet so that Kreida would not have a chance to escape. The last couple of days had been full of her complaining that marriage would be prematurely restrictive on her life. Bouts of ill-temper made it difficult to get her ready. They called on Tesra for help, and after the Mother of the Academy took her into a side room for a few minutes, she came out much more compliant. Yanbre served in place of her father and Laerah, wife of Tomius, in place of her mother. Tomius, as the leader of the Genazi, officiated the ceremony.

Kreida had little time for self-pity as hundreds of people sought a moment to congratulate her and Treybal. Veranna and Karsten saw to it that everything went smoothly, the empress silently signaling the servants to replace most of Kreida's drinks with grape juice with only a tiny amount of wine. The flagon of deep red wine she had already downed was quickly manifesting itself.

It was amazing how Treybal had learned to control her antics with an understated glare. He had to calm her down after an especially pretty, young woman took more than a reasonable share of time to give him her blessings on his marriage. Kreida's instincts sent her into a threatening, violent mode that caused the young woman to blanch and hurriedly melt back into the crowd.

The celebration went on well into the evening with many songs and dances. Near the end a group of Genazi men gathered and offered a traditional Genazi rite to Treybal called the 'Ten Terrors.' Each of ten men would stand and warn the groom about something bad or dangerous in his new wife. It was intended to be humorous and often ended up with the bride getting involved in skirmishes with the men. It was considered a great way to work her up for the honeymoon.

Fortunately, Kreida took it all in good humor. She laughed and yelled that the men had obviously been castrated and denied her attentions.

Treybal stood, emptied his flagon, and lifted Kreida in his arms. He shouted a good night to everyone and then walked quickly out and down the hall to his chambers. Kreida pretended to be taken against her will and cried out for help. The people laughed and toasted their marriage as her screams faded down the hallway.

An hour later, Veranna and Karsten decided to retire for the night. Tesra walked along with them and was strangely silent. When Veranna asked her what was troubling her, the venerable Mother paused and sat down in a chair in Veranna and Karsten's receiving room.

"Oh, it is a number of things, I suppose. I have not seen my son for a while, and I always worry about the Academy when I am gone. Also, as much as I may complain about Kreida's irritating ways, she does know how to dispel boredom in her own manner. I hope her marriage does not extinguish such a fire in her."

Veranna and Karsten made comic grimaces and groaned, each commenting on how marriage might make her worse. Veranna's look turned to one of loving concern as she took Tesra's hand in her own.

"Mother, there is something else lying heavy on your heart. What is it?"

Tesra looked down and spoke softly. "The contest; I have such a sense of foreboding about how it ended. It was not like you to agree to the death of someone in such circumstances. Certainly you had the right to expect such an end, but mercy has been your trademark. I fear serious consequences over this difference."

The older woman's voice and demeanor sent a wave of pity and regret through the young empress. "I am very sorry over that also, mother. I hope that you will find some comfort for your heart and mind before you travel back to Clarens. I will admit that I felt a certain savage satisfaction at Weston's demise. It was like finally striking back at a bully who has molested you for years. The Erains will think twice before they try something like that again."

"Just make sure that you save your savage moments for the right occasions. The Erains had to give up one of their own for their folly. Your's may be a similar fate. Maybe *consequence* would be the better term."

Karsten tried to set both women at ease. "Let us all be thankful that the Erains and Gelangweils have been set back for a while. In losing the duel they have lost a good deal of face. Some of their allies may be thinking them unworthy of allegiance and come over to our side. The next Council of Lords meeting should evidence a change. In the meantime we pray for mercy."

Veranna smiled and spoke confidently. "That is right mother, let's use this opportunity to our advantage." She looked at Karsten, longingly. "I am not ready to give up one of my own, especially Karsten. It is so wonderful to be home and in his arms again."

Tesra gave them a brief smile and stood up. "I am tired; I think I will get to bed. May I take the strange book from your nightstand? I want to study it while I am still here in Tolemera."

"Of course, mother; anything you wish." She handed the book to her and kissed her goodnight. She closed and locked the door, then turned to Karsten and started removing her clothes. "As for my savage moments, I am experiencing one now."

Tesra walked to her room and readied for bed. Sitting back against the headboard she pulled a lamp closer and opened the book. It opened to the middle. She drew a sharp breath when she saw that only half of the pages were written on. The right page held one short set of lines:

The righteous suffer punishment and grow in the knowledge of their Creator. Severe and lasting shall be their correction, leading to the collapse of pride. The leaders shall be made an example to all and help them grow. The Creator's will may be resisted by ours, but it shall be done.

She closed the book and wept for Veranna and all of the people of the Seven Lands. Praying fervently, she begged for mercy for them all.

Outside, behind the clouds, the moons missed alignment and shined in sickly hues. A shooting star zipped by, flared out and then reappeared in a blaze far in the east.

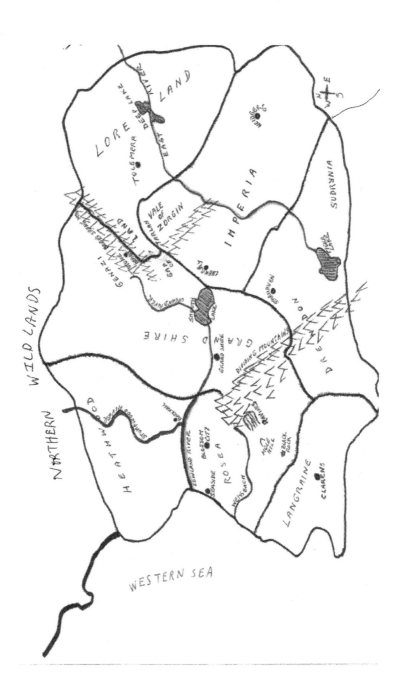

9597529R0019

Made in the USA
Charleston, SC
26 September 2011